THE SURVIVOR

Also by Tim Champlin
in Large Print:

Colt Lightning
Dakota Gold
King of the Highbinders
Summer of the Sioux
The Last Campaign

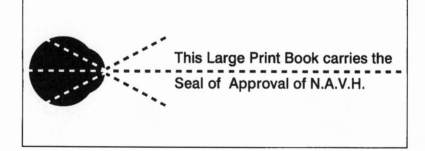

THE SURVIVOR

Tim Champlin

G.K. Hall & Co.
Thorndike, Maine

Published in 1997 by arrangement with
Golden West Literary Agency.

G.K. Hall Large Print Western Collection.

The text of this Large Print edition is unabridged.
Other aspects of the book may vary from the original edition.

Set in 16 pt. Plantin by Rick Gundberg.

Printed in the United States on permanent paper.

Library of Congress Cataloging in Publication Data

Champlin, Tim, 1937–
   The survivor : a western story / by Tim Champlin.
    p.   cm.
   ISBN 0-7838-1672-3 (lg. print : hc : alk. paper)
   1. Large type books. 2. France. Armée. Légion étrangère —
Fiction. 3. Western stories. gsafd. I. Title.
   [PS3553.H265S8 1997]
   813′.54—DC21   97-24018

For Alice and Harry Hosey

Chapter One

Marcel Dupré was slowly starving to death. This fact came to him in a flash of clarity as he pushed aside the small loaf of dry bread and tipped the tin mug of water to his lips. He was a very small man who required little food to subsist, but he had eaten nothing at all for thirty-six hours, and worst of all he had absolutely no appetite for any kind of nourishment. Here in his solitary cell on the island of Saint Joseph in the penal colony of French Guiana, this nourishment consisted of bread and water two days out of three. On the third day he was given soup, a few vegetables, and bread. In addition, for a few *sous*, he might bribe a guard to bring him some sweetened coffee and bananas. But now he was out of money. Not that it mattered. Having lost his appetite for anything at all, he knew it was only a matter of time. How much time? How many days could a man live without food? Ten? Twenty? In his weakened state he knew it would not be long enough to finish his sentence in solitary. Without even looking at the tiny scratches he had made on the stone wall of his cell, he knew he was in his fifty-sixth day of a ninety-day sentence.

He sighed deeply and picked up the tiny, cylindrical tube that lay beside him on the bare-board cot suspended from the wall. He unscrewed the tube in the middle and carefully tapped out one cigarette paper, the last few crumbs of tobacco, and a tiny match head. He had been hoarding this for the past three days to give himself something to look forward to, but now decided to go ahead and smoke his last cigarette. The small tube was a rectal suppository and was known as a "plan." Most of them were made of a non-corrosive metal. His own was a much nicer one made of smooth ivory which he had purchased from another convict. Before leaving the disciplinary barracks on the mainland, he had carefully rolled up a few francs and packed them tightly into this plan, along with some tobacco, thin cigarette papers, match heads, and a tiny folding razor. In such a device most of the prisoners kept what money they could get their hands on through some small graft. Only by carrying this plan inside one's own body could a convict be sure of its safety, since most of the men had no pockets, often no clothes, and definitely no place to store valuables. Even then, if a particularly ruthless convict knew another had money and wanted it badly enough, he could get it. The guards, unlocking the barracks in the morning, would often find a bloody corpse in the latrine. And it wasn't just money that provoked these knifings. Just as often the murders were a result of grudges of one kind or another, sometimes brought on by jealousy over a homosexual partner.

Brutal guards often extracted plans from prisoners by forcing the convict to drink a laxative, or just by a vicious kick to the gut. Dupré had somehow learned to survive in this degraded atmosphere since he had debarked from a French ship at the pier in Saint Laurent in May, 1863, twenty long years ago. It seemed like an eternity. Several thousand men had been condemned to the equatorial colony since then, and about an equal number had died, maintaining the population of the place at approximately the same level. But somehow he was one of those who'd survived.

He struck the match head against the damp stone wall. It left a mark but didn't light. Then he very carefully struck the remainder against the sharp edge of his tin cup handle. The sulphurous flame flared up, burning his fingers, but he held it long enough in spite of the pain to light the crimped cigarette. As he inhaled, he automatically listened for the footsteps of the guard overhead on the iron-grated catwalk. The walkway ran along the top of the wall that separated the two rows of twenty-four solitary cells. The armed guard, by glancing to one side or the other, could look down into the individual cells that were roofed only with bars. To keep the tropical sun and rain off prisoners, a peaked tin roof had been nailed to a wooden frame that ran from one end of the cell block to the other, about twenty feet above the catwalk. The guard, by reporting any minor violations such as smoking, talking, or hanging by the hands from the bars, could extend a prisoner's time in solitary.

Actually he had been lucky, Dupré reflected as he took one long last puff and dropped the tiny coal to the floor, kicking it quickly to scatter and snuff out the fire. He had been sentenced to only ninety days — thirty days each for insulting a guard, for allegedly swearing at a doctor who failed to order him to the hospital, and thirty for speaking out in court and irritating his judge. All in all a light sentence, considering he had just been caught and returned from his latest *cavale* — his seventh attempt at escape. The usual penalty for this was two to five years in the solitary cells, but he had pled his own case with desperation and what he thought was eloquence, in spite of the inept attorney who had been assigned to represent him. The attorney had simply mouthed the routine, "I beg the court's indulgence", and let it go at that. Dupré had told the judge that he had tried to escape because he knew certain death awaited him in the jungle camp if he stayed — from malarial fever, parasites, dysentery, and anemia. Other captured *evades* used this defense, and it usually didn't work but, for some reason, the judge had looked at his frail body and pleading eyes and acquitted him, while sentencing his companions to harsher terms. The judge, apparently to save face, had tacked on a thirty day sentence of his own to bring the total to ninety.

Dupré had left the courtroom of the T. M. S. — the Tribunal Maritime Special — with a sense of relief. After vegetating in the stench of the disciplinary barracks for two months until the next semi-annual meeting of the tribunal, he had drawn a sentence of only ninety days! He could do ninety days on the island and survive. But two to five years would have been out of the question. Men routinely died or went mad while serving time here where every hour was like a day and every day was like a year. There was absolutely nothing to do to pass the time.

He heard the measured footsteps of the guard approaching along the catwalk and fanned away the remaining smoke of the cigarette. He got up and pressed his back against the wall almost beneath the catwalk so as to be out of sight. The footsteps paused just overhead, and there was silence for a few seconds.

"Having a smoke, are you, Dupré?"

Dupré didn't reply, hoping the man would lose interest and go on. But he didn't.

"You know I could report you for this and get you an extra fifteen days," the grating voice continued.

Finally, Dupré stepped out and looked up at the dark face of the Corsican guard, peering down at him from under his dark blue kepi. The man's name was Mulette, and he was one who took a great delight in making the prisoners' lives ever more miserable.

"I don't have a cigarette," Dupré replied in a tired voice.

A grin split the lean, dark face. "There's only

one man close to you, and he is asleep. No, your addiction to tobacco has done you in again." He made it sound as if he had surprised Dupré committing a major crime.

Marcel sighed and dropped his head. He was so weak he hardly cared what the Corsican said or did. He knew that anything he uttered in his own defense would be worse than useless. He had already broken the rule of silence by speaking at all. He had dealt with this man before. Mulette had been a guard at Charvein jungle camp from where Dupré and three others had made their last escape. As a result of their successful *cavale*, Mulette and one other guard had been suspended without pay for thirty days. Dupré waited for the axe to fall.

"Not talking, eh, Dupré? Well, I'm not making any report against you for smoking."

Dupré looked up in surprise.

"You won't survive your original sentence, so why give you more?" The Corsican chuckled as he leaned on his elbows on the iron railing. "The turnkey told me you haven't eaten in two days. You look like you couldn't weigh more than a hundred pounds. At that rate you'll be food for the sharks soon enough." A rumbling laugh broke from him as he straightened up and resumed his pacing under the tin roof.

Chapter Two

Jay McGraw had always been extremely uncomfortable in the presence of great wealth. He was feeling this uneasiness now as he fingered his cravat and eyed the tables of formally-dressed men and women in the huge dining room of the Palace Hotel in San Francisco. In spite of the exquisite, several-course meal he had just consumed, he fervently wished he were in Boyle's Saloon, sampling the free lunch and enjoying a mug of steam beer. The surroundings there were more to his taste. But he was here at the invitation of his close friend, Fred Casey, a detective on the San Francisco police force who was helping provide security at this formal dinner being hosted by U. S. Senator William Sharon in honor of the visiting French ambassador. Since Casey's promotion from uniformed policeman on the Chinatown squad a few months earlier, he had been free on most evenings to take part-time plain-clothes security jobs such as this. In addition to being paid for his services, he was given two complimentary tickets to the dinner so he could bring a friend. He was to mingle inconspicuously with the several hundred guests while keeping an eye on things.

"You only invited me because you and Joyce

had an argument," McGraw grinned at him across the table over a rich dessert of cherries jubilee.

"That's not entirely true," the black-haired Casey replied, signaling a white-coated waiter for a refill of his coffee cup. "You were just back from your Chicago run, and I thought you might enjoy a good meal. Besides," he gestured expansively, "who could afford all this if either of us had to pay for it?"

Jay nodded, unobtrusively easing his belt out a notch. The meal had been superb, from the smoked salmon salad with artichoke hearts to the turtle soup to the rare, tender beef with mushrooms and wild rice and dry, red wine to the dessert he was enjoying now, all of it served on sparkling China with glittering silverware on snowy linen tablecloths by ghost-like waiters. The biggest and grandest hotel west of the Mississippi River was a proper setting for an event like this, he reflected, glancing around at the palm plants and the ornate, gaslight chandeliers that illumined the vast dining room. Satin and silk-gowned ladies with diamond and sapphire necklaces, immaculately coifed, contrasted sharply with the drab, black-coated gentlemen. Jay likened the scene to a lot of penguins scattered in a field of bright flowers.

McGraw had recognized several dignitaries in the crowd, including at the head table Mr. Lloyd Tevis, president of Wells Fargo & Company, his own big boss. In addition he had earlier identified

Mark Hopkins and Charles Crocker, two of the millionaire owners of the Central Pacific Railroad, James ("Slippery Jim") Fair, silver magnate of the Comstock Lode, and an assortment of lesser dignitaries. Jay felt totally out of his element. The whole thing had an air of artificiality that increased his uneasiness, but at least Fred Casey was here for a practical purpose.

"After all this food, you probably couldn't move if you had to stop some trouble," McGraw remarked.

"Not much chance of that happening in this crowd," Casey replied, dabbing at the edges of his mustache with a linen napkin. "Only had one serious problem since I've been working these affairs. Couple of gents got into it in the barroom after a few whiskies. It was an older man who accused some fella of seeing his young wife. They had a few words and, before I could get there, the old man had pulled a hide-out gun and shot the younger one. Killed him with a single slug to the heart."

"Strange. I don't remember that."

"I think you were back in Iowa, visiting your parents. Besides it was pretty well hushed up. I'm guessing considerable money changed hands to keep the scandal from busting wide open. The old man was a well-known financier but a mighty rough customer in his younger days as a miner. The younger fella was a sort of dandy. Whether or not he and the young wife really had anything going, I don't know, but the old man was never arrested or indicted. Self-defense, backed up by several witnesses."

Jay pushed back from the table. "I guess it's about time for me to slip out before the festivities begin."

"Oh, no you don't," Casey replied, taking a small glass of brandy from a silver tray proffered by a waiter. "You're about to have to pay for all this food by listening to a few long-winded speeches. If I have to stay, you have to stay."

"Well, if you insist. . . ." McGraw unbuttoned the bottom of his vest. "I'll just doze a little. Punch me if I start to snore."

The after-dinner speakers paraded to the podium at the head table, one after another, their pomposity exceeded only by their girth. Their words droned in Jay's ears without his hearing any of them. Allegedly the purpose of this occasion was to welcome the French ambassador on a tour of the United States, and the preliminary speakers were lavish in their praise, not only of the United States but also of the great relationship this country had enjoyed with France from LaFayette during the Revolution to the present day.

Jay was nodding when Senator Sharon left the stand to polite applause, and the French ambassador finally began to speak. He was a short, stout man of middle age. His brown hair was thinning on top, and his face looked fuller than it was, due to the muttonchop whiskers. His speech proved to be full of the same, high-flown generalities as all the others, albeit delivered with a French accent. McGraw was totally insensitive to political and diplomatic subtleties. He stifled a yawn as he noticed Casey leaning forward to catch every word.

"Pretty boring, if you ask me," he said in a whisper. "What's he talking about? Got any ideas?"

"It's a plea for money and support for his government," Casey answered in an undertone. "And he seems to be emphasizing how good French justice is, and how no one should flout authority. I don't really get the point of all that. I don't think anyone would disagree with that."

The speech finally ended with an eloquent plea for cooperation between the two great governments of France and the United States, and the ambassador bowed formally to a standing ovation from the assembly. Jay McGraw was back in his room at the boardinghouse and asleep by half past eleven.

Chapter Three

Marcel Dupré stopped his agitated pacing after a time. The soles of his bare feet had softened in the constant dampness, and he couldn't stand to walk on the cement floor for very long. Besides that, he was aware of how quickly his strength was fading now.

The afternoon had grown oppressively hot, and he stripped off his cotton jumper and trousers that were made of bleached flour sacks, let the board bunk back down in place, and stretched out to rest. The clothes he rolled up for a pillow. Shut away in this cell on an island nine miles from the mainland, he had no need to wear the usual prison garb of red and white vertical stripes, since he had no need to be identified as a convict.

The sea breeze did not reach him in his cell, but the humid heat did. The blazing sun beat down on the tin roof overhead, and the afternoon heat settled down like a damp blanket.

His eyes had long since accustomed themselves to the dimness of the nine-by-twelve-foot cell. There was nothing in the enclosure except the board bunk, a blanket, a pail to use as a latrine, a tin cup for water, and a wooden bowl and metal spoon for whatever food he was given. By design, the punishment in solitary confinement was as much psychological as physical. There was nothing to read, nothing to write on, no one to talk to or share ideas with. Silence was enforced. A man was thrown completely on his own thoughts and devices.

In the weeks past he had devised methods of occupying his mind and hands in order to keep his sanity. He had early on asked the turnkey for a broom so he could sweep the cell himself. With the frayed bundle of straw he was given, he would sweep the cell very carefully. Then he would get down on his hands and knees and examine all the cracks and corners to be sure every speck of dust was out of the crevices. Then he would sweep the cell again before his soup was brought to him. Before he ate, he would take the tiny razor he had packed in his plan and cut his bread into small slices. Then he would polish his spoon until it shone with a bit of earth and dust he had saved up from his constant sweeping.

After eating, he would take off his clothes and examine them for any frayed threads. He picked the threads off one by one, separating and counting them. His eyes had grown so accustomed to the dim light that he could see almost as well as a cat. He made a game of the threads. Each new thread he found became a momentous discovery.

Night followed day with an eternal sameness. Aside from making tiny scratches on the wall beside his bunk to mark the passage of the days and watching the green mold spread along the cracks, he was lost in his own world of thought.

And these thoughts, more often than not, turned from past to future. The past was set and unchangeable; the future was hope and unlimited possibilities. In his mind he was living in freedom in Paris or New York. He was eating at a sidewalk cafe. He would spend hours deciding just what to order; he would linger over what drink would go with what dish, and how much to tip the waiter. He pictured himself in a new suit of clothes, sitting in the bright sunshine, waiting for a beautiful woman to come and join him. He would glance at his watch, impatient for her to arrive. She was always beautiful, sometimes a brunette, sometimes a blonde, smiling and affectionate, attentive to his every word. They would linger over a glass of champagne, planning their afternoon together as if they had plenty of leisure and plenty of money.

He lived in this dream world, and it became so comforting to him that he was actually irritated when the turnkey came to bring his slight ration of food or to empty his latrine pail. After an interruption he could hardly wait to begin recreating the spell of the dream world he had wrapped himself in, where life was good and freedom abounded. All that had been in the past. It had enabled him to kill most of the fifty-six days he had spent here. With death quickly coming down the road toward him, the harsh reality of his surroundings had returned, and it was more difficult for him to escape into his fantasy world.

He became aware that the afternoon light had dimmed even more, and he heard the sudden thunder of tropical rain drumming on the tin roof about thirty feet above him. He smelled the rain, and the dank odor of decaying vegetation outside. The downpours did not refresh him or cool the air; they just made the hot air more oppressive afterward when the sun returned.

The first three weeks he had been confined here, he had been bothered at night by visits from vampire bats. He often awoke with some blood crusted on his bare ankles from the tiny puncture wounds of the painless bites. Shoes, socks, and underwear that might have given some protection from these pests had long since disappeared from his life in the prison colony. Socks, underwear, and handkerchiefs were not issued. Shoes were sold or traded for extra food or tobacco. But of late the bats had not bothered him. Maybe in his anemic condition the blood-sucking night raiders were now attacking juicier prey. He smiled grimly at the thought.

At least he had never contracted malaria, even after all these years in this fever-ridden region. Why he hadn't was a mystery to him. Maybe he could persuade the doctor to send him to the hospital to study this phenomenon. It was a vain hope. No medical research was done in Guiana. With the number of sick and dying men constantly in the prison colony, it was all the doctor could do to administer the limited medicines to the worst cases and grind his teeth in frustration at the impossibility of his job.

The tropical rain shower passed, and silence reigned once more, except for the sound of dripping water and the distant booming of the surf on the rocks below the flat hill where the cell blocks rested. It was like being in a damp, airless mausoleum. He felt very weak and tired and closed his eyes, drifting into a dreamless sleep.

He awoke to a demented scream ringing in his ears. He was disoriented for a few seconds and then realized the sound was coming from somewhere near the far end of the cell block. Another one would shortly be removed to the third cell block that housed the insane. Another heart-rending scream wavered and died with a choking sob.

He swung his feet to the floor and sat up. While he had slept, the night had fallen and his cell was in blackness. The only light visible anywhere was filtering through the overhead bars from a dim oil lamp high up under the tin roof above.

He slipped into his trousers and pulled the jumper over his head. The screaming started again, and he heard the guard's slow steps approaching. Then his faint shadow passed across the top of the cell wall. No one was going to the aid of the man whose mind had apparently snapped. After all, that was the whole idea of solitary confinement — punishment. It was intended to break those who had been classed as incorrigible — "incos," as they were called. These were men who refused to be cowed by the penal administration, those who would not resign themselves to the degradation of prison life. They were the rebellious and ungovernable ones who repeatedly tried to escape.

Marcel Dupré's skin did not tingle with a chill at the sound of the maniacal wailing, as it had done the first time he had heard it years before. It was now just another fact of life, one of the natural sounds that surrounded him, like the screeching of the monkeys in the nearby jungle. Besides, he was so far gone himself that all he could do was take note of the screams; they produced no emotional effect on him. For every screamer he wondered how many went quietly away, slipping their moorings to reality and drifting off into some other world — in effect, dying before their physical existence ceased on this earth. He himself had done much the same thing with his hours and days of fantasy. But he had done it deliberately, and had been able to return at will. He had done it to preserve his sanity, to give his mind something to focus on.

He fumbled about in the darkness until he found the crust of bread and tried to force himself to gnaw off a piece with his toothless gums. It was dry and hard. He located his mug of water and soaked the end of the bread. Then he tried again. The tasteless ball of dough in his mouth caused his stomach to retch. He spat out the bread into his pail. It was no use; he could not eat. His body had shut down and was continuing on its downward slide toward death. Why was it so hard just to let go and accept it? It couldn't be all that painful. Compared to what he had already been through, it would have to be a relief. At least he would be done with this living hell.

But a small, steady flame burned deeply inside him — a flame that animated his wasted body and refused to be quenched. Somehow, a combination of cunning, patience, and luck had allowed him to survive these last twenty years. And he was not ready to give up just yet. One last desperate gamble remained. Tomorrow, when the turnkey came to leave his food and empty his latrine pail, Dupré would use the only material thing of any value he had left — his empty ivory plan — to bribe the Arab turnkey to bring him a tiny vial of sulphuric acid from the infirmary. Then he would make his last bid for survival.

The Arab turnkey brought the tiny, glass-stoppered vial of sulphuric acid late the next day just before dark, unlocking the sliding panel in the door and silently passing it to Dupré. The doctor was due to make his weekly rounds of the solitary cell blocks the next day. By the time the doctor arrived, he would have gone without food for three days. He carefully placed the vial of acid under his bunk and lay down on the hard board to rest. He was feeling light headed and very weak and slept only intermittently, awaking often with disturbing dreams. The night seemed endless, but finally he sat up on the edge of his bunk and put his mind in neutral, awaiting daylight. It finally came, creeping into his cell from the open grill above, dispelling the blackness. He drank some water and waited. The light grew to its usual mid-morning dimness.

Just after the turnkey came to empty his latrine bucket, he took the vial and poured the sulphuric acid into his spoon. The acid began to react with the metal. He cautiously sniffed the fumes rising from the spoon. The searing smoke burned his nose, and he turned his head away, coughing and wiping his watering eyes. Then he carefully inhaled the fumes several more times before hiding the spoon and the vial under his bunk.

Just before midday he heard a key grating in the lock, and his cell door swung outward.

"You said you wanted to see the doctor," the Arab grunted, motioning him outside.

Dupré had to steady himself against the wall of the corridor as he preceded the man toward the room just off the inner courtyard of the quadrangle the doctor used for an examining room. Because a convict had once attacked and killed a doctor in one of these rooms, all convict patients were required to come before the doctor completely naked so no weapons could be hidden. Dupré knew this and stopped outside the door, stripping off his jumper and dropping his pants, leaving them on the floor as the turnkey opened the door and waved him inside.

The doctor got up from the small table and came over to him. Dr. Rousseau was a tall man with graying mustache and sidewhiskers. He wore a white cotton jacket and tan trousers. Dupré knew this medical man only by hearsay, and he stood nervously as the doctor ran a professional eye over his thin body.

"Hmm. . . ." He placed a big hand on Dupré's shoulder and turned him around. "What seems to be your problem?" he asked brusquely.

Dupré coughed and wiped the back of his hand across his runny nose. "Don't know. Been coughing a lot. My chest feels bad."

Dr. Rousseau grabbed Dupré's chin and turned the small man's head toward the light, looking intently into his irritated eyes. Then he took the stethoscope that hung around his neck, placed it in his ears, and pressed the other end to Dupré's chest. "Take a deep breath."

Dupré inhaled and exhaled.

"Again."

He moved the stethoscope to several other spots and repeated the process. Then he flipped the instrument out of his ears and picked up a pencil on the table and wrote something in a notebook.

"Remove this man to the hospital," he commanded the turnkey without looking up. "He has bronchitis."

Dupré nearly collapsed with relief. His ruse had worked. If he couldn't be sent to the hospital because of anemia or starvation, at least he could escape the cell because of a phony condition he had created himself. The fumes had caused enough rattling in his chest temporarily to fool the doctor.

A quarter of an hour later two guards escorted Dupré and five other convicts down the hill to the boat landing for the trip across the intervening strip of sea to the infirmary on Isle Royale. In a building at the foot of the hill each convict was given a slip for the hospital on Royale.

The twenty-four-foot longboat arrived at the stone quay, and the five were herded onto the middle thwarts between six big, strong-armed oarsmen. Two armed guards sat near the stern and one at the helm. Without ceremony the lines were cast off, and the oars dipped into the water, the boat gliding out past the stone jetty. Then they hit the gentle heave of the open sea as they passed the end of the island. It was only a few hundred yards across to Royale, but a stiff, on-shore breeze was blowing and the boat began to leap and plunge, causing the rowers considerable trouble. Dupré clung to the thwart, feeling giddy. He shut his eyes against the stabbing points of light caused by the sun flashing off the cresting waves like a million brilliant jewels.

By the time they were half way across, three of the convicts had become seasick and vomited into the bottom of the boat. The oarsmen were cursing them as they attempted to bring the boat head-up into the wind and waves. Dupré's stomach tightened, and he silently retched a time or two, but there was nothing in his stomach to bring up.

The boat finally slid into the lee of Isle Royale, and the sunburned, sweating oarsmen brought the boat to the landing. Dupré stumbled getting out of the boat. He was terribly weak, and the hot afternoon sun was beating down on his bare head like a hammer on an anvil. One of the other convicts took his arm and helped him up the pebbled path toward the white administration building at the top of the hill. They had to stop and rest twice before they got there. Dupré looked at his helper, a big man named René Arnette. He knew him only in passing but, like himself, René had been classed as incorrigible. He smiled his thanks as he sank to the ground for a few moments' rest. The sunny hillside and the palm trees swam in his vision as tears filled his eyes. He had won. Somehow he was still alive. He was in the fresh air and sunshine and among people again. Whatever happened from here on, even if he died from his ill treatment, he at least would die in better surroundings, and he would go out knowing he had fought the penal administration every step of the way.

The flame did not go out. It flickered feebly several times during the next few weeks, but Marcel Dupré survived. Much of the time during the first few days he slept. The phony symptoms of bronchitis quickly disappeared, and the doctor who had ordered him to the ramshackle wooden hospital on Isle Royale finally realized what Dupré's problem really was. Dr. Rousseau checked on him daily, ordering the convict attendants to feed him a little milk, alternating with a little broth until Dupré's stomach could tolerate it. Then, very gradually, he worked him up to tapioca, a small piece of bread, then bananas, and finally to other solid food. His system began to function once more, without the vomiting and dysentery. He was able to walk around a little, and each day grew stronger and began to take an interest in his surroundings again.

The remaining days of his ninety-day sentence ran out and expired. Since hospital time counted as time served, he would not have to return to the solitary cell. The hospital, primitive as it was, still looked like heaven compared to what he had been used to. The long, white wooden building had twenty-four beds on each side. The beds consisted of three boards on a frame, topped with a thin, palm fiber mattress and one sheet. The glassless windows were open to the outside with only wooden shutters that were always propped open. The wooden floor was sprinkled with creosote once a week. The strong smell of this chemical mingled with the stench of latrine pails, carbolic acid, and sour vomit.

One of the doctors made the rounds each day. As the weeks passed, Dupré gradually grew stronger and put on weight. When he had first been able to get up and totter to the latrine pail at the foot of his bed, he noticed the looks in the eyes of some of the other patients. It was a look of detached curiosity that said — "I wonder how long this one will last?" But he ignored them and continued to eat more and make good progress until even a convict attendant remarked how he had filled out the hollows of his skeletal frame. Dupré estimated he gained about twenty pounds during his stay in the hospital.

A man was brought and placed in the bed next to him. The newcomer was gaunt and shaking with an attack of malarial fever. Dupré could see that it was nearly over with him. He appeared to be getting help too late. He had no physical reserves to call on to rally.

Just at daylight one morning as Dupré was using the latrine pail at the foot of his bed, he heard the man's breath rattling and then suddenly cease. The patient on the other side was out of bed in a flash and snatched the man's shoes. Another convict hobbled over and ran a hand under the mattress and took a small sack of tobacco and cigarette papers. A few minutes later an attendant came down the walkway between the beds.

"Better check on Jean," one of the patients told him.

The attendant looked closely at Jean then took a small mirror from his shirt pocket and held it before the man's face. There was no breath. He pulled the sheet over the dead man's head and then ran his hands under the mattress and looked under the bed. Finding nothing, he stalked off with a grim face and yelled for two convicts to haul the body out. The attendant had been too slow and had missed the spoils of the dead man's few belongings — things that would normally have been his as a result of his position as infirmary attendant. If the body contained a plan, it would be retrieved before Jean, wrapped in an old sheet, was rowed out at sunset to mid-channel between Saint Joseph and Isle Royale and slid overboard. The sharks in the area were used to regular meals and would be waiting. It would be a rare occurrence if the rocks that weighted the sheet hauled the body to the bottom before the sharks tore the corpse to shreds. Sometimes the feeding frenzy was so great that several attacked at once, causing the body to bounce on end across the water in a macabre dance. The convicts who were assigned to burial detail invariably came back ashen faced and shaken, having just seen the fate that awaited them.

Dupré was finally discharged and, since his sentence was up, he was returned to the prison compound on the mainland. During the trip aboard the forty-foot sloop, he breathed in great lungsful of the fresh sea air and thought optimistically of the future. The doctor, at Dupré's request, had written an order that stated he was to be given only light duty due to his frail constitution. He would be set to work in the bakery, or as a clerk, or at some other such task that would take the place of his being returned to one of the jungle camps. This written order would undoubtedly save his life. No more would he be required to go out into the jungle each morning, naked as the day he was born, with an axe on his shoulder to sweat all day chopping trees with wood so hard it would turn the edge of the sharpest axe, all the while being constantly wet and tormented by clouds of mosquitoes. Inadequate food, hard labor, parasites that laid eggs under the fingernails and toenails, malaria, and the lack of any sanitation that caused every small cut and abrasion to become quickly an infected, open wound — these were the things that killed even strong men within a few weeks or months. A constant turnover of convicts sickened and died as they labored in these camps that were isolated from each other and from Saint Laurent on the Maroni River by several miles of jungle footpaths.

Upon his return to Saint Laurent, he was again clothed in the familiar red and white stripes and confined to the barracks where he was greeted warmly by a dozen old friends who had feared he would never live through his sentence on the Isles du Salut, the so-called Healthy Islands, named by the early settlers because it was there they took refuge when fever was raging on the mainland.

Before Dupré was even assigned a new duty, he was already quietly planning his next attempt at escape.

Chapter Four

The morning after the banquet for the French ambassador, while the fog was still muffling the city in a cool, damp silence, Jay McGraw walked from his boardinghouse to Market Street where he caught a cable car to the Ferry House. Across the bay at the Oakland railroad terminal was a train that, in less than two hours, would start its run to Chicago. He would be aboard, locked inside the Wells Fargo express car, guarding whatever valuable cargo the company had acquired for this trip. During the past two years he had gotten so accustomed to this run that he no longer had pangs of regret at having to leave his adopted city, even for the two weeks or so it would take the express to run to Chicago and back.

As the cable car neared the· foot of Market Street, Jay pulled out his gold-plated pocket watch and popped open the case. Still plenty of time, he didn't need to hurry. Not that he could do anything about hurrying the Oakland ferry boat. He slipped the watch back into his jacket pocket, fingering it with loving care. He didn't need to open the back of the case to read the inscription; he knew it by heart. Wells Fargo & Company had presented him with this watch seven months earlier as a token of appreciation for his defense of the express car in a wild gun battle with robbers who had attacked the train in Wyoming. The terse inscription on the back of the watch gave only a clue to the full story. It was more than just a robbery attempt — much more, as it turned out. That had all happened last fall — October, 1883. How long ago it already seemed! He had been treated and fêted as a hero. But, after a time, his adventures became old news, and he learned the ancient lesson that fame is fleeting. The one thing that had endured was the increase in pay the company had given him, and he could just about name his own work schedule. He had asked his boss not to have to start any runs east on weekends, if at all possible.

His wish had been granted, but now it was a foggy, damp Monday morning, and the train to Chicago awaited him across the bay. Something he thought of, though, as he swung down from the cable car at the Ferry Building was the fact that the company now regarded him being so valuable as a messenger that he might be stuck in this job and never get offered any higher position. This didn't particularly bother him, even though he was approaching twenty-seven years of age. He loved the outdoors and adventure and physical activity. The last thing he wanted at this point was to be cooped up in some office or bank ten hours a day, six days a week, filling out vouchers or keeping ledgers, even in one of the coveted positions as a Wells Fargo agent. He might eventually come to that, but for now this was enough. He breathed deeply of the cool fog before he entered the Ferry Building.

"Jay!"

The sound of his own name snapped him out of his reverie. "Bill Strunk. What are you doing here?"

It was another of the Wells Fargo messengers. The young man strode toward him through the flowing crowd of early-morning ferry passengers. He wore the short jacket and stiff-billed railroad cap with the brass Wells Fargo name in front.

McGraw gripped his friend's hand. "What's up?" he asked. "I didn't know you were on the schedule today."

"I am now," the lean, blond man replied. "I'm taking your run to Chicago."

"What? Why?" McGraw's head was in a whirl. What could have happened? Was he being fired? He thought frantically of something he might have done to warrant being let go. Bill Strunk was one of the junior messengers who had been with the company less than a year.

Strunk shrugged. "All I know is, I was told to head you off here this morning and tell you to report to Anthony Artello's office right away."

McGraw's heart sank into the pit of his stomach. Artello was the district superintendent for Wells Fargo & Company. He was the top man in this area, and nobody went to see him, especially a lowly messenger, unless something was gravely amiss.

"I've got to go get my ticket. The boat'll be loading in a few minutes," Strunk said. "I can't wait to get back and find out what the big news is."

"News?" McGraw's mind was still in a fog.

"Why they pulled you off your run to go see the big boss." He grinned and slid off into the crowd.

Jay stood pondering the situation for a few moments, then he shook his head and retraced his steps to the street and headed for the nearest cable car.

Jay McGraw sat in the outer, oak-paneled office, turning his cap nervously in his lap and wondering if he should have removed the shoulder holster and the Colt Lightning he carried near his left arm under his jacket. But there had been no time. Strunk had told him to report immediately, and he had done so, taking the cable car directly to the Wells Fargo headquarters building on Montgomery Street. He tried to distract himself by glancing admiringly at the profile of the secretary who sat at the desk across the room, working at one of the newest model Remington typewriting machines. She wore silver-rimmed spectacles, a high-necked, starched shirtwaist, and her dark hair was done up on top of her head, giving her a rather severe appearance. Even though there were a few streaks of gray in her hair, Jay guessed from the firm, fine-textured white skin of her face and neck that she was no older than her early thirties.

McGraw had just begun to calm down when the door to the inner office burst open and a man in a dark suit came out. Jay recognized Anthony Artello.

"Ah, Mister McGraw! Good of you to come so quickly. Come in, come in." He ushered Jay into his office and closed the door behind them. Motioning Jay to a red leather armchair, he walked around behind his desk and sat down.

McGraw sat stiffly, his cap in his lap, and waited.

"Cigar?"

"No, thank you."

The short, balding man with the heavy eyebrows selected one for himself from the humidor on his desk, clipped the end off with a penknife hanging from his watch chain, struck a match, and lighted it, blowing a cloud of smoke toward the ceiling. Then he leaned forward, resting both elbows on his desk top.

"Wells Fargo normally doesn't operate this way . . . I mean snatching employees off the job without prior notice. But this company was founded and grew because the men in charge were not afraid to seize opportunities when they presented themselves."

McGraw nodded, having no idea what the regional superintendent was getting at.

"We have such an opportunity now." He paused to puff on his cigar. "Have you ever heard of a man named Marcel Dupré?"

McGraw searched his memory quickly. "No, sir."

"He is an escaped convict from the penal colony in French Guiana on the coast of South America. He somehow made it to this country and has taken refuge in an old mission church south of here. He will not come out of this sanctuary until he is assured by the U. S. authorities that he will be given asylum in this country and will not be turned over to the French or deported. As you can probably imagine, this has created all kinds of diplomatic maneuverings. This would normally be only a minor diplomatic incident that would be handled routinely by the politicians. But the problem is, this Marcel Dupré has brought with him a huge, handwritten manuscript that he wrote while a prisoner, detailing all the horrors and brutality of that penal colony."

Unable to sit still, Artello got up and paced around the desk, puffing on his cigar. He stopped and stared out the window that overlooked Montgomery Street. "He has let it be known through the priest at the mission church that he wants to get this manuscript to a publisher. As you can imagine, this would be a great international embarrassment to the French government. In fact, this has happened at the worst possible time for the French. I don't know if you follow French politics at all, but since Eighteen Seventy-One there have been many changes of government in France. The Republicans are currently in power, but there have been many revelations of scandals in high places. The upper classes, the clergy, and the professional army officers are all opposed to the current regime. Because of this nearly all the energies of this current government are being expended to ensure their own survival. In fact, that's the main reason Charles Lacroix, the French ambassador, is in this country . . . trying to pry money out of Congress to prop up their shaky regime. Officially, though, his trip to the States is a good will tour to help strengthen relations between our two countries, and so forth . . . you know the old political horse shit. Lacroix spoke at a dinner here in San Francisco last night."

"Yes, sir. I was there."

"Oh?" Artello turned from the window, arching his heavy brows.

"I was the guest of a police detective friend of mine," he hastened to add, squirming in his chair, and wishing he had kept his mouth shut. He suspected that even District Superintendent Artello had not been invited to this high-class affair.

"As I started to say, this business with the fugitive convict has put a very wobbly French government in a delicate position with the U. S. government. If our country decides to give political asylum to Marcel Dupré, his book will almost certainly be published and cause untold damage to the French regime because it could reveal a totally corrupt, inhumane penal system the French have espoused since Eighteen Fifty-Eight.

"If, on the other hand, we turn this convict over to the French to be sent back to prison in Guiana, the French officials will be very pleased, but our government will be criticized by many for knuckling under to pressure from the French and going against our own principles of freedom and fair play. In the meantime Marcel Dupré is claiming the ancient right of sanctuary in a church, and even the French would not dare touch him while he's there."

McGraw nodded, silently, trying to absorb all this and assumed the black-mustachioed superintendent would finally get around to telling him how he would fit into it.

"Now, then," Artello continued, taking a final puff and stubbing out his half-smoked cigar in a brass ashtray on his desk, "here's where Wells Fargo comes in. If we can somehow get Marcel Dupré's manuscript from him and transport it safely to a publisher in New York, we can reap an enormous amount of good publicity for the company. We have a great reputation already, but we will become known as the company that is safer than the U. S. mail, a company that can be entrusted with any valuables for safe and sure delivery to any destination. If we can pull this one feat, it would mean many thousands of dollars' worth of free publicity."

"When are the diplomats going to decide what to do with him?" McGraw asked.

"Forget all that," Artello said, waving his hand impatiently and returning to the chair behind his desk. "All the political wrangling between governments has nothing to do with Wells Fargo. We are in the express and banking business. Until a political decision is made, there is nothing illegal about someone from Wells Fargo trying to get this Dupré to let us have his manuscript for safe transport to a publisher."

McGraw had a sinking feeling about who this someone from Wells Fargo was going to be.

"That's why you're here. Mister Tevis has instructed me to put the best man we have on this project. He suggested you and, of course, I thought that was an excellent idea." The superintendent paused, leaning back in his chair and eyeing McGraw for his reaction.

Even though he had seen it coming, Jay was as stunned as if he had just stopped a fist from James J. Corbett. Lloyd Tevis, the head of the famous Wells Fargo & Company, had personally requested that he, Jay McGraw, a lowly express-car messenger with only two years of service be assigned such a job! Since he had been with the company, though, McGraw had gained a measure of fame and brought his employers public praise. He wondered if he really had a choice in the matter at hand. His express messenger job was getting very dull and routine again. This, at least, would provide a little variety.

"It is strictly voluntary, of course," Artello said, when McGraw didn't reply immediately.

41

"What do I have to do?" Jay asked cautiously.

"Go south to the San Antonio de Padua Mission church, meet with Marcel Dupré, somehow persuade him to let you have his manuscript, bring it back here for shipment to New York. You'll accompany it, of course, in the express car. It depends on how he reacts, but you might also want him to sign something giving you or Wells Fargo permission to act as his literary agent in selecting a publisher. This manuscript may be so poorly written it's not publishable in its present form. It may have to be totally revised, and I know it'll have to be translated from the French. But I have a feeling the book will cause a sensation when it's published. I understand it even contains an exposé of brutality in the French Foreign Legion. And Wells Fargo will reap the reward of a great publicity coup for delivering it safely into the hands of a publisher." He grinned under his thick mustache. He tapped an antler-handled letter opener on his desk pad and glanced toward the window then back at Jay McGraw. He had hardly stopped moving since Jay had come into the room and still seemed nervous.

"Why do I get the feeling there is more to this than just running an errand for the big boss? If it's only a matter of picking up a package, there is probably a Wells Fargo agent closer to that mission than I am." Jay disliked talking to his superiors as an equal, but he had put his life on the line for the company before and felt he deserved to know the whole, unvarnished truth. If he strongly suspected he was being used or deceived in any way, he would have to give a firm, but polite "No" to this offer and leave.

"Well, there will be some diplomacy involved," Artello said, rising from his chair and walking toward the window again. "You'll have to show him that you're not out to steal his preciously-guarded manuscript. And there may be a communication problem, since I don't know if he speaks any English, or if the priest at that mission church can translate." McGraw waited for more. Artello stood still, staring out the front window, his back to him. The silence stretched out to a full minute or longer. "Oh, there is one other thing you should probably be aware of," Artello finally continued. "We have heard some rumors . . . unconfirmed, of course . . . that the French authorities have secretly hired some killers to eliminate Dupré and destroy his manuscript so it will never see the light of day."

This announcement was delivered in the same matter-of-fact way, and he did not turn around, so Jay could not read his expression. *So that was it,* McGraw thought. *More in the line of undercover police work than the job of a courier.*

"He must have known he was in danger or he wouldn't have sought sanctuary in that church," McGraw put in thoughtfully.

"Perhaps," Artello nodded, moving back toward his desk. "But you must remember that this man has been imprisoned for years and is not likely to be too trusting of any government officials, even those in our country. So taking sanctuary in a church may be his way of making sure he'll get political asylum here before turning himself in."

Possibly, Jay thought, *but not very likely. The man would probably not have fled to the United States in the first place if he had been afraid of being sent back.* But there were just too many things he didn't know to make any kind of a judgment.

He questioned the district superintendent further but found that Artello could add little more to what he had already said. Now it was up to him to decide.

"Time is critical," Anthony Artello warned. "If you are going, you must start this morning. If not, we must find someone else quickly."

McGraw hesitated only a second. "I'll take the job."

For the first time that morning Artello seemed to relax. A huge smile spread across his broad face. He thrust out his hand. "Good! Good! I'll have my secretary type a letter of introduction for you. If you can pull this off successfully, there will be a nice bonus in it for you."

A chill went up Jay's back at this. Bonuses were not paid for routine work. A strong premonition of danger clung to him like his sweat-damp clothing even as he emerged once more into the foggy street. He hoped he would return alive and well enough to collect that bonus.

Chapter Five

From his earliest days in the prison colony, Marcel Dupré had classified the convicts into two categories. One group was composed of those individuals who had made new lives for themselves inside the prison by force or submission. They would never try to escape. They had given themselves over to licentious homosexual behavior, or to gambling, or to some sort of graft, or to all three. The *forts à bras,* literally strong arms, were the physically powerful, unscrupulous criminals who dominated the weaker ones around them, fought with other *forts à bras* to establish their own circle of influence, like jungle cats establishing a territory, bribed guards, bought and sold any luxury they wanted with money stolen, gambled for, extorted, or obtained by graft. These were the feared ones who actually ran the prison from within. They could often literally get away with murder, since most quarrels and feuds were settled with homemade knives in the darkness of the midnight barracks or blockhouses and, even if there were a dozen eyewitnesses, no one dared speak up under questioning of the authorities, or his life was forfeit to the killer's friends at the next opportunity. These *forts à bras* kept the weaker ones in line and, like it or not, the weaker men had to give in and go along.

The other major category of convicts was the one to which Marcel Dupré himself belonged. He agreed they were the incorrigibles. They were the ones who had never allowed their confinement to break their spirits. They tried to survive their present circumstances with something of their dignity and humanity intact while thinking of nothing but escape. Thoughts and dreams and plans of escape occupied their minds every waking hour. It was the only thing that gave them hope and saved them from total despair. In his twenty years in Guiana, Dupré had attempted to escape seven times. All of these had ended in failure. Twice he had tried alone, but the other attempts had been with from two to nine companions. These *cavales* had lasted from only a few hours to one of six months when he was actually safe in Venezuela. He was working at a laborer's job when the dictator of that country, due to a murder committed by an escaped French convict, decided to round up all French convicts he could find and deport them to the prison colony at Guiana. Before he could get away, Dupré and a friend were caught in this net and put on the next ship to Saint Laurent. After that one he had almost fallen into despair. He had let himself become careless, or he might still be a free man. As the days of his freedom had stretched into weeks and then months, he had allowed himself to believe that his freedom would last the rest of his life. Thus he was not as wary as he might have been when the foreman of his road work crew called him away from the span of mules he was using to drag the roadbed level and began asking some questions about his past. Just as he realized where the questions were leading, he bolted for the woods but was quickly overtaken and put into chains, awaiting the arrival of the Venezuelan police.

The depression he had experienced after arriving back in Saint Laurent was profound and lasted for almost a month. For this attempt, his seventh, he was locked in the blockhouse to await the next semi-annual sitting of the Tribunal Maritime Special. This confinement in the blockhouse was punishment in itself. The men here were not allowed to go outside to work. They were fed only the bare minimum, with alternating days of bread and water. Forty of them were crowded into a stone building sixteen feet wide, forty feet long, and twelve feet high. Barred windows were eight feet above the floor and admitted the only light and air. They were tormented by swarms of mosquitoes that feasted on their near-naked bodies at will. At night the men slept on bare-board bunks that let down from the walls on each side. They slept with their heads to the wall and their feet to the center. A long bar, called the "bar of justice," was run down the length of the building from front to back. As the bar was slipped into place at night, each convict took the end of it and passed it through the metal ring that circled one ankle. When the bar on each side connected all the convicts, it was pushed through a hole in the back of the building and locked from the outside. Thus each man slept with one ankle locked to one of two iron bars each night. The hours from dusk to dawn were filled with the incessant clicking sound of these ankle rings rattling against the iron bars as the men moved and turned in their sleep. There was the usual snoring, muttering, groaning, and men talking disjointedly in their slumber. Many were the sleepless nights that Dupré spent swatting mosquitoes as he lay on his back and stared up into the darkness — a darkness softened only by the dim oil lamp suspended from the ceiling and barely illumining the narrow center aisle. The fetid atmosphere — with the smell of unwashed bodies, cigarette smoke, unemptied latrine pails, along with the lack of food and exercise — was debilitating. Except for the company of other men in the blockhouse, it was almost as bad as the solitary cells on Saint Joseph.

It was during this two-month wait in the block-house for the T. M. S. to sit that he witnessed his first formal execution. Half crazed by starvation and brutal treatment, a prisoner in one of the jungle camps had attacked and killed a guard with his axe. For this he had been sentenced by the T. M. S. to lose his head to the "widow-maker" — only one of many names for the guil-lotine. The condemned man, whom Dupré did not know, spent the last few weeks of his life in confinement. From all reports through the prison grapevine, these were weeks of contentment. The gossip around the gambling blanket in the block-house was that the man had gone insane. But the more perceptive of the convicts offered the opinion that the man was not crazy. By comparison to his life, death on the guillotine was actually something to look forward to — a quick escape from this earthly hell to an unknown, but hopefully better, existence. Whatever the case, the night before the execution was a sleepless one in Dupré's blockhouse. The men sat up, smoking and talking and telling tales of friends and acquaintances long dead and of adventures experienced or heard. As each man's story ended, another took up the thread and started a narrative of his own. A restlessness pervaded the place. Death showed its many gruesome faces in Guiana several times each week. Yet there was something so awful and so final about the guillotine that these hardened men drew together in an unspoken bond to celebrate life as if their all-night vigil could somehow push back what was coming with the dawn.

Before sunup, just as there was light enough to see, they could hear the executioner and some turnkeys putting the final touches to the guillotine that was set up just outside in the courtyard. The sun was just gaining strength, but the heat of the day had not yet set in when the men in the blockhouse heard footsteps, voices, and the clang of an iron door in the blockhouse across the courtyard.

"They've come to get him," one of the smaller men reported. He was sitting on the shoulders of a *forts à bras* and grasping the bars of one of the high windows. "*Mon Dieu!* He's walking outside like he's going to a picnic."

There were muffled voices from the courtyard.

"What are they saying?" one of the men below whispered urgently.

The man at the window strained to hear. "It's the administrator and six guards. They told him it was time. And he said it was a beautiful day, and he was ready to go."

There were some low whistles from the men below the windows.

Marcel Dupré sat on his bunk with his back against the opposite wall. He wanted to know nothing of the details of this. It held no fascination for him, and he tried to think of other things.

Just then a key rattled in the lock of the iron door. The door to the barracks swung open and two guards appeared. One had a paper in his hand from which he read aloud.

"Champlain, Paquette, Dupré. . . ." Ten names he read off. Then: "Outside!"

Dupré's heart fell. By random choice he had been selected as one of twenty — ten from each blockhouse — to be an official witness to this execution. Even though the sun was barely up and its rays were just touching the tops of the buildings, Dupré slitted his eyes at the relative brightness of the outdoors as he and the nine others filed out under the eyes of the guards.

Bang!

Dupré jumped at the noise of the heavy blade slamming down as the executioner tested the machine. The widow-maker loomed gaunt above them as they were formed up on either side of it and ordered to kneel on the hard cobblestones. Dupré's thin body was covered by a ragged pair of pants, shredded off just below the knees, and a half-sleeve cotton shirt tied together in front with two pieces of string. The hard stones dug into his knees as he went down in line with his companions.

The condemned man was brought out, flanked by two guards. He looked around at them, half smiling. "Why the long faces? Don't be sad for me." He took a deep breath. "Isn't it a beautiful morning? I'm going to a much better place." He stopped at the foot of the instrument of death and looked up at it. A shadow crossed his face, but he quickly recovered himself and turned to the executioner. "C'mon, let's get this over with."

The guards led him up, bound his hands behind his back, and stretched him full length on his stomach, his neck across the notched board.

"Make a quick, neat job of it, my friend," the man said to his executioner.

"Arms across your chests!" the guards ordered the kneeling witnesses.

They all obeyed immediately. The guards stepped aside, and the executioner took his place.

"Heads bowed!" a guard barked.

Thankfully, Dupré bent his neck and looked down at the stones, his forearms crossed against his chest. Total silence reigned. Everyone seemed to be holding his breath.

Ssshhhuunnkk!

"C'en est fait!" — "It's over!" — the men at the blockhouse windows cried.

Dupré looked up. A bloody head lay in the basket, and a red stream flowed from the trunk that jerked spasmodically. Nauseated, he dropped his eyes, breathing heavily.

He had never forgotten that sight. The condemned man had probably been correct — he had left them to a fate worse than his own. All of Dupré's seven escape attempts had ended in failure and had been punished by periods of solitary confinement and extension of his sentence until he knew he would never leave Guiana alive unless it were by his own wits and luck. Several dozen men he could name who had attempted to escape with him were now dead — some killed in the attempt, some killed by the merciless jungle, some drowned, some dead of fever and dysentery, some killed by guards or other convicts, two killed by the Indian tribes in the jungle, and three who had lost their heads to the guillotine.

The years and the terrible existence had taken

their toll. He knew of only four or five men he considered friends who were still alive after many years of confinement in that hell. The rest of his friends were dead or were younger men who had come here in more recent years. His next escape attempt would be with some of these younger, stronger men, the few he felt he could trust. He would lend them his vast store of experience gained by many failures.

On the surface everything was the same. He had come and gone to his daytime job outside the prison compound at Saint Laurent to work as a clerk in one of the offices of the penal administration. He had been given the task of cleaning out a huge storage room containing boxes of inactive files that needed to be sorted, put in some kind of order, dusted, and shelved. It was the neglected accumulation of years. The job was not taxing on his strength. In fact it was proving to be very interesting, almost like browsing in a library all day by himself. This job afforded him the opportunity to do something he had been wanting to do for a long time. He had begun making a written record of his life in Guiana and the Foreign Legion before that. Each day he retrieved several loose, blank sheets of paper from the many boxes of files. Each night in the barracks after supper he propped himself up on his bunk and wrote. He dredged things from his memory he had almost forgotten. As he wrote, impressions and incidents flowed from his pencil. He covered page after page with bold script as the story of the legion and the penal colony took shape.

Darkness came and the head gambler rattled his dice in their cup, as a signal for the men to gather around the blanket spread on the floor of the center aisle to begin the nightly game. Dupré would then light his candle on a scrap of tin and continue to write by its flickering glow. His personal history, experiences, and observations burst from his pent-up heart and mind.

Over a period of six weeks the manuscript he kept wrapped in oilskin under his bunk grew to be more than three inches thick, and he was still adding to it. Finally, after he had written himself out, he went back and re-read it, correcting, changing a few details, rewording, smoothing out the story with all its horror and corruption. Nowhere in it, he noted sadly, was there a hint of joy or laughter. What a way to have spent one's adult life! Besides his own experiences he added the stories of other convicts he knew to round out the story of the colony. He related tales of murder and madness, death in all forms and moral corruption, both among convicts and among many of the penal administration. Everything he committed to paper was as accurate and detailed as he could make it. Even though he had lived it, Dupré was struck by the horrifying and depressing picture it presented after he had read it for the second time. It was certain to be a shock to someone who had never experienced this existence. The entire penal colony was a blot on the face of French justice. It was much more inhumane than the dreaded Penal Battalion of the French Foreign Legion.

Dupré found only one problem with his job of records librarian — it allowed him no opportunity to accumulate any money. And he would have to have money to prepare for his next *cavale*. Each man in a *cavale* had to contribute something, usually money. Besides cunning, experience, and luck, money was the primary necessity for any successful escape. It was the most essential ingredient for bribes, a boat, forged papers, clothing, food, and any number of other things that might be required.

He had to find some way of accumulating a few hundred francs. The nightly gambling games in the barracks were a good source of money, but those games were held by the toughest criminal, whoever he might be at the time. If Dupré were a cook or a middleman in some kind of distribution chain, he would be able to skim off a little extra for himself. Even the convict who made the coffee for the men in the barracks was able to water it down and later sell the extra beans he saved for a little money.

Dupré automatically raised his arms to be searched by a turnkey before entering the prison compound each evening. Most of the prisoners who were not confined to the jungle camps, blockhouses, or the islands, held jobs outside the prison compound in Saint Laurent as street sweepers, servants, cooks for the civilian authorities or the families of the penal administration. For these jobs they were paid only pennies a day, and the *liberés* competed for these same jobs. However, the convicts always won out because the *liberé* could not afford to work as cheaply, since he had to support himself. The *liberés* were men who had finished serving their sentences and been released. However, since they had no money or any means of acquiring any, they usually clustered in Saint Laurent, subsisting on handouts, drinking cheap rum, and earning a little by loading and off-loading the infrequent ships that docked there.

A few of the more ambitious *liberés*, who were forbidden by French law to leave Guiana until they had been free as long as they had been prisoners, made some money by going into the nearby jungles every day with butterfly nets and catching some of the rare and beautiful insects that were common to that region. King among these butterflies was the magnificent Blue Morpho. By accumulating collections of these butterflies, mounting them, and selling them to passengers on ships that called at Saint Laurent, these *liberés* were able to make just enough to live on.

Convicts working in Saint Laurent were not closely guarded. Twelve hours after failing to answer roll call, they were officially listed as missing and were assumed to have escaped. But walls and bars were not the detaining forces in this prison colony. The remoteness of the colony and the hundreds of miles of jungle and sea surrounding it on all sides were the real deterrents against escape. Those, and the ever-present diseases that took such a fearful toll of the ill-fed prisoners.

An idea had gradually evolved in Dupré's mind. He knew two *liberés* who had been friends of his prior to their release. They had not fallen into the trap of hopelessness. They shared a hut on the edge of town and hunted the butterflies in the jungle each day. Dupré knew they were saving their money toward a possible escape. He also knew they were both from Paris and had no experience with boats, large or small. The next afternoon he left his job of sorting, dusting, and filing records nearly an hour early.

"Have to go into town and buy some cigarettes for a friend," he said to the sleepy official who questioned him on the way out of the building.

The official nodded. Dupré was one of the few who labored daily through the heat of the early afternoon when most others in this tropical climate were napping, so the official knew the administration had gotten its day's work out of Marcel Dupré. He went down two dirt streets and cut back toward the edge of town, praying that his two *liberé* friends were at their hut. They were and preparing for an early supper. Two small lizards and some chopped coconut, Dupré noted with disgust as he peered in the open door.

"Marcel! Come in quickly. What are you doing here?" asked the shorter of the two men, dropping a half-skinned lizard and wiping his hands on his ragged trousers.

"Hello, Marcel," the taller, leaner man nodded, gripping his hand.

"Jacques, Phillipe, you're planning a *cavale*. Am I correct?" Dupré said quickly with no preliminaries.

They glanced at one another.

"Aren't half the men in this colony?" the tall Phillipe asked defensively.

"How did you know?" Jacques inquired.

"It's not hard to figure out, the way you're living, in spite of those collections of butterflies you've got over there."

"You're right," Jacques admitted in a lower voice, glancing out the door to make sure no one was within earshot.

Phillipe held a half-empty rum bottle toward him, but Dupré shook his head. He knew these men drank sparingly and that was one reason he had come.

"I'm here on business. If you're planning an escape, I'd like to be in on it."

The two *liberés* glanced at each other and then back at him.

"We heard you were in solitary on Saint Joseph," Jacques said. "Are you sure you're ready for another *cavale* so soon?"

Dupré quickly gave them the details of his confinement and hospitalization. "I've been back on the mainland for several weeks, and they've got me working in the penal administration's records room. I've been resting and eating well. By the time we're ready, I'll be as fit as ever."

"Are you sure you want to try again?" Phillipe asked. "You've already failed seven times. You're a legend in the colony."

"Better to fail another seven times than to remain here. My sentence has already been extended to life."

"But, if you're caught again . . . *mon Dieu!*" exclaimed Phillipe, taking a swig of the rum bottle he still held. "You could get three to five years on Saint Joseph, and that would surely kill you. You were lucky last time."

"I would attack a guard and go to the guillotine before I'd die by inches in those solitary cells," Dupré whispered grimly. "But never mind that. Can I be included in your *cavale?*"

"Marcel, you're a good friend. Certainly you can come with us. We have failed before, but this time, God willing, we will be free men."

"Or dead men," Phillipe added dourly. "One way or another, I'm not coming back from this one."

Chapter Six

Jay McGraw did not own a horse. He had found it an unnecessary expense since coming to the city almost two years before. He had sold his horse and wagon at that time to afford food and lodging until he could find work. It had been more convenient to rent a saddle horse or a rig whenever he was in need of one. And this he intended to do now.

Before he paid a visit to the livery, though, he walked the several blocks from the Wells Fargo office to the Mission Dolores, knocked at the small rectory next door, and asked the house-keeper to see the resident pastor. The house-keeper disappeared, leaving him standing on the front step. A minute later a tall, white-haired priest in a black cassock came to the door.

"May I help you?"

"Father, I need some information. What can you tell me about the Mission San Antonio de Padua?"

The priest furrowed his brow. "Not much, I'm afraid. But come in off the street. I was just having a late breakfast after Mass. Will you join me?"

McGraw shook his head as the priest held the door open for him and then led the way into a small rear kitchen. The warm aroma of coffee dispelled the smell of the chill fog outside.

"I might have a cup of coffee, if you don't mind," Jay said as they sat down at the small kitchen table.

"San Antonio de Padua was one of the original twenty-one missions founded by the Spanish *padres* in the late Seventeen Hundreds," said the priest who had introduced himself as Father William Holding. "The last I heard, it had pretty much fallen into ruin after being abandoned for quite a number of years. This church next door here was also one of those original missions. But, as you can see, it's been kept up, probably because there was more need for it in the city."

McGraw nodded, sipping the coffee the priest had poured for him, his mind racing ahead. "Did you say it was a ruin? You mean there's no priest or congregation there? It's not an active parish or anything?"

"It's been seven or eight years since I was down that way, but at that time there was nobody there but a few Mexican families, keeping some goats and sheep and living in what was left of some of the outbuildings. The roof of the church had partly fallen in and the walls around the place were beginning to crumble. It's a shame to see that historic old place go to ruin like that. The Church or some organization of laymen should try to save it and restore it, if it isn't too far gone already."

McGraw was getting nervous. "But is it still

considered a real church?"

"The Blessed Sacrament was not being kept there, if that's what you mean. But the buildings and the property belong to the Church. What's your interest in this old mission?"

McGraw briefly explained the situation with which he was faced. "But I'm afraid, from what you tell me, that this Marcel Dupré might already be gone or dead if this ruined church is not considered a sanctuary and there is no resident priest present."

"I read about that situation in the newspaper," Father Holding said. "But I don't believe the piece mentioned he was at the Saint Anthony mission. Wish I could be of more help, but I don't really know what state that old church is in now."

McGraw thanked him and left. He went back to his boardinghouse and hurriedly packed a change of clothes, his razor, and toothbrush. Lastly, he took off the holster he wore under his left arm that contained his nickel-plated .38 caliber Colt Lightning. It had been his constant companion for two years since it had been given to him by an Arizona rancher as a reward for saving his daughter's life. He had carried it on all of his messenger express trips, and it had served him well when he really needed it; but lately the double-action mechanism had been giving him trouble, and a gunsmith had not been able to keep it in adjustment. It was Colt's first attempt at a double-action revolver, the gunsmith had told him, and it was a complicated piece of machinery that easily malfunctioned. On impulse, he tucked it away in a drawer. He would buy an old reliable single-action Colt to take along.

He had to hurry if he wanted to be out of the city by noon. The fog had burned off to reveal a warm summer sun, and the breeze off the bay was fresh and clean as he left his boarding house with his few belongings rolled into a blanket and a rain slicker. He rode a cable car to the J. Tompkinson Livery on Minna Street where he rented a long-legged bay gelding and selected an old-style, deep-seated California mission saddle with a slim horn and plain leather *tapederas*.

"I don't know how long I'll be gone . . . maybe only a few days, but here's a deposit. I'll settle up with you when I get back," McGraw told the hostler, handing over some greenbacks and accepting his receipt.

He stopped at Fred Casey's station house to give his friend the news, but Fred had gone to investigate a robbery. Jay scribbled him a note, explaining where he was going, and left it in care of the desk sergeant.

His next stop was at Lunenberg's Gun Shop. Robert Lunenberg greeted him and helped him pick out a good, used rig that consisted of a tooled Mexican leather gun belt with cartridge loops and a blued, single-action Colt .44 with a 4.75 inch barrel and ivory grips. Even though used, Lunenberg assured him, the gun was in excellent condition. McGraw confirmed this as he noted the almost-new finish and tested the smooth, crisp action. Since McGraw was a good customer, Lunenberg knocked off a few dollars from the price.

"I need to get rid of this rig," he said with a grin when McGraw paid him. "It's been in here too long,"

As he buckled on the gun belt and turned to leave, McGraw's eye caught a Winchester carbine in a rack of long guns. On impulse he picked it up and examined it. It, too, had been used but well cared for, with only a few scratches on the walnut stock. It had an octagonal barrel and was also a .44-40 caliber.

"How much for this?"

"Well, since you bought the Colt, I'll let you have it for twenty dollars."

"Throw in a couple of boxes of cartridges, and it's a deal."

"It even comes with a saddle scabbard."

"Good. I'll need it."

Jay paid him and left the shop. He felt a little self-conscious as he tied the leather scabbard on the left side of his saddle and slid the Winchester into it. *Why was he arming himself like this? There was no logical reason for it,* he decided as he dropped the boxes of cartridges into the saddle bags and mounted. It had been pure instinct, but he had learned to trust his instincts.

He pulled his horse's head around and started south.

It was just over a hundred miles to the Saint Anthony of Padua Mission, Jay estimated, studying a map he had brought. For everyone's convenience the *padres* had founded the original missions in California about a day's travel apart. The first night he stopped at a hotel in San José, putting his horse up at the livery. The second day he rode south, avoiding towns and villages, and late in the afternoon passed the old mission of San Juan Bautista. That night he picketed his horse along a grassy stretch of the San Benito River and rolled into his blanket under the stars, using his saddle for a pillow.

He was not used to the hard bed and slept poorly, awaking before daylight with a crick in his neck from the saddle. He was mounted and on his way by five-thirty. His breakfast consisted of some dry bread and cheese he munched as he rode and water from his canteen. The farther south he got, the more he had to resist the urge to push faster. He didn't know the endurance of this rented animal. Consequently, he was careful with him. He didn't want to wind up afoot.

He turned his horse southwest, keeping the jagged peaks of the Pinnacles on his right, and angled toward the Salinas Valley. The hot summer sun rose in a clear sky and began baking out the pungent smells of dry grass, tarweed, and dust. Sweat was soon trickling down his face from under the leather sweatband of his hat, but McGraw was enjoying the peaceful solitude of this ride. Toward noon he struck the sandy riverbed of the Salinas River, choked with cottonwood and willows. The late summer heat had nearly dried up its sluggish flow, but to Jay it was a green oasis of shade and refreshment. He got down, unsaddled, and put his horse on a long picket rope to let him roll and drink while he made himself a snack of biscuit, cheese, and dried beef from his saddle bags.

He lingered for an hour or more before saddling up and heading south, following the river. About six leisurely miles brought him to King City, a town founded some fifteen years earlier as a focal point of the ranches in the area. There were few people on the streets in the heat of early afternoon except for a few old cowboys loafing in the shade of the general store's verandah. They paused in their talk to spit tobacco juice into the dusty street and watch him ride past without stopping. Just out of town he encountered a wooden sign so weathered he could barely read it. It contained one word: **JOLON**. He turned right and splashed across the shallow ford of the Salinas River and rode almost directly south by the sun. If his map was correct, the Saint Anthony Mission was somewhere off to the right of this road, about a dozen miles farther on and about six or seven miles this side of the tiny hamlet of Jolon, in the sequestered Jolon Valley.

The afternoon heat rose in shimmering waves ahead of him. He eased his horse along at a walk, pushed his hat back on his head, and wiped his face with a shirt sleeve. He met no one on the road. The road itself was rough, brush-choked, and appeared little used. The absolute solitude and stillness made him wonder if there was really anything to this story Artello had told him. Jay had not read anything about this affair in the *San Francisco Chronicle*, but there were many days when he missed reading a newspaper altogether. He half expected a lot of people, maybe curious spectators, reporters, politicians, or someone to be around, as he approached the mission. Maybe Marcel Dupré had already been captured or had left the mission church. *Maybe I'm too late,* Jay thought. He mentally kicked himself for not pushing his horse and arriving the day before. If he missed this opportunity by taking his time, it was very possible he could be fired. He shoved this thought to the back of his mind and kept his mount going at a steady walk.

He estimated he had ridden about twelve miles when he came to a rutted wagon road that turned off to the right. He reined up and considered. This should be about where the cut-off to the mission was located, but there was no sign. He could see no farther than a quarter mile down the road where it disappeared into a copse of oak trees. On impulse, he decided to try it and turned his horse into the new road. He was probably on somebody's ranch, and this road led to the house. But he had to find out. He rode for about fifteen minutes along the faint wagon track through an oak-studded valley when he suddenly reined up and stared ahead. There, about a half mile ahead, was the mission. He scanned the layout carefully, wishing he had thought to bring some field glasses. The place appeared to be deserted. Even from this distance the dilapidated state of the buildings was evident.

He urged his horse forward at a walk, eyes darting here and there as he went. Brown, bare hills rose behind the mission while it was fronted by a half mile or more of grassy fields. His eye caught a movement, and his hand went to the butt of his Colt, loosening the rawhide loop from the hammer of the weapon. His heart began to race as he reined up. Then he saw the movement was only a few goats grazing near the long row of tile-roofed arches that formed a walkway to the left of the church building. These animals were either domestic goats gone wild, or he was on someone's ranch land. Father Holding had said the mission was Church property. These animals must belong to the Mexican squatters. But he saw no Mexicans or anyone else. He saw no horses, wagons, or humans, no tracks that anyone had been here recently. The peaceful pastoral scene belied what he had been told about a state of siege existing here. He wondered if maybe Artello had steered him to the wrong mission.

He kneed his horse forward at a walk. Nothing moved but the grazing goats. Silence prevailed. The late afternoon heat rose in shimmering waves, making the image of the mission church waver in his vision.

As he approached to within a hundred yards, the plastered brick loomed much larger. The façade was intact, but he could see where part of the roof had fallen in and a portion of a side wall collapsed. The church had a long-abandoned, forlorn look. McGraw began to wonder what he would do if he found the ruin deserted. How would he get word to Anthony Artello? He would have to ride to a town large enough to have a Western Union office.

His thoughts were suddenly interrupted by the crack of a rifle. The slug tore into the grass a few feet ahead of him. His horse reared at the loud report. McGraw slipped from the saddle, grabbing for the Winchester in the scabbard but missing as the horse plunged in fright. It was all he could do to hold the reins and try to maneuver the horse between himself and the unseen gunman. No more shots came, and he could see nothing but a little white smoke drifting from a grove of trees about eighty yards away. He yanked his Colt while holding the horse's head near the bit with his left hand. Then he turned his mount and began walking him slowly back the way he had come. He crouched slightly to keep his head behind the animal. The grassy field was wide, and there was no other place to hide. The unseen gunman had missed him by several yards. *He must be a very poor shot,* Jay thought. But, since there was no additional firing, maybe it had only been a warning.

He kept his eyes on the trees but held his fire, since he was out of effective pistol range anyway. Whoever it was had probably moved by now. He carefully walked his horse about two-hundred yards until he was well out of sight and range of the grove of oaks. Then, mounting up, he rode off the faint wagon track to make a wide circle around the area where the shot had originated to see if he could spot the ambusher. The valley floor was grassy with intermittent clumps of trees, and he rode slowly and carefully, his Colt drawn but not cocked. He rode for nearly a half mile without seeing a living thing. A rifle shot cracked nearby, and McGraw's horse reared again, nearly throwing him.

"Whoa, boy! Whoa!"

Jay regained his balance as the horse danced in a circle. When the horse turned, McGraw saw a man standing about twenty yards away, holding a Winchester pointed loosely in his direction.

"Raise that Colt up over your head and unload it . . . very carefully."

Still holding the reins in one hand, Jay raised the Colt, half cocked it, flipped open the loading gate, and began turning the cylinder, allowing the cartridges to drop out, one by one.

"Okay, holster it and get the hell outta here." The man worked the lever of the rifle to emphasize the command.

McGraw slid the revolver back into its holster but made no move to leave.

"Who are you?" he stalled. "Am I on some-body's private land?"

The rifleman smirked. "Private. Yeah, that's it. No trespassing. Now git on outta here."

"I was just passing by," McGraw persisted. "Saw that old church and thought I'd stop in to light a candle and offer a prayer." He hoped his voice sounded innocent.

"Huh!" the man grunted. "That ain't no regular church. That old mission's been a ruin for years. You'd best ride on to the next good-sized town. I reckon they'll have a church."

"No priest here?"

"Naw."

"Then you haven't any call to be shootin' at me for goin' inside to look around."

"Look here, mister, this here church building is now on Mister Dean Atherton's private forty-three-thousand-acre spread, and he's hired me and some others to keep off squatters, trespassers, and vandals. I aim to earn my money by doin' just that. Already had to run off some Mexicans who had took up residence in some of them outbuildings."

Keeping the rifle steady by tucking it under one arm, the man reached his free hand into the pocket of his plaid shirt and pulled out a black plug of tobacco, gnawed off a corner, and replaced it. He was silent for a few seconds while he worked the chew into one cheek. He spat the first juice to one side without taking his eyes from McGraw.

"Are you deef, mister? I told you to git on down the road. I ain't tellin' you again."

Jay realized there was nothing more to be gained here so he pulled his horse's head around and spurred him to a trot. He had a strange feeling between his shoulder blades until he was well out of sight. He didn't think the man would shoot him in the back, but he hated the idea of someone holding a loaded rifle on him.

The guard appeared to be lying. But, what now? Jay had come this far, and he wasn't about to let some lean, gap-toothed gunman keep him from getting a look inside that mission. The village of Jolon was only about six or seven miles farther down the road. He would head for it and then consider his next move. When well out of rifle range, he slowed his mount from the jolting trot to a walk and proceeded to reload his Colt from the cartridges in his gun belt.

An hour of easy riding brought him to the edge of Jolon, as the late afternoon shadows were growing long. It was a poor excuse for a village that straggled out ahead of him along one main street. Jolon consisted of a few vacant buildings, weeds sprouting up through the broken boardwalk. There was a general store and a school that appeared to have dismissed its last pupil some years before. The low sun was striking the weathered wooden belfry of a small clapboard church at the far end of the street.

There were not even any loafers in the chairs on the porch of the mercantile, and no dogs in the street. Jolon had definitely seen better times. The only thing stirring was a driver whose stage-coach was preparing to depart from the front of an adobe building about half way down the long block. The driver helped a middle-aged woman up into the coach and slammed the door behind her. He climbed to the box, released the brake, and took up the lines.

"Yeeaahh!" The whip cracked over the backs of the four-horse hitch and the Concord coach lurched into motion. Down the street it rumbled, its wheels churning up the dust. In less than a minute it had reached the end of the street and disappeared around a curve in the road, headed south.

Jay rode down the street, looking for the inevitable saloon. *It should be a good place to start,* he reasoned. Maybe he could get some information about the mission. But he saw no saloon. He reined up at the spot vacated by the stagecoach in front of the largest building in town, a two-story adobe with a wooden balcony reaching out over the boardwalk. A faded sign proclaimed this simply as the **Adobe Hotel**. A fine film of dust lay over everything, including the green leaves of the grapevine that climbed up and partially shaded the upper verandah.

McGraw dismounted, stiff and tired, and tied his horse, making sure the reins allowed the animal to reach the algae-green water in the wooden trough next to the hitching rail.

Inside, the front desk was unmanned. A pendulum clock on the back wall measured the silent seconds with a loud ticking. The murmur of conversation came from a room that opened off to his right. McGraw stood for a moment, allowing his eyes to adjust to the dimness. Then he went through the doorway. Voices stopped when he entered the room, and heads turned to watch him stride to the bar. The place was a combination barroom and dining room for the small hotel McGraw realized, as he ordered a beer and slapped the dust from his clothes with his hat. He laid a ten-cent piece on the bar and sipped at the luke-warm foam while he studied the room behind him in the mirror on the back bar. He could see six men — four at one table and two at another, nursing drinks and playing a desultory game of cards. Jay feigned indifference to the glances they shot in his direction and didn't meet their eyes in the mirror. The Adobe Hotel was obviously the stage stop in this nearly deserted hamlet. *The hardcases must be staying at this hotel,* he reasoned, since he had seen no other horses at the hitching rail out front.

The bartender had retreated to the far end of the bar and resumed reading a magazine. He was a middle-aged man with pouches under his eyes, an enormous mustache that hid his mouth, and a creased, pale face that had seen little sun. He didn't look particularly friendly, but McGraw decided he had to make the effort to draw him into conversation if he was going to find out anything about the Saint Anthony Mission. He didn't want to approach any of the men at the tables. He took his beer mug and slouched along the bar a few feet toward the bartender who stood, leaning on his elbows, perusing a copy of the *Police Gazette*.

"Do you know where the desk clerk is?" Jay asked. "There was nobody out front when I came in."

The bartender looked up owlishly. "I reckon he's around somewhere. Just go out there and give a holler." He went back to his magazine.

McGraw hesitated and then unconsciously lowered his voice slightly. "Do you know anything about the Saint Anthony Mission up the road?"

"What about it?"

Jay thought fast. "I'm down from San Francisco to look it over. A group of citizens is looking into the possibility of restoring it. They sent me to have a look at the property. How would I get in touch with the owner? I've been told it's on somebody's ranch now."

The bartender straightened up and glanced at the men in the room over McGraw's shoulder. The room had gone quiet behind him.

"How long since you seen a newspaper?"

Jay shrugged. "Been a while. Why?"

"Don't you know what's going on out there?"

"At the mission?"

"Yeah. It's been the hottest topic of conversation around here for a week. Reporters swarmin' all over the place. There's some escaped convict holed up out there. He's a Frenchman from someplace outside the country. The French want him back, and there's been a helluva powwow about it. But, I know one thing . . . my bar business has fell off considerable since those politicians were in here a few days back."

"Really?" Jay feigned wide-eyed interest. "Why doesn't the law just go in after him?"

"He ain't wanted by the law here. The convict wants our law to give him protection from being deported to the French authorities. But, as long as he's in that church, nobody can touch him. Something called 'sanctuary.' "

"I thought that's what they called the space up around the altar of a church," Jay grinned.

"I dunno. It's some word like that anyway."

McGraw was aware that the men in the room were all listening to the conversation, even though he was keeping his voice low and was blocking their view of the bartender.

"Think I'll ride out there and see what's going on. Maybe we could use all this publicity to raise money to get the old mission restored. If we wait many more years, there won't be anything left to restore."

"I don't think this would be a good time to go messin' around out there," the bartender said uneasily.

"Won't hurt anything to ride out there and have a talk with this Frenchman," Jay said lightly. "Maybe I can talk him into leaving so I can get on with my business. Is he there by himself? Does he speak English?"

"Better do like the man says and forget it," came a voice from behind him.

McGraw had wondered how long it would take for one of them to speak up. He turned to face the man, leaning his back against the bar, sipping his beer. He was suddenly aware of the tied-down, tooled Mexican holster and the weight of the Colt on his hip, making him look like anything but the innocent he pretended to be.

Jay looked at the speaker, curiously, waiting for him to continue. The man was only about twelve feet from him. He had a massive bulk, a big, round head with black curly hair, and a two-day growth of stubble. He was riffling a deck of cards in his huge hands. A walnut-gripped Army Colt hung in a plain black holster at his side. His clothes looked trail worn. No frills. Strictly business. He looked back up at Jay McGraw.

"You don't want to get mixed up in this. Just ride on back to San Francisco and come back another time."

"Who're you?" Jay asked.

"They call me Waterloo Williams. But that ain't the point. The boys and I have been hired to capture that Frenchman as soon as he shows his head outside that church. And that's what we aim to do. So don't go poking your nose into anything that doesn't concern you."

"You working for the law?" Jay asked indifferently.

Waterloo Williams eyed him up and down, taking in the gunman's rig low on his hip, apparently trying to decide to whom he was talking before he replied. "We're working for the law, right enough. French law." The five men nearby grinned and nodded.

"What Frenchmen hired you?"

A look of profound injury came over Williams's face. "Now, is that a gentlemanly thing to ask? Did I ask who your boss is? Or did I ask who those concerned citizens are who sent you here to see about fixin' up that old church? Hell, I didn't even ask your name . . . mainly because I don't care."

His companions nudged each other and winked, grinning.

"Is he out there by himself?" McGraw asked, as if trying to get this whole picture clearly in his mind.

"You another reporter?" Williams asked suspiciously, sliding his chair back to face McGraw more directly.

"No. Just curious."

"You know what curiosity did to the cat."

The men behind him guffawed and slapped each other.

Thus buoyed by his friends, Williams grew a little more expansive. "There's some priest out there and an old Indian caretaker. But I've got men watching the place. Ain't nobody else goin' in or out of there. We'll see to that. And they haven't got any food. He'll be ready to give up before long."

"What if our government decides to give him protection?" Jay asked, hoping to keep the man talking. This might be his only chance to find out what the situation really was.

"The government didn't hire us. We're bein' paid to do a job, and we'll do it. Ain't nobody goin' to get in our way." He glared at McGraw, as if daring him to say any different.

Jay merely downed the rest of his beer and set the mug on the bar. "Well, it's been nice talking to you gents, but I'd best be gettin' on." He picked up his hat from the bar and started toward the door.

"Tell your friends they can do anything they want at that mission as soon as we have this little French bastard in our hands," Williams said, hitching his wooden chair back around to the table and taking up the cards once more.

McGraw was a few feet from the door when the door frame suddenly lurched sideways in his vision, and he staggered. He felt the floor shudder under his feet and for an instant thought his drink had been drugged. But then came the crashing of glass and wild yelling behind him. He felt a sudden concussion in his legs and clawed for his holstered Colt as he lost his balance, fell sideways against a table, and hit the floor.

Chapter Seven

Jay McGraw was on his back on the floor, his senses reeling, Colt clutched in his hand. The six men went thundering past him, boots booming on the wooden floor as they headed for the door. Then they were gone outside into the street, and it grew suddenly quiet. He heard the crash of a last bottle breaking, and the bartender was cursing.

McGraw shoved an overturned chair out of his way, got to his hands and knees, and then stood up. The room was empty except for himself and the bartender who was just emerging from a crouch at the end of the bar.

"Damn!" the barkeep breathed, taking in the shattered mirror above the back bar and the depleted shelves where his liquor bottles had stood only moments before. "That was the hardest one yet!"

Dust was sifting down from the overhead beams that supported the wooden floor above.

"What happened?" Jay asked automatically yet already knowing. He had experienced the same thing in San Francisco numerous times in the past two years.

"Earthquake," the barkeep said, stepping gingerly over the broken glass behind the bar. The air reeked of whiskey and dust, and — Jay hated to admit it — his own fear. The room's only window, that looked out front, had been broken.

Another tremor shook the building, and they both grabbed for the bar to steady themselves. There was a loud crack overhead, and McGraw jumped back, looking up. One of the beams supporting the low ceiling had split diagonally and was sagging at a precarious angle. "Let's get out of here," he said.

The bartender nodded, and they headed for the door.

"It's been about two weeks since we last had one of these," the barkeep said as they emerged where the six men stood in the middle of the street, their eyes wide and looking at the buildings and trees around them. Jay almost laughed. Hardcases they might be, but nature had temporarily put the fear of God into them, including Waterloo Williams.

A thin man wearing a black vest and a boiled shirt was also standing there, white faced and gaping. The desk clerk, McGraw guessed. Apparently the small hotel had no other guests at the moment, since no one else had appeared.

A man had also run out of the mercantile across the street, looking wide eyed and scared. McGraw's knees were still a little weak as he walked to his horse and spoke soothingly to the animal who was pulling back on his tied reins and walling his eyes. Jay took hold of the halter and stroked the bay's neck, never letting on to the others that he was as shaken by the quake as they were.

When the horse was sufficiently calmed, he untied him and mounted. He had changed his mind about staying under a roof this night with the earth trembling. The nine men afoot scattered to avoid the fractious bay who was sidling sideways and kicking his heels as Jay tried to get him under control.

Waterloo glared at McGraw as he passed. "I hope to hell you ain't goin' out to that mission!"

Jay ignored him and urged the bay to a canter to work off his energetic fear.

"Damn you! You'll never get in!" Waterloo Williams shouted after him.

McGraw never looked back and gave no indication that he had even heard.

"You ain't here about restorin' no damn' church building!" Williams shouted. "I figured it was mighty funny you showin' up just now, after that place's been abandoned for years. You come here about that convict!"

As McGraw rounded the turn at the end of the street and started up the road he had come in on, he heard the leader yelling something to his men. He glanced back, but they were cut off from view. He wanted to urge his horse to a gallop but knew the bay was tired and couldn't run any distance. On the other hand, if Williams and his men were coming after him, they would have to retrieve their horses, which were nowhere to be seen on the street. By then, Jay would have a decent head start. He presumed these men, who had laid siege to the mission, were making their headquarters at the Adobe Hotel. He had not looked to see if there was a livery stable in town, but the half-starved look of Jolon didn't indicate it could support one. With any luck the earth tremor had spooked their animals, and they would have some trouble catching and saddling them.

Jay eased the bay to a walk after a half mile. The horse's fear had run itself out, and he was blowing and sweating. McGraw cursed himself for not carrying out his ruse to the end and amiably insisting he was on his way home to the bay area. But the arrogant attitude of Waterloo Williams had galled him into making a foolish mistake. Now they assumed he was headed for the Saint Anthony Mission.

It seemed as if the six and a half miles back to the ruin was twice as long as it had been. He wondered if Williams and his men knew a short-cut that he was unaware of. Where were all the politicians who were supposed to be deciding this convict's fate? Probably arguing in the safety of their offices in Washington and the consulate. Who had been the politicians the bartender re-ferred to? Were they local, or were they higher up in government? He wished he had had time to question him further. Since this had become a stand-off, the reporters had apparently gotten their stories and left some days before. This would only be newsworthy again when the stalemate was broken, and something happened.

He wondered how Anthony Artello had found out about the French hiring these gunmen. But Artello had insisted it was only rumor. Something like that would be hard to keep a complete secret. Unproven rumors about their real intentions of killing Dupré would be bound to leak out.

The sun had set, and dusk was creeping into the valley. For that McGraw was thankful. He slid the Winchester out of its scabbard and made sure it was fully loaded. If it came to a running fight, he wanted to be sure he was ready. He cursed himself for letting things come to this; he could have somehow gained access to that mission by being more circumspect. On the other hand, he had no way of knowing in advance that the men in that barroom were the hired guns the French had put in charge of taking care of Marcel Dupré. There was no way they were just going to capture and turn him over to the French consul for deportation to the Guiana prison colony. More than likely, Dupré would just disappear without a trace or, if explanations had to be made concerning his death, they could always concoct some story about an attempted escape or of self-defense. One way or another, Jay felt certain, Marcel Dupré was slated for death and his incriminating manuscript for destruction. He was also sure they would have no scruples about doing away with him or anybody else who interfered with their plans.

He nervously glanced over his shoulder, half

expecting to hear hoofbeats and see riders overtaking him, but the road was deserted. He almost wished he would meet some other traveler so he could ask for help, but the road was apparently little used, except by the stagecoach that traversed the Jolon Valley. The freshly-cut wheel tracks and hoof prints were apparent. The stagecoach was the only thing keeping the weeds and brush down and the road open.

By the time he reached the turn off to the church, it was so dark he almost rode past without seeing it. He reined to a stop and listened intently. He heard nothing. The sky overhead still held pale light, but he could see and hear nothing as he cocked his head this way and that and peered into the trees where the single-rack road wound out of sight. If there was going to be a moon tonight, it had not yet made its appearance in the darkening sky. He had to get to the church under cover of darkness before it rose. He saw there would be no clouds to obscure any moon.

He climbed down stiffly, slipped out the Winchester again, and walked the tired bay into the sparse oak trees parallel to the faint road and toward the mission. He was glad he wore flat-heeled boots to ease his walking and no spurs to make noise. Every sense was alert. Would the same guard be on duty? Was there more than one guard? Maybe Waterloo Williams and all of his men had taken a short-cut and were waiting in ambush for him now. Not probable, but he had to work on that premise. A lack of caution could cost him his life. Should he just walk across the vast open field to the church, or should he mount up and ride like hell, hoping to catch any guard by surprise? If he did that, he risked being shot by any watchers inside the mission. Maybe he could circle around and come in on the side where the wall had collapsed. But he had not scouted this route in the daylight, and it would be too chancy in the total darkness. If there was debris in the way, his horse could easily break a leg. Besides, the more vulnerable side of the ruin would likely be defended, if any defense was being made at all other than the sanctity of the church itself. The mission was backed by some high hills of one of the coastal ranges. No chance of coming in that way in the dark without some knowledge of the terrain.

All this went through his mind while he led the horse as quietly as possible through the scattered trees, keeping the faint, overgrown road in sight. In spite of his caution, it seemed to him the bay was making an uncommon amount of noise. With the coming of night, the hot breeze that had been blowing all afternoon stopped, leaving everything very still. The birds had gone to roost, and a few crickets had set up their soothing noise. But, like watch dogs, even they ceased at his approach. He wondered briefly what kinds of perils the first Spanish missionaries had faced many years before when they first came to this area. Probably no danger from the Indians, since the poor natives were not like the war-like tribes of the plains or the deserts. Only under extreme provocation had they later revolted against the *padres,* at one or two places. The deadly danger now in this civilized part of California was from other white men. Jay smiled tightly in the darkness at the irony of it.

Suddenly, almost before he realized it, he was on the edge of the vast, open field fronting the mission church. He stopped to look and listen — only the crickets chirping in the distance and the stars winking overhead in the vast vault of blackness. Good. He would try walking quietly across the open field and hope he could gain the security of the mission walls before anyone was the wiser.

Just as he took the first step, he heard a horse whinny somewhere to his left. Before he could clamp a hand over his bay's nose, the animal lifted his head and whinnied loudly in return. There was a human shout of surprise, quickly followed by the crack of a rifle. The lucky shot in the darkness almost got him as the bullet snatched off his hat and threw it over his back where it hung by its leather thong.

Before the sound of the shot had even died away, Jay vaulted into the saddle and was kicking the bay in the sides with his booted heels. The startled horse leaped forward, almost throwing him off backward as he tried to hang onto his rifle and the reins, while the stirrups were flopping free of his toes. He leaned over the horse's neck and rode for his life. The horse responded as if shot from a gun. He showed no sign of fatigue. Someone was shooting at the sound of his hoofbeats, but to no avail, as the bay covered the distance to the mission in fast time. McGraw sensed, rather than saw, the walls looming up and at the last second reined up, skidding the bay on his haunches and pulling his head to the left as he leaped from the saddle. Still holding the rifle in one hand, he pulled the horse through one of the low arches in the wall that extended to the left of the church.

Something moved near him, and he swung the rifle to bear, jacking a round into the chamber, his heart leaping into his throat. But he held his fire just in time as he heard the bleating of goats he had disturbed. Two more shots rang out somewhere behind him, and a bullet knocked a chunk from the adobe wall not five feet from his head. He pulled the trembling, sweating horse into the cover of the wall. He was breathing hard as he let down the hammer of the Winchester. No point in firing back. He had made it. Now to get under some secure cover and figure out just where he was. He slid the rifle back into the saddle scabbard and started to turn.

"Stop right there, *señor*, or you are a dead man!" a voice hissed, and he felt the pressure of a gun muzzle in his side.

Chapter Eight

Jay McGraw's heart skipped a beat, and he froze in his tracks, half-turned, his left hand holding the reins. He felt a hand slide his Colt from its holster.

"I should shoot you now for violating this church, but I will take you to Father Stuart. He will decide what is to be done with you."

McGraw stood still, waiting for further instruction. He felt the gun barrel jab him in the back.

"Go."

"Where?"

"Through the door beside you."

The night was so black he could see no door. Apparently they stood under the shelter of the tile-roofed walkway whose series of arches opened to the front and a parallel unseen wall on the other side of the walkway a few feet away. Jay assumed the door was somewhere in this back wall. He shifted the reins to his right hand and reached out with his left, taking a step or two forward, hoping to encounter the door. His fingers brushed a smooth adobe wall. He ran his hand along until he encountered a break and a rough wooden door.

"Here?"

"Yes."

"What about my horse?"

There was a pause, as if his captor had not considered this. McGraw took advantage of the hesitation to say: "There were men shooting at me back there."

"Bring your horse down to the end and inside. I will follow you, so go slowly and always know that a gun is at your back."

McGraw could just make out the faint outline of the arches by the starlight and started down the walkway, away from the church, keeping the open arches to his left, tugging the tired animal after him. He passed more than a dozen arches, the bay's shod hoofs ringing on stone, before he suddenly came to the end of the walkway and stopped.

"Turn right," the voice behind him ordered.

He complied, leading his bay into an open field that was part dirt and part grass, as he could smell the dust being kicked up by his boots. He saw a yellow shaft of lamplight streaming from a square window in the wall they were now behind.

"Turn your horse loose. He will be safe here."

McGraw slipped the bit from the gelding's mouth and dropped the reins, letting the horse search for browse.

"Move ahead of me to that light."

McGraw did as he was told. As he came nearer the window, an arm came around him and opened the door just to the right of it. Light flooded out.

"Inside."

McGraw stepped inside and was temporarily blinded by the sudden light. He was aware of someone else in the room and then could hear the breathing of his captor crowding in behind him. The breath reeked of tobacco.

"What was that shooting about, Santiago?" a voice asked.

McGraw focused on a man seated at a wooden table, his back to the wall. The man wore the cassock and collar of a Roman Catholic priest. He looked up calmly from the breviary he had been reading under the coal-oil lamp.

"I caught this man, Father. He rode in very fast. Someone was shooting at him, but I think it is a trick. The shots were only to make us think he was being chased, so he could get inside. He is one of them."

"Be sure he is not armed, Santiago," the priest said.

McGraw felt rough hands moving up and down his body from behind and checking his boots for a knife or other hidden weapon.

"I have taken his only weapons, Father," the man said, stepping back and to one side, so that McGraw got his first glimpse of his captor. Santiago was an ancient Indian with the skin hue of mahogany. He had a heavy nose and thick lips. The broad face was as seamed and cracked as a dry-lake bed. He was one of those ageless individuals who could have been anywhere from fifty-five to eighty-five. His iron-gray hair was pulled straight back from the broad forehead and tied with a rawhide thong at the nape of his neck. His eyes were mere slits in his face as if they had spent years squinting into the sun. Whatever his age, he was heavy-boned and still appeared to be hard muscled. One callused hand held an old 1860 model Army Colt percussion revolver trained on Jay's midsection.

The priest, his face in the shadow above the hooded lamp, studied McGraw for a moment and then said: "I believe you can safely put your gun away, Santiago. He is disarmed."

The old Indian looked suspiciously at Jay McGraw, but gradually lowered his weapon.

"You can leave us alone," the priest continued. "I want to talk to him. You can go back to your post."

Santiago edged toward another door that led out into the roofed walkway. "I will be close by, Father, if you need me," he said, still eyeing Jay McGraw. He lifted the latch and was gone from the room in one silent motion.

Jay let out his breath in a quiet sigh and relaxed.

The priest got up and came around the table. "I am Father Charles Stuart. And who might you be?"

He did not offer Jay a chair, although there was a chair and a small wooden bedstead against the opposite wall. The floor was large, flat fieldstone. A small, homemade crucifix hung on the cracked adobe wall above the bed.

"I asked your name," the priest repeated, a little sharply.

"Uh, Jay McGraw, Father."

"Since your name obviously means nothing to me, I should have asked what you are doing here."

McGraw had made it inside the mission. Now all he could do would be to make a clean breast of his intentions and hope the priest approved of what he had come to do. He briefly explained who he was and why he had come to the San Antonio de Padua Mission.

"Apparently my boss's information was correct," Jay concluded. "The men I met in Jolon are trying to get their hands on this escaped convict."

The priest did not reply immediately. His face was impassive. Only a narrowing of the eyes gave McGraw an indication that the priest disapproved of a plan to take the refugee's manuscript away from him. Father Stuart dragged the plain wooden chair from behind the table to the center of the room and sat down. He motioned to the chair near the bedstead.

"Sit."

Gratefully, Jay pulled up the chair and lowered himself onto it. He was tired.

"I have become a fairly good judge of men in my fifteen years as a priest," Father Stuart said. He paused and looked intently at Jay McGraw. "I feel you are probably telling the truth. I could be mistaken, but I don't think so. But, first of all, do you have anything that identifies you as the person you claim to be?"

Anticipating he would have to convince Dupré of his identity, Jay had brought along not only his Wells Fargo badge but also the letter typewritten by Anthony Artello's secretary and signed by the superintendent. This letter stated that the bearer, Mr. Jay McGraw, was an authorized representative of Wells Fargo & Company and gave his badge number, stated his age, and gave a brief physical description of him as being five-feet, ten inches tall and weighing one-hundred sixty-five pounds with dark brown hair and brown eyes. The letter further noted he had a one-inch scar on the back of his left hand. Father Stuart examined the badge and the letter in silence and then handed them back and reached to examine McGraw's left hand.

"The description fits. Except for that I would say you could have stolen the badge and forged the letter."

"It's a Wells Fargo letterhead."

"You wouldn't believe the ruses these amateurs have tried to get our refugee," the priest said. "In the past ten days someone has come to the mission nearly every day posing as the local sheriff, whom I happen to know, as a U. S. Marshal, and as an immigration officer. There was even one who said he had been sent from Washington by the vice-president himself to escort Marcel Dupré to our nation's capital to get all this settled." The priest chuckled wryly. "This high-placed official of our government had obviously borrowed the suit of clothes he was wearing, since it was several sizes too small. And he looked like he was more comfortable in a slouch hat than the silk top hat he was wearing. So you can't blame me for being careful."

McGraw nodded. When the priest said nothing more, Jay pushed ahead. "Then Marcel Dupré is here? May I see him?"

"All in good time. First of all, tell me what has been going on outside. I have been virtually a prisoner here since Dupré came to me sixteen days ago. Just as I had finished saying Mass in the church here, he came up and begged for sanctuary. He told me someone was trying to take him back to that terrible prison colony of French Guiana. The man was a walking bag of bones. I didn't think he could survive another day. But Santiago, the old Indian sexton who looks after this ruin, and I took him in and cared for him, giving him a little food and water.

"And, sure enough, another man came looking for him only a couple of hours later. I declared that Dupré had sanctuary in this church and would not be given up by me or anyone else until he was ready and willing to leave on his own. Except for a few reporters and politicians . . . and, of course, our friends out there . . . that's where the matter has rested until now. But we have been cut off from all outside news. What has been done . . . what is being done . . . to get this man safe passage to wherever he wants to go?"

"I have to confess I haven't got all the details myself," Jay answered. "I'm a Wells Fargo express-car messenger, and I was on my regular run from the West Coast to Chicago when all this occurred and was written up in the newspapers. I'm afraid I pay little attention to the daily scandals and crimes of my fellowman that passes for news, so I wasn't aware of the situation until just a few days ago when I attended a dinner in San Francisco honoring the visiting French ambassador." He went on to relate what Anthony Artello had told him, and what had happened when he tried to enter the mission earlier that day.

"I heard that shot," Father Stuart said. "But, by the time I looked out front, I didn't see anyone. Santiago said he saw someone leading his horse away."

"That was me."

"I knew they had at least one or two guards posted around to make sure no one got out without being seen. Apparently they are also keeping anyone from getting in."

"This can't go on much longer," Jay said. "If this fugitive is really a diplomatic prize, some legitimate authority from Washington will show up here with the force of law and grant him asylum. They'll lift the so-called 'siege' these hired guns have on this mission. Surely our government won't let these bandits have Dupré and won't turn him over to the French authorities to be returned to Devil's Island, or wherever he came from. Even if some of our politicians don't have a sense of fair play, I believe their constituents will force them to give this man political asylum. Besides that, I think our government officials are too stubborn to let any other government tell them what to do."

"I wish I could be as sure of that as you are. Besides, even if some legal representative of the U. S. government showed up here, I don't believe Marcel Dupré would consent to go unless he had a firm assurance that he would be given permission to remain in this country indefinitely. Remember, it's Dupré's choice if he stays in this church or leaves. Sanctuary cannot be violated."

"Where is this refugee I've been hearing so much about?"

"He's sleeping. He was very weak when he came here, and I've been trying to feed him small amounts at frequent intervals to build up his strength and weight. He's a very tiny man. That's probably what helped him survive. Some of the tales he told me of his past would make your hair stand on end, but the problem with feeding him is that we have very little food stocked here. I don't live here, even though I've stayed here for just over ten days now. I usually come here only on Sundays and holy days to say Mass for anyone in the area who wants to attend. Even though this property was returned to the Church by private owners in Eighteen Sixty-Two, no effort has been made to restore it to a permanent, regular place of worship. Santiago has spent nearly his entire life here at the mission. He considers it his home, and he looks after the buildings and grounds as best he can. His parents were mission Indians and were the caretakers here before the days of secularization. His wife is dead and his children grown and gone. He stays out of loyalty. What little food we have here is Santiago's and, now that we're under siege, we haven't been able to bring any more in."

"You have water?"

"Yes. The early *padres* tapped the San Antonio River about three miles above here, impounded the water with rock dams, and brought it down into the mission grounds with aqueducts where it was stored in reservoirs. They used it to turn the grist mill, supply a fountain . . . even a bathing pool. All that's gone now. The reservoirs are empty, but Santiago and some work men cleaned and reopened one of the stone aqueducts a few years ago, and we have a continuous flow of water through the mission grounds. I'm afraid, if these men get desperate, they'll somehow shut off the water. I'd store a supply, but the reservoirs are too leaky, and there're no containers larger than a small pan to collect it in."

"Can't you leave to get supplies? Surely they wouldn't hurt a priest."

"I could probably leave without harm, but I doubt they would let me back in. I've chosen to stay close to this man." He took a deep breath.

"Providence has left him in my care. If Dupré were left alone . . . even for a short time . . . anything could happen. I seriously doubt that his sanctuary would be respected by those men out there." He gestured toward the adobe front wall as he got up and restlessly moved around.

McGraw looked closer at this heavy-shouldered priest with the thick, curly hair and mustache. He appeared to be no older than his late thirties. Jay noted the eyes were red-rimmed, probably from lack of sleep. A several-day growth of beard covered his full cheeks. Jay felt amazement at the coolness of this man who had sat calmly reading the canons of his office while gunfire was erupting outside.

"They've been shooting at you?" McGraw was incredulous.

"Not at me. Now and then someone puts a few bullets into the walls . . . I suppose just to let us know they're still there . . . and to keep us from getting much sleep." He smiled tiredly. "Nothing to get excited about. That's what I thought they were doing when they were shooting at you."

"How long have these men been trying to keep everyone out of the mission?"

Father Stuart leaned against the table, folding his arms across his thick chest. "About eight or nine days, I think. Just after that last reporter from Los Angeles talked to Dupré."

Jay struggled to pull it together in his mind and to make sense of it. How could this be happening in a civilized section of California in the year 1884? A gang of hired gunmen laying siege to an old church that contained a political refugee? What had become of the forces of law and order? Surely somebody knew what was going on. If the French were really serious about getting their hands on Dupré, why not just order these gunmen to come in and take him? Probably for the same reason they were afraid of Dupré and his manuscript — bad publicity. Amazing what a threatened loss of face could force a man, or a government, to do. The hot light of bad publicity was a powerful tool.

"I think our local sheriff is intimidated by the reputation of this Waterloo Williams. And, technically, the gang has broken no laws . . . yet. If there is some shooting on private property away from town and nobody complains, the law can't arrest them."

McGraw voiced the question that was uppermost in his mind. "But where are the politicians, the diplomats who are supposed to be resolving this dispute? Are they just leaving you here to protect this man and face these gunmen?"

The priest shrugged. "I wish I knew. Early on, the sheriff and a federal marshal were here and got Dupré's story. Since then, except for a few reporters who were allowed in briefly and for the men keeping watch on this place, I've seen nobody until you showed up."

"You did know these gunmen are working for the French?"

Father Stuart nodded. "That's what one of them told me when he came to the door about the first day. Tried to convince me I was doing wrong and violating justice by harboring an escaped criminal. He said they would be sure he was turned over to the French authorities for deportation."

Jay eyed the priest. "You didn't know they actually plan to kill Dupré and destroy his manuscript to avoid international embarrassment to the French government?"

"No!" Father Stuart shot a sharp look at Jay McGraw. "How do you know this?"

McGraw admitted he had no factual proof but only a strong rumor.

"Hmm. Guess I'm not really surprised. Explains why they are so determined."

McGraw suddenly felt drained. After a long, hot, stressful day and no supper, he was feeling the effects. "Looks as if I'm in here with you now," he said. Without giving the priest a chance to reply, he continued: "Since you know I'm no enemy, I'd like to get my gun back."

"I'll have Santiago bring it to you."

"I also need to see to my horse. And then I'd like to meet Marcel Dupré."

The priest nodded his assent as Jay went to the door where he had entered.

A pale moon was rising to give McGraw just enough light to find the bay, cropping the short grass. The moonlight from above the hills behind the mission showed two or three gaps where the wall had crumbled, but the tired animal was making no effort to escape the quadrangle. Jay unsaddled him and rubbed down his sweaty back and flanks with the saddle blanket. Then he put him on a long picket rope and pin he carried in his saddle bags.

He dropped the saddle on the ground near the adobe wall and draped the damp saddle blanket over it. He paused to gaze at the moon and inhale deeply of the perfume of the night air. The drowsy droning of the crickets and dim outline of the horse grazing in the silvered quadrangle gave a sense of peace and tranquillity that belied the situation they were in.

Jay reëntered the room with his carbine and saddle bags. Father Stuart handed him back his Colt. He checked to be sure it still held five shells and holstered it, slipping the safety thong over the hammer to hold the weapon in place. Santiago was nowhere to be seen.

"Where is Dupré?"

"Sleeping."

"May I see him?"

Father Stuart hesitated. "Can't it wait until morning? He's still a little weak and needs all the rest and nourishment he can get."

Jay wanted nothing worse than to cave in and sleep for several hours himself. Athlete that he was, he was built more for speed, agility, and coordination than for long endurance. Nevertheless he said: "I'd really like to see him now, if you don't mind. There's not much telling what could happen before morning."

"All right. This way." The priest took the coal-oil lamp from the table and led the way through a plank door to an adjoining room. "I made him a bed on the floor in an alcove off the main church in case there's some question about him not actually having sanctuary in the church building itself."

McGraw, in spite of his fatigue, felt excitement building as he prepared to meet the man who had created an international dispute — a dispute that promised to turn deadly before it was over.

Chapter Nine

The wavering light of the smoky, untrimmed lamp cast eerie shadows on the cracked walls as they passed through two musty rooms. McGraw's eyes caught the darting movement of a mouse along the floor as it skittered away from the disturbance. Apparently the Mexicans who owned the goats hadn't taken up squatters' rights in this part of the old mission complex.

Father Stuart stopped at a door that was solid planks strapped with long, wrought-iron hinges. He lifted the latch, and the door swung out on squeaky, rusty hinges. They went through the doorway. As the priest held the lamp high, Jay saw they were in what had apparently been a baptistery in an alcove just off the ruined nave of the main church. On the floor in one corner a figure stirred on a blanket and sat up, blinking at the light. A tin cup and plate were on the floor beside him. The man known as Marcel Dupré was not an imposing sight. As he stood up, Jay saw he was short and thin, clad in an old cotton shirt and trousers with sandals on his bare feet. Short brown hair, sprinkled with gray, covered his head, and his lean cheeks were clean-shaven. McGraw was struck by a burning intensity in the man's eyes that was reflected in the lamplight as

Father Stuart introduced them.

"*M'sieur,*" Dupré murmured, "let us walk as we talk. Night is the only time when I can get some exercise without being seen."

The three of them went through the arched doorway into the large church. The front of the building was reasonably intact, the original, plain façade having been protected by a *companario* built onto the front at some unknown time in the past. As they walked through the vacant structure, Jay noticed a sprinkling of stars winking through a gap in the roof toward the sanctuary end of the building where part of the wall had also collapsed.

"This place was stripped of all usable material years ago . . . pews, pulpit, altar and statues," Father Stuart said, pausing to hold the lamp aloft. "I'm afraid most of it probably went for firewood."

The church looked even larger empty. At the edge of the light Jay could make out some pieces of rotted ceiling beams on the floor and some small piles of adobe bricks scattered here and there.

"I set up a temporary altar to say Mass down there in the corner and brought in what I needed. Santiago had pretty well cleaned up the debris in here and stacked those fallen bricks, but that jolt we got this afternoon shook down some more. Hope it didn't weaken the walls."

The priest turned down the wick and then blew out the lamp, plunging the place into total darkness. They were standing near a side door, and he led them out into the moonlit quadrangle. Jay couldn't help but notice, as they stepped outside, that a rifleman stationed in the hills behind the mission would have a clear daytime view of anyone in the quadrangle. But it might be out of effective range of a Winchester. Maybe a Sharp's would do it. Even as the thought crossed his mind, he doubted whether anyone would try to kill the diminutive Dupré while he was still inside the mission grounds. The gunmen would wait until they could get their hands on the manuscript as well as its author.

"They have a watcher in those hills," Father Stuart said, reading McGraw's glance. "I've seen the sun glint off field glasses or a rifle barrel a few times."

The trio strode across the quadrangle past McGraw's horse that still grazed quietly. Jay wasted no time on preliminaries. He explained clearly and simply to Dupré why he was here and what he hoped to do about taking his manuscript to a publisher in New York. He hoped Dupré had a good enough grasp of English to understand what he was proposing, but he needn't have worried on that score. Dupré spoke very good English, albeit with a pronounced accent. And he understood it just as well.

He did not answer the question directly. "*M'sieur* McGraw, it took me many months to reach this country even after we finally escaped to Trinidad. It has long been my dream to come here where there is real freedom and justice. I had no idea I would be treated as an escaped criminal."

"What happened? How do you know you are to be sent back?" Jay asked.

"After leaving Trinidad in a new boat furnished by the British authorities, we encountered stormy weather and were blown off course. My companions forced me to land on the first island we saw, which happened to be Martinique. Only one friend and I escaped capture by the French. We put to sea again in our open boat without a compass. After many perilous days of suffering from heat and thirst, we finally reached Panama. Here we were able to lose ourselves in a group of Frenchmen living in Panama City. They provided us with false identifications, and we were able to find jobs as menial laborers. The demand for labor is high because of the thousands of Frenchmen who are in Panama working for Ferdinand de Lessups, whose French company is digging the new canal to connect the oceans.

"I worked at various light jobs around a hotel until my health and strength returned, and I saved a little money. Then I made my way to the West Coast and was fortunate to stow away on an American steamship that was in port. I spent three days of blackness in the cargo hold without food and came on deck only at night to drink rainwater from small puddles. I slipped ashore when the ship docked and found myself near Los Angeles. I walked into the city and asked for the nearest police. When they took me to an official, I told my story and asked for asylum in this country." He paused in his walking and faced Jay McGraw in the pale moonlight. The soft gurgling of the stone-channeled watercourse sounded close by, near the wall. "I was locked in jail for a day or two, and then some more officials came and questioned me about my escape and what I had done to be in prison and what I intended to do in this country. I think I made a mistake by telling them what I planned to do with my manuscript. I have seen many officials in my years, and I felt these were like the others although not as brutal. They wanted to find a way to keep me in jail and get rid of me as soon as possible. They talked of sending a telegraph message to the French consulate in Washington. My heart sank when I heard that. I wanted to get away, but they locked me back in jail. They were going to take my manuscript from me, but I told them I would write another one because every line of it was burned into my brain. I also told them I would go to the newspapers with my story as soon as I was able. I have heard that the newspapers are a very powerful force in this country since they are not controlled by your government. So they let me keep my manuscript. No one there could read French anyway.

"The next day an American official came again and told me he had received a message from the French consulate asking that I be held until they could come to California. This official told me I would probably be deported as a person who was not desirable." He stopped talking for a moment and drew a deep breath. "Do you happen to have a cigarette, *m'sieur?*"

Jay shook his head.

"No matter." He started walking again in the shadow of the wall. Jay McGraw and Father Stuart fell in beside him.

"I am disappointed. I had hoped to find freedom of expression in America."

"Politicians are the same the world over," Jay commented. "They are usually looking out for themselves and their own public image. If they have any moral principles, they're not going to stand up for them if it makes them unpopular. There are a few exceptions, but I don't know of many."

"Oh, I believe most of the people would favor allowing you to stay in this country permanently," the priest told Dupré. "The common man champions the underdog. It's the public officials who are afraid to offend a friendly country by harboring you here and allowing your book to be published."

Marcel Dupré nodded. "I have spent most of my life suffering in penal institutions, dreaming of freedom, dreaming of coming to the United States. That is why I set myself to learning English years ago, associating first with an English prisoner and later with an American one. Even my first attempt to come to this country might have succeeded if I or some of my companions had known how to speak English."

"How's that?"

Dupré related how he and a squad of men in the Foreign Legion had deserted while on a campaign in Mexico in 1863 and tried to escape to the United States but had encountered a group of deserters from the Confederate armies just before they reached the border. Because of the language barrier, Dupré said, the legionnaires were not able to explain where they were going. The Confederates mistook the legionnaires' uniforms for some unit of the Mexican Federales and shots were exchanged. Before the confusion of languages could be straightened out, a company of Mexican troops had arrived and surrounded them all. These troops were loyal to Maximillian and had turned the deserters over to the corps.

"I often think that if we had been able to explain our situation to the Confederates, we would have been quickly on our way. The border was no more than five miles away."

"Fate has a way of working itself out," Jay said. "If you had made it, you might have been caught up in our Civil War and killed. Who knows?"

"*Oui*. Perhaps it is best that I am just now arriving. I am still alive and in fairly good health, even if I am forty-two years old."

McGraw was shocked. This man was only forty-two? He looked to be sixty, if he were a day. But he managed to hold his tongue. Considering the life he had led, it was little wonder he looked old. He had lost all his teeth; his small body had an emaciated look; his skin was blotched with brown age spots, and his neck was as wrinkled as a turkey's. Only the eyes were young. Young and alive and defiant. The man's spirit shone through those eyes. This man had survived both the mysterious French Foreign Legion and twenty years in the dreaded penal colony of French Guiana, not to mention the harrowing escape that had finally brought him here.

"Tell me more about your life," Jay said as they made another circuit of the quadrangle, walking near the wall. He had forgotten all about his fatigue as they sat on the edge of the low stone aqueduct where the water gurgled quietly, and he listened to the Frenchman talk.

"It is a sad tale, I'm afraid," Dupré sighed. "My great mistake was made in Paris when I was a young man of nineteen. The mistake that sent me on the road to hell!" He passed a hand over his face and was silent for a few moments. "I was in love with a beautiful girl named Claudette. We were planning to marry, but I had no job nor any skills to speak of. But I had one other consuming passion then . . . a thirst for adventure. I did not want to settle into a dull routine of married life with some low-paying job until I had tasted some excitement and seen some of the world. You are a young man. You know what I mean, yes?"

Jay grunted his assent in the darkness.

"Well, I finally decided that Claudette could wait. Even though she argued and objected and begged me not to go, I was determined to wear the white kepi. I signed up for a five-year enlistment in the *Legion Étrangère* . . . the French Foreign Legion. My enlistment was really illegal, since only officers are supposed to be native-born Frenchmen. Ah, but I was so eager to join that I would have done anything. Lying to the recruiting sergeant was nothing to me. I told him that I spoke French well because I had been born in Belgium and had been brought to Paris as a small child. He did not question my statement and passed me through, although I was undersized. They were not particular in those days.

"At last I was a legionnaire . . . a brother-in-arms to those who, with thousands of others over the previous thirty years, were giving the corps a reputation for valor and swaggering adventure and more than a hint of mystery about the men who filled its ranks. In my eagerness I had read everything I could find on the corps. King Louis Philippe, by royal decree, on March tenth, Eighteen Thirty-One, had sanctioned the formation of all the bands of mercenaries left in France after the Napoleonic Wars into one military body to be known thereafter as the *Legion Étrangère*. This new fighting force was sent south to conquer Algeria, and the tradition was born.

"I was processed into the ranks and departed France through the massive stone walls of Fort Saint Jean in Marseilles. Then I was shipped south with the other recruits to begin my training in North Africa. After a few months of training I was assigned to a regiment stationed at Sidi-bel-Abbes, Algeria. As luck would have it, this was a week before my unit was ordered south by forced march to engage some rebellious Arab tribes in battle. Very quickly I learned the meaning of the legion's saying, 'March or Die.' Never had I experienced anything like it. Only my youth and physical conditioning saved me during some of the fifty-mile-per-day marches with rifle and full pack in the desert heat. Blisters formed on my feet. My legs and back ached fearfully. I dropped on the ground in an exhausted stupor at every infrequent rest stop. I could have drunk ten times the amount of warm water in my canteen. At the end of the march we were attacked from ambush and forced to fight for hours with no rest. It required two days of battle to subdue the Arabs, but it was finally done.

"I survived my first combat without injury but learned a valuable lesson: the corps places no value on human life. The foot soldiers, who are nearly all foreigners, are expected to throw themselves into battle on the orders of the non-coms and officers without regard to their own safety. Maniacal charges were routine. The slaughter was usually fearful, I was told by older legionnaires, in any encounter. And I had seen some of that myself. But the corps usually prevailed against the desert tribesmen because of greater discipline and a fiery zeal that bordered on fanaticism. It was almost as if these men joined the legion to die. I was appalled. I wanted to live.

"The men in the corps came from all types of backgrounds and a variety of countries . . . Germany, Holland, Spain, Sweden, and I heard many Middle and Eastern European languages spoken around me. There were even a few Englishmen. Most of the men spoke or understood only the minimum amount of French to be able to respond to commands. Under those blue and white uniforms were criminals, professors, clerks, cobblers, men escaping situations they fancied to be worse, and men simply seeking adventure, as I was.

"The corps did not care how many men perished, as long as the troops carried the day. There were always plenty of new recruits to fill the ranks of those who died gloriously in battle. After all, these men were foreigners. They owed no allegiance to France, even though they fought like madmen, and France owed them nothing but their pittance of pay. They all joined voluntarily. If they left their bones under the desert sands by the hundreds, what of it? No one came looking for them. No relatives questioned their whereabouts or their fate. It mattered not whether they died of fever, a bullet, heat stroke, venereal disease, suicide, or were tortured to death by Arab women after being captured in battle.

"My eyes were opened to the reality of this life early in my enlistment. I knew I would have to be very careful and very lucky to survive my five-year obligation. But the odds seemed stacked against survival . . . the terrible desert heat, the grueling forced marches, the temptation to escape this misery in alcohol when we got leave to go into the Arab towns." Dupré paused in his narrative to scoop several handsful of water from the flowing aqueduct to drink. "But one of the greatest terrors of life in the corps was a condition known as *cafard*," he continued.

"What's that?" McGraw asked.

"Literally the word means 'bug' but is a slang term that can mean anything from a mild bad mood to a serious sickness of the mind. It is usually brought on by heat, boredom, stress, alcohol, or all of these things working on personalities that are not stable to begin with. I saw several episodes of sudden madness among my barracks mates that the older hands blamed on *cafard*. One man shot an officer during an inspection in front of the entire regiment then turned the gun on himself. One man hanged himself from a balcony. Another ran naked into the desert, screaming gibberish, and one went quietly mad, insisting that he was a prince and was to be addressed as royalty and waited on hand and foot in his barracks room.

"Of course, all this was enough to disillusion even the most foolish romantic . . . which I was. Ah, but *cafard* was only one of the hazards of the corps. The sergeants were the worst danger . . . worse, even, than the enemy. Sergeants in the legion are delegated almost total power. They are treated like officers and live apart from the men. They are promoted from within the ranks and are usually the most hardened individuals. The sergeants have complete charge and a free hand when it comes to enforcing discipline. Keeping some of the hardcases in line by force is necessary, but many non-coms seem to glory in excessive punishment. As a result many of them are hated and feared, and more than one has died in battle from a legionnaire's bullet rather than from enemy fire.

"Some of the on-the-spot punishments made up by the sergeants were burying a man up to his neck in the sand under a broiling sun and leaving him for several hours, solitary confinement in the blackness of a tiny guardroom with only a thirty-minute airing in the prison yard each day, tying a man upside down between posts in the sun with his head just off the ground. Then there was the more common sentence of eight days in the prison compound that meant no pay, no wine ration, harder work, and longer hours. Also there was the *plute* . . . forcing a man to march around the prison courtyard in step and regular formation for nine hours per day with a seventy-pound sack of sand on his back. These punishments were for such things as failure to salute a superior, a button missing from a uniform, a dirty rifle, a dirty mess kit. Cursing a sergeant or an officer could bring severe flogging that could result in death.

"Two forms of punishment were usually reserved for desertion. *Silo* was given to a man by making him stand in a cone-shaped hole in the ground in the sun where he could not sit or lie down. At the end of a day or more, the man had to be carried to his bunk as often as not. The other was *crapaudine*. This torture consisted of tying a man's wrists and ankles together behind his back until his body resembled a drawn bow. After being left like this for many hours, a man was usually unable to walk.

"Very severe infractions like murder, treason, or desertion in battle usually brought a sentence of death by firing squad from a formal court-martial. Assaulting an officer, a murder of passion while in the grip of alcohol or *cafard*, could bring a sentence of several months to several years in the dreaded *Bataillon Correctionel* . . . the Penal Battalion. The French, for some reason, have a penchant for cruel and unusual punishment, as some of your more barbaric Indian tribes have. The Penal Battalion was an example of this. As bad as the normal daily life in the corps was, you can imagine how much worse this place was. It was located far south in the desert of Algeria, near the Moroccan border at a place called Colomb-Bechar. And many a man took a one-way trip there. Thank God I was never sent there, but I have seen men who survived their sentences come back to serve out their enlistments. They were never the same. Often they were discharged, broken in body and spirit, wrecked for life. The Penal Battalion was the corps' equivalent of the civil government of Guiana.

"I gathered enough of the lesser punishments to make me hate my life in the legion more with every passing week. In fact, I was making plans with two friends to desert when our regiment was ordered to march. But this was not to be a desert campaign. We went north to the nearest seaport on the Mediterranean where we took ship for Mexico. I had been in the legion for sixteen months and had taken part in several battles. Now I found myself embarking for a country on the far side of the Atlantic where I and my comrades were to help maintain the Emperor Maximillian on the throne of Mexico.

"Before we even landed, six men and I were making plans to desert and go to the United States. Little did I realize at the time that our attempt to desert saved our lives. Sixty other men who went into battle that day near the village of Camarone made legion history by being slaughtered. They were in a house surrounded by Mexican irregulars and held out for a whole day but were eventually cut down to the last man. Captain Danjou's severed hand lay next to his body when legionnaire relief finally arrived. The severed hand was saved and later preserved and placed in a hall in France where it was revered as a symbol of legion valor. As far as I know, it is there yet. The date of the battle, April thirtieth, Eighteen Sixty-Three, has been celebrated every year since as a sacred day. It is somehow fitting that the corps should celebrate the heroism that resulted in death, since death seems to be what the corps is all about. In all, more than forty-two hundred officers and men were killed during their futile attempt to keep Maximillian in power.

"By missing the battle at Camarone, my companions and I undoubtedly saved our lives, but we were captured by Mexican troops loyal to the emperor and brought back. Instead of being punished simply as deserters, we were court-martialed for cowardice in the face of the enemy. We somehow escaped the death penalty because we had deserted before we were actually in battle. We were sentenced to five years of hard labor in the Penal Battalion instead. Since the regiment was not scheduled to return to Africa for some time and the troops were constantly in the field, a problem arose as to how or where we should be confined. A bargain was finally struck with the French civil authorities in Mexico that the convicted prisoners would be put aboard ship and transported through the Gulf of Mexico and down the northern coast of South America to serve our time as prisoners in French Guiana.

"That's how I came to be transported to that terrible penal colony where my five-year sentence stretched into twenty. At the time, though, I was secretly relieved at going to Guiana instead of the African Sahara, since it put me out of the hands of the legion and into a tropical paradise from which there would surely be easy escape. Then I thought I would make a quick return to France as a stowaway on some ship, assume a new identity, and take up my life once more, after less than a two-year absence. I would get a job, marry Claudette, and settle down to write, under a *nom de plume*, an account of my thrilling experiences. It would all work out even better than I originally planned." He gave a short, bitter laugh. "How little I knew as I lay seasick in the hold of that stinking navy ship that was rolling off the Maroni River awaiting the high tide to land at Saint Laurent. Little did I think that it would take me eight attempts and twenty years and so much suffering finally to reach this country."

He paused in his long narrative and seemed to sag. Jay did not interrupt, and Father Stuart also remained silent. The moon had set, and the quadrangle was in darkness but for a sprinkling of stars.

McGraw was caught up in this tale and wanted to hear of life in the penal colony and of this man's obvious success on his final attempt. It was a life and a world beyond anything he had ever imagined, and here before him was living proof that such things existed. Father Stuart had heard this tale before but, Jay guessed, not in the detail they were getting now. Jay estimated the time was well past midnight, but he wasn't even sleepy.

"What happened in Guiana?" he prompted when, after a time, the small man did not go on with his story.

"It was a terrible existence," he replied.

"Hardly human. But, if you wish to hear it, I will tell you."

At Jay McGraw's urging he went on to relate in considerable detail his acclimation to the life in the colony, and his instinct for survival. His first three attempts at escape had been overland, through the jungle where he nearly lost his life to head-hunting Indian tribes in the rain forest. Only his rabbit-like quickness and ability to hide saved him. He had finally given up when starvation threatened him. On another try he and four companions had skirted the coastline, trying to travel along the beach. But, after a few miles, they found their way blocked by the tangled roots of a mangrove swamp that extended several miles inland. The third overland attempt had resulted in two of his companions killing a third for his food ration. Since none of them knew how to survive in the jungle, the brutish pair had wound up roasting and eating the flesh of their victim. Marcel Dupré had feared for his life more then than at any other time, but they finally blundered into one of the timber-cutting jungle camps and were captured.

As the years passed, he gradually gained a reputation as an honest, single-minded man who could not be forced into anything by either fellow inmates or the administration. He even gained a grudging admiration from some of them since he made no enemies and bothered no one. He was finally left alone, except for a few close friends he had made. He brought his rapt listeners at last to his solitary confinement on the islands where he very nearly died.

"I can't believe you came back alive from that," Jay McGraw said when the older man paused for another drink of water from the stone aqueduct.

Dupré wiped his mouth with the back of his hand. "When I was returned to the mainland, I was given a job as a clerk cleaning up and putting in order the records storage room of the penal administration. This was a job I could do, and it gave me a chance to write down everything about my life in the legion and Guiana. I had time, and there was plenty of paper I could steal a few sheets at a time. This room was like a garret that had not been attended to for years and was full of dust and boxes of folders on convicts long dead and forgotten. I learned much about the history of the colony as I sorted and put these records in order.

"During the several months I was writing this manuscript in the barracks at night, I was also planning another escape with two of my friends who were *liberés* in Saint Laurent."

Chapter Ten

"And that escape was finally successful?"

"*Oui.*"

"After all those failures and all those years, how did you finally get away?"

When Dupré did not reply immediately, Jay prodded: "If it is too painful to talk about . . . ?"

"*Au contraire.* It is a joy for me to tell . . . ," Marcel Dupré said, his voice trailing off with the remembrance. "I can still hear my friend, Jacques, the day I visited his hut on the edge of Saint Laurent. He was flaying a lizard for supper when I came in. 'One other man is going with us — a *liberé*,' he told me. Then his friend, Phillipe, spoke up."

McGraw could well visualize the scene the Frenchman began to create.

" 'How much money can you add to this?' Phillipe asked, rolling and lighting himself a cigarette. 'We've been at this butterfly catching for several months and have saved only the equivalent of one hundred U. S. dollars. Most of the time we have to go through traders, and don't get much for them. I'm sure they're making a big profit on the other end.'

" 'Of course.' I hesitated. 'I have only a few francs. I can add nothing to this *cavale*.' I held up my hand as Phillipe started to object. 'I know. Each man must put in his fair share. This is too desperate a business for friendship to get in the way. I have something besides my experience to offer you.'

"Jacques dropped the skinned, headless lizard into a blackened pot and looked up curiously.

" 'Is this attempt to be made by sea rather than by land through the jungle?' I asked.

" 'Yes.'

" 'Do either of you know how to sail a boat?'

"The two *liberés* looked at each other. Jacques finally shook his head. 'We'll just have to do the best we can. I think André, the other *liberé*, has worked an outrigger fishing canoe some. We're planning on him doing most of the sailing until we get north to Trinidad.'

" 'That's what I have to offer you,' I told them. 'I'm an excellent small-boat sailor. I learned many years ago, and I have piloted several dug-outs in my earlier escape attempts.'

"Jacques grinned, showing several gaps in his front teeth. 'Marcel, my friend, that is the best news we've had today. Not only can you sail and navigate, but you're small and won't take up much room in the boat.'

" 'Do you have a boat yet?' I asked.

" 'No. We are waiting until we have everything else in readiness before we get one. If we can't buy a decent one that is big enough and has a good sail, we'll have to go upriver a ways and see if we can steal one from some of the Indians. If you're going to steal one that's worth a good amount of money, it's best not to do so until just before leaving,' he added with a grin.

"We parted then, agreeing to meet later to work out the details. For four more weeks I worked at my job of sorting records while life in the penal colony went along as usual. At the end of four weeks, the *liberés* acquired a dugout canoe through a Chinese merchant in the town. Where the merchant got it, no one asked, but it cost the *liberés* the remainder of their savings.

"One sweltering afternoon I slipped away from the dusty storeroom while the clerk dozed at his desk and met the *liberés* at a prearranged spot near the edge of the jungle. They led me by a circuitous route about two miles to the hiding place of the canoe. It was perfectly concealed with rushes and overhanging branches in a small creek that fed the Maroni River.

"I gave it a minute inspection. On this craft would depend all of their lives. It was about sixteen feet long. A somewhat shorter spar, wrapped in a sail, lay across the thwarts. The sail was cotton shirts and mattress covers, crudely sewn together. The material was thin and would probably tear under any kind of strain.

" 'Maybe we can strengthen that,' I mused aloud, straightening up. If there was anything in short supply in the colony, however, it was good cloth. 'If you can get some wood, we need to add a few inches of freeboard along each gunwale,' I informed them. The craft was broader of beam

125

than the average dugout, I noted with satisfaction. And the craft was not old and had none of the visible cracks that many of them were prone to develop. I could tell it was not waterlogged the way it rode lightly on the surface.

"I slid down the muddy bank into the craft and inspected the rudder and tiller. Strong and well-fastened. With the help of Jacques and Phillipe I stepped the mast through the hole in the forward thwart and fastened the forestay and shrouds to hold it. Then I practiced raising and lowering the loose-footed sail and inspected the cordage for weak or rotten spots. Satisfied, I wrapped the sail around the mast and they helped me unstep the spar.

" 'Well, the Chinaman exacted a high price, but he gave us a good boat and good gear, except for that sail,' I said, accepting a hand up onto the bank once more and helping pile the rushes over the boat. 'Be on the lookout for some kind of canvas at the docks or somewhere that we can make a better sail of.'

"The two *liberés* looked at me with respect. 'You're a godsend, Marcel,' Jacques said as we walked back toward their shack at the edge of town. 'You were the one missing ingredient in our escape formula. We really needed a seaman who knows boats, and you showed up.'

"I nodded but did not reply. No ordinary sailor, however skilled, would normally go out on the open ocean in such a narrow, shallow craft without even an outrigger loaded with four grown men and provisions and then attempt a voyage of at least a fortnight with no charts to an island they knew only the general direction of. But this was not a normal time or place. And desperation made brave men of many. They had to make do with the best they could buy, steal, or devise.

"Traditionally, serious escape attempts by sea were made in the month of May, when sea conditions are calmest. From long experience the guards and administration also knew this and consequently were more vigilant during this time.

" 'Is everything else ready?' I asked them.

" 'We'll go over the list when we get to the hut,' Phillipe replied. 'Just a few more food items that won't keep we can steal at the last minute.'

" 'When do we go?'

" 'May sixteenth. There will be a quarter moon that night if it's not cloudy. The outgoing tide won't be pulling as strong, but a full moon would be too bright for us.'

" 'I hope there's a good breeze or a strong enough current to get us clear of the shoals at the mouth of the river before the tide turns,' I said, 'or we'll be capsized and drowned, or piled up on the Dutch coast and find ourselves back in the blockhouse in a day or two.'

"I continued working as if nothing was happening, but I had a difficult time concealing my excitement. I had been through this several times before and knew the odds against a successful escape were long indeed. But, somehow the thrill of the gamble, the clandestine preparations, the danger of discovery, the anticipation, but most of all the hope still stirred my blood.

"The sixteenth of May was only six days off. I would be ready when the day came. I would go to my job as usual that day and leave at the normal time in the afternoon but, instead of returning to the barracks in the prison compound, I would meet Phillipe and Jacques in the jungle near their hut on the edge of the village. I would be missed at roll call just before the evening meal, but no search would be made. If I was still gone at morning roll call, some twelve hours later, I would be officially reported as escaped. I would have to depend on the *liberés* to furnish all the food, since I could hide nothing on my person except the new metal plan I had acquired and carried inside me. I had no personal items to carry anyway, except the ragged red and white striped cotton prison clothing I wore, a wide straw hat, and of course the oilskin-wrapped manuscript, which I had smuggled a little at a time to my work place.

"But the night of May fifteenth proved disastrous. I should have seen it coming, but I was so caught up in my own thoughts and plans I paid no attention when a loud argument broke out around the gambling blanket that was spread, as usual, in the middle aisle. Arguments were a nightly occurrence there. Sharp curses and threats were hurled back and forth before the game finally broke up for the night and the candles snuffed out. The regulation lamp burned dimly from the ridgepole of the room. It was well after midnight before I was able to relax enough to fall asleep. I knew I would need my rest since I would get none the following night.

"But the next morning the body of a man was discovered in the latrine. His throat had been slashed. The gambling argument had been settled in a permanent way . . . a way that would only spark reprisals from the victim's friends and continue the feud. I was more irritated than horrified by the bloody murder. After removal of the body, the barracks was locked and the convicts questioned one at a time by the guards. No one was allowed outside to work that day.

"I was nearly in a panic. I would miss the *cavale*. There was no way the *liberés* could know what had happened to me. Would they go without me, thinking I had backed out at the last minute? Who would sail the boat if they did? André? I had met this fourth man only once . . . a short, dark, taciturn man in his late twenties. I had taken an instant dislike to him. The man seemed to be bursting with repressed hostility and arrogance that were directed to everyone around him.

"But it would make no difference what André was like, if they all left without me. Jacques and Phillipe were trustworthy friends, but they were considerably younger and less experienced than I and might be pressured by André to go ahead.

"I spent the long, hot day sweating in the barracks with the other convicts, trying not to show my impatience. There was no one on the outside I had contact with that I could trust to send a message to my friends. The men who brought their meager rations were new since my solitary confinement and unknown to me. I dared not give away the secret by trying to bribe one of them to carry a message.

"I ate the soup, bread, and weak coffee they served for supper without really tasting it. As expected, the guards found out nothing about the murder, even though they were required to go through the formality of questioning each prisoner. Even those who might have seen something dared not talk for fear of losing their own lives. I had been awakened by a muffled scream the night before but hadn't moved from my bunk. I wanted to know nothing of this.

"The long day of confinement passed, and night came on. The gambling blanket was spread and a rather subdued game commenced. I lighted my stub of candle from the regulation lamp and sat on my bunk. My manuscript was already stashed in the storeroom where I worked and beyond my reach until the next day. A quarter moon became visible through the barracks window and, with a sinking feeling, I realized that the dugout was probably gliding out of the creek into the Maroni River and headed for freedom. I closed my eyes and tried to think of something more pleasant. My depressed mood finally wore me out and I fell asleep, my tiny candle still burning.

"The next morning I ate my hard bread and coffee at six o'clock and, when the turnkey unlocked the barracks door, dragged myself out of the compound through the quiet, dusty streets of Saint Laurent to the storeroom behind the main administration building to take up my job. I would have to start all over again planning an escape. My heart was heavy. The day dragged as if it would never end. I shuffled and stacked documents and official reports, sneezing now and then as I breathed the paper dust.

"Finally, I could stand it no longer. During the heat of the early afternoon rest period I took my manuscript and quietly slipped out through the outer office where the administrative clerk was sound asleep in his chair. On an impulse I stopped and slid open the side desk drawer. The loaded revolver was in its usual place, and I promptly confiscated it and slipped it under my shirt.

"I walked quickly down the deserted dirt street, turned a corner and, my heart pounding, made my way quickly to the hut of the *liberés* with no one seeing me. The hut was empty. Maybe they were out hunting butterflies. But I immediately knew that was not the case since the hut had been stripped bare of everything except the crude furniture. My heart sank. I would have to hide the revolver before I went back to my job and deny any knowledge of it if I were questioned, but I still had some time. I refused to acknowledge that the *liberés* had left me behind. It would be a while before I would be missed by the clerk, so I determined to go the two miles through the jungle to the creek where the canoe had been hidden.

"I jogged down the dim jungle trail, gripping the manuscript I had tied up in oilskin. The raucous calls of the brightly-colored tropical birds and the occasional screech of a monkey accompanied me. Sweat was streaming from my body in the humidity. No breeze penetrated the green twilight of the jungle floor. I had never quite conquered my instinctive fear of the unknown dangers lurking in the jungle, even though three of my escape attempts had been overland.

"I alternated jogging and walking, watching carefully for snakes on the faint path as I went. By the time I neared the creek bank, I was breathing heavily and I slowed to a walk. The canoe was still there, and uncovered! I stopped, confused. But just then Jacques and Phillipe materialized out of the foliage a few feet away. I jumped back, my heart in my throat, and then a flood of relief engulfed me as I recognized my friends.

" 'We were just trying to decide if we should go without you,' Jacques said. 'Where were you last night?'

"I explained the reason for the delay.

" 'Are you ready to go?' Phillipe asked.

" 'Yes, but we'll have to wait until dark.'

" 'What do you have in the package?' the one

called André asked, emerging from behind the tall Phillipe.

" 'Just some personal papers,' I replied.

" 'Pretty big package,' André said.

"I said nothing.

" 'You the navigator?' André asked.

"I nodded. I was looking at a fifth man, standing back to one side. He was a huge, hulking brute of a man. 'Who's that?' I asked.

" 'Larique,' Jacques replied. 'He's a friend of André's.'

"I motioned for Jacques to step away from the others and walked a few paces down the path with him.

" 'I thought this was supposed to be a four-man party. The boat's not really big enough to hold another man, especially one his size.'

" 'He's a friend of André's, and André insisted he come along. He threatened to stay behind and give away our plans if we didn't let him come,' Jacques said. 'Besides, his size and strength might be useful if we get into a tight spot.'

"I had a sinking feeling in the pit of my stomach. This escape had started badly and didn't show signs of getting any better. I glanced in the direction of André and his huge friend, who were staring back at me.

" 'What's all the whispering about?' André demanded. 'There can't be any secrets if we're all in this together.'

" 'We were just discussing how five of us are going to fit into that canoe,' I said casually, as if

133

I were not aware of the edge in André's voice.

" 'Well, he's coming, and that's it,' André stated flatly.

"I shrugged and turned away toward the boat, feeling the reassuring pressure of the gun in my waistband under my shirt. I went to examine the canoe again. I paced off its length along the bank. I had underestimated earlier. The dugout was over seventeen feet long. It might hold all of us, if we placed the big man near the center to balance the weight. The mast had been stepped, but I could see it would have to come down until we were out of the creek, since its fourteen-foot height would never clear all the overhanging branches.

" 'Marcel is in charge of the sailing and the navigation of the boat,' Jacques was saying as I turned back to the group. 'That must be understood. The safety of all of us depends on it.' He paused as I came up to them. 'We'll go as soon as it's dark. The moon should be up by the time we reach the river.'

"I nodded. 'I'm glad to see you got an old coal-oil tin and some charcoal for a fire. Do you have some matches?'

" 'Right here. Sealed in wax. We've also got several gallons of water in some kegs lined with tar. We even got some wood added to the gunwales to give us more freeboard, just as you suggested.'

" 'Good. What about the sail?'

"Jacques shook his head. 'We couldn't find

anything better. But we did get some strong thread and needles in case we have to repair it.'

"I groaned inwardly at this but did not show it. If that sail started to go in a strong wind, it would probably be blown to tatters. But I made no comment. It couldn't be helped. We walked down to the boat with Phillipe and three of them examined the food they had collected, item by item. I also noted that there were three strong paddles.

"After they had gone over everything thoroughly, we sat down in the shade to rest and await nightfall. I stretched out on my back with my manuscript package for a pillow.

"I awoke to the sting of mosquitoes biting my sweaty neck. I swatted them away and sat up in the jungle twilight. Phillipe was asleep, and Jacques and the big man, Larique, were both dozing, backs against a huge tree. André was staring off into the jungle, smoking a cigarette.

"I woke the others, and they gathered everything together and placed it in the canoe and then unstepped the mast, lashing it along one gunwale. Then we positioned ourselves in the dugout, I at the tiller, and pushed off down the creek.

"By the time we had gone a hundred yards, the twilight had slid down into darkness, and we proceeded by feel and instinct. Pushing off with the paddles, stroking the black water, occasionally fending off a low-hanging vine or branch, we glided downstream toward the river. The eerie

135

sounds of night prowlers began a cacophony in the jungle growth all around us.

"I sensed that the stream was getting wider and tried to keep the craft in the middle of the channel. We had to be getting close to the river. Finally, the dank jungle wall fell away from us abruptly and the canoe glided to a stop in the black water, bobbing gently, before the current in the big Maroni River began to nudge the bow. I eased the tiller over and started downriver to the sea, several miles away.

"We fumbled around in the dark, getting the mast up again, and the stays fastened in place. By the time we finished crawling over each other, untangling the lines and setting the rigging in place, cursing softly, tripping and stumbling into things, I estimated that more than an hour had passed.

"Jacques and Phillipe sat nearest me and stroked steadily with the paddles, helping the current and the outgoing tide speed our flight to the unseen ocean somewhere ahead. The moon rose, shedding a quarter of its light on the Maroni. I kept the boat in the middle of the river, and the paddlers made as little noise as possible.

"We passed several wooded islands, the largest of which contained the isolated leper colony. To add to the horror of the place, leprosy had made its appearance among the convicts two years before and a dozen of the poor wretches were now banished to this island while their bodies slowly rotted away until death finally released them from their misery. Saint Laurent slid past on our right. Only a few lights were showing.

"At the mouth of the Maroni we hoisted our patchwork sail. The land breeze was coming over my right shoulder. The canoe slid out over the muddy shoals and began to dance on the water like a log . . . the log it once had been. I picked out the star in the clear sky that would guide us north and brought the canoe about. The change in direction caused the chop near the mouth of the river over the shoals to slop over the sides of the boat. The canoe carried seven or eight-hundred pounds and was not as buoyant as it might have been. Even with the addition of the planks along the gunwales, the craft had none too much freeboard.

" 'Damn water coming over the side already!' Jacques spat, grabbing a bailing can, while Phillipe began moving the wrapped packages of food away from the water in the bottom. I sat with my wrapped manuscript tucked safely behind me. A fair following wind was coming over the port quarter, and I let the sail full out to starboard. The breeze drove us offshore at an angle, but I and the others were continually looking back, dreading that an overtaking sail would show up in the pale moonlight. But there was no pursuit. The night passed quickly and, when the sun came up out of the sea in a glorious fireball, the ocean swells looked friendlier in the light. Only a few gulls watched our progress. The Guiana coast was only a dim line on the horizon.

I squinted over my shoulder but wasn't sure I could even see the land at all. Maybe the dim line was only the base of a cloudbank.

"André busied himself making a charcoal fire in the empty coal-oil tin and shortly we were brewing some strong tea, laced with raw, brown sugar to revive our flagging strength. We all talked with nervous jollity, happy to be free of French Guiana at last. Even Larique was talking, and André seemed to be in a good mood for a change.

"We made steady progress all day. Jacques confided to me that we would have carefully to ration the food due to the extra man. We were totally at the mercy of the implacable sea, but I felt happier than I had in a long time. Every hour was carrying us farther away from the suffering of my former life in the penal colony.

"The sun went down that evening in a welter of reds and golds. It was almost as if we could hear the hissing of the fireball being put out in the western ocean. About eight o'clock the wind began to blow, coming out of the southwest off the continent behind us. Cloud cover blotted out the stars as the force of wind continued to increase. The canoe with its human cargo tore along through the sea, faster and faster, the sail bellied out stiffly against the starboard shroud. The waves began to grow in front of the mounting wind. Higher and higher the foamy crests grew.

"I was planning to be relieved at the tiller, but

the others had waited too long to make the switch. Then it became too dangerous for anyone to move in the dugout, so I kept the helm. Nothing in my sailing experience had prepared me for anything like this. Fear caught in the back of my throat like a lump I couldn't swallow . . . a primal fear of primal forces. The only way I could conquer this fear was to force myself to concentrate solely on what I was doing at the moment and to shut out everything else. All through the long night I dared not let my attention wander or the dugout would have broached and capsized in a second.

"I was glad I couldn't see the huge waves as they roared up from behind, lifting the slender dugout by the stern higher and higher as we shot forward at a breathtaking speed. Then the foaming, hissing crest passed in a blaze of phosphorescence, and the boat slid down the back of the passing wave. The sail snapped taut, straining, and then flapped uselessly as we dropped into the trough out of the wind. I was afraid the mast would carry away, but we needed the sail to provide some steerage and control. The other four men hung on until each crest passed and then bailed madly until the next wave caught up with us. Fear gripped me as this terrible, impersonal power of the sea took control. But as the hours wore on, my fear was slowly dulled by fatigue, and I steered automatically, old habit taking over. The night seemed endless . . . an eternal hell of roaring wind and sea.

"Finally the gray dawn crept up over the flying spray gradually to reveal the windy, smoky hills and valleys of the sea. But, as if on cue, the rising sun signaled a drop in the wind, and the waves subsided until the great wilderness of water was only moderately rough. By mid-morning nature was smiling benignly as the sky had been swept clean of clouds, and the sea was a sparking blue all around us. We were shaken and white but quickly recovered our spirits, seeing we had survived intact. We set about bailing the dugout dry, inspecting the stores for damage, and hanging our clothes on the stays to dry. Some of the bread had gotten soggy, so we apportioned it out and ate it first with some hot tea Phillipe brewed.

"Even with the wide straw hat I had stuffed under me and managed to save, the tropical sun, climbing higher in the sky, began to burn my exposed skin. I turned the tiller over to tall Phillipe and then dropped, exhausted, to the bottom of the canoe. I was asleep almost immediately.

"I awoke about four hours later with the sun burning the side of my face and a terrible thirst in my throat. I sat up, rubbing my gritty eyes, and asked for a drink of water. Salt water had somehow penetrated the fresh water keg. It was still drinkable, but had a brackish taste even when made into tea.

"The patched sail was ripped in several places, and Jacques was taking advantage of the calm to stitch it. The combination of several shirts and an old mattress cover had worn thin in places,

140

and Jacques had to double the material here and there to make it sufficiently heavy to sew.

"We saw no sign of a ship all day. The tropical sun and the glare off the sea burned every inch of exposed flesh. The sores on our legs, inflicted first by iron bands that were welded about our ankles during the early years of imprisonment and aggravated by the constant rubbing of shackles in the barracks, began to open and run and burn under the intermittent soaking by salt spray. My hands were swollen and blistered from gripping and pulling on the tiller for many hours, so I gave up the steering chore to Jacques as the third night came on.

"Cramped together for two and a half days, we men began to get on each other's nerves. The euphoria of the first few hours of our escape was gone. Each man began to find fault with his neighbor. Every minor irritation became a major one. Raw nerves were chaffing as we could not get away from one another, even to squat briefly on the latrine pail. I was nothing if not patient. I had seen this several times before during my previous escapes, so I held my tongue and endured my discomforts stoically.

"As darkness came down, the wind began to blow once more, and the sea began to rise in response. Jacques was very nervous, but I sat in front of him, quietly instructing him on the art of helmsmanship. As the waves grew and the troughs deepened, Jacques started to panic. 'I can't do it! Here, you take it!'

" 'No. Just brace your feet and get a good comfortable grip on the tiller. There, now. No! Don't look back. Keep your eyes straight ahead. You can feel them coming. Just keep the boat pointed straight. Let them push us.'

"I knew that even helmsmen on square-riggers were told never to look back at a following sea in a storm. The sight and sound of those mountains of water bearing down are enough to make the stoutest heart quail. With me there to push or pull when a correction was needed, Jacques little by little began to get the knack of anticipating the waves rolling out of the blackness.

" 'Yes. That's it. You're getting it!' I shouted encouragingly as the boat went surfing briefly along the crest at racehorse speed before the thunderous comber passed on, and the canoe slid back into the trough. He was definitely getting the feel of it. I could sense his confidence growing.

"The night proved to be just as wild as the night that preceded it. The only blessing was that a hard rainstorm accompanied this blow and we spread our shirts and pans and tried to catch as much of the fresh rainwater as we could. Several gallons were somehow collected this way. It later proved to be slightly brackish due to the continuous salt spray, but it was better than nothing.

"The storm passed with the night, and morning found us all stiff, sore, wet, thirsty, hungry, and dispirited. We had not been able to hold any kind of course with no stars and no compass. It was all we could do to keep from being capsized.

" 'We'd better turn in toward the mainland and get some fresh water,' André said, sipping his tea and making a face. 'Drinking this salty stuff will kill us or make us go mad.'

" 'We've been gone only three days!' I answered. 'And you're already talking of turning in toward the coast. We can live on this water.'

" 'We're probably off Demarara,' André continued. 'I'd rather take my chances in the jungle. At least there's plenty of fresh water to drink.'

" 'I told you when I started I would not turn back,' I attested.

" 'We don't want to turn back. We just want to get some good water, and then we can start again.'

" 'No. We'll be wrecked landing in the surf. Or the Indians will capture us, or some natives will turn us in for a reward to the French. No. We stay at sea.' I was by far the smallest of the five men, but I tried to make my voice as commanding and confident as I could. After all, I was the sailor in the group and was not as intimidated by the sea as the others.

"The four said nothing for a time but then began to argue that turning shoreward was the best alternative.

" 'Better than being drowned or going mad from drinking salty water in this terrible sun,' André insisted.

"But I was adamant. 'The jungle is impassable. I know. I've tried it. Our best chance is right here. If we reach Trinidad, we'll be safe. The British will not turn us in. The British are a sporting people. I've heard from others that they let escapees rest there. Then they furnish supplies for them to go on. Sometimes they even furnish a better boat for the trip.'

"But their courage and resolve were failing them. Four sullen, defeated faces stared back at me. Even my friends, Jacques and Phillipe, looked as if they were ready to give up and turn toward the coast. They grumbled some more but were not willing to press the point when they saw I was determined. At least for now the sea was fairly calm, and they had just eaten a little food to make up for the lack of sleep. For the moment the world apparently did not look as bleak as it had.

"But it didn't help that the fourth night was increasingly cruel. The dugout, in spite of its load, demonstrated what I thought were amazing qualities of buoyancy. Time after time, just as it appeared we would be buried under tons of roaring water, the frail craft would almost magically rise up over a foaming crest, quiver for a moment, and then plunge at a sickening angle down the back of another wave.

"We somehow lived another eight days and nights. The nightly storms abated somewhat, although the sea remained lumpy. It was a nightmare of hunger, thirst, constant wettings from salt spray, and day after day of blistering sun. We sat in a stupor most of the time. I dozed at the tiller, my straw hat gone, trying my best, during intervals of consciousness, to keep the dugout pointed in the direction I thought would bring us to the island of Trinidad.

"Even though the dugout was narrow, with no outrigger, it had no tendency to roll or tip when sailing. Because of its short rig, the wind merely pressed the slightly heeled boat down into the water as the hull sliced forward.

" 'We'll never reach Trinidad,' André grumbled one morning after the last of the meager rations had been consumed. Tea and some waterlogged tobacco were all that remained, along with the brackish water. 'We should have been there by now. With all these storms, there's no way we could have kept a true course. We've probably passed it in the dark.'

"Larique, the huge silent one, growled his assent. I said nothing, not wanting to antagonize him. I had heard it all before, many times, in the past few days. The sun was high, and the canoe rode the heaving green billows on a broad reach as the trade wind blew across them from the starboard side. Now and then I noticed a triangular fin cutting the water briefly, twenty or thirty yards from the canoe. The sharks had been coming closer and more frequently the past two days. The others had noticed it too, and I felt this increased the fear I knew was gnawing at their innards.

" 'I think we've all had enough of this, Dupré,' André said, glancing around at the others for

145

support. 'I say we turn toward the coast.'

"To my surprise, Phillipe nodded. 'I'd rather take my chances with my feet on solid ground.'

" 'It'll give us a chance maybe to find some bananas or coconuts to eat,' Jacques added.

"I was losing them all. But I held the tiller and kept the boat on its northwest course.

" 'Put that tiller over!' André ordered, seeing that he now had the majority.

" 'No. We'll be safe in Trinidad, but this is the Venezuelan coast. If we land there, we'll be turned over to the French authorities for sure. How many times do I have to tell you that? Do you want to go back to the blockhouse and solitary on bread and water?'

" 'We're going to land,' André said and started to crawl toward me. As he reached for the tiller, Jacques grabbed André and pulled him back. André swung at him, and they fell, locked together, against the gunwale. Water sloshed over the side as the canoe was overbalanced.

" 'You idiots! You're going to capsize us!'

"The big Larique tried to get past Phillipe to help his friend. Phillipe tried to stop him and caught a fist on the side of the head for his trouble. He dropped without a sound, and Larique kept coming, crawling over the bodies. I reached inside my shirt and drew the revolver that I had carried hidden in my waistband. I raised the gun and cocked it. The big man stopped, a look of wonderment on his face as he stared into the black muzzle.

" 'I'll shoot every one of you if I have to, but we're not turning toward the mainland,' I grated in deadly earnest.

"Jacques and André stopped struggling and sat up, looking at me. Larique backed away.

" 'You can't stay awake all the time,' André said. 'We'll get that gun away from you sooner or later.'

"I didn't want to hurt any of them. As I looked at their unshaven, sunburnt faces and salt-reddened eyes, I knew they held no personal animosity toward me. It was only a desperation born of fear . . . fear of sharks, of drowning, of dying of thirst and exposure.

"André rubbed a hand across his face and turned away. Then he came to his knees and pointed excitedly ahead. 'Look! Look! Land! There's land ahead!'

"I didn't move. It had to be a ploy to catch me off guard so someone could snatch the gun and overpower me. Jacques and Larique were craning their necks to see, while Phillipe was just regaining consciousness and rubbing the back of his head.

"My view forward was obscured by the low sail so I eased the bow to port a few points as the canoe rose up on a swell. And there I saw, against the horizon, high green mountains outlined against the blue sky. The sight wiped out all animosity, all arguing. I slipped the gun back under my waistband. I pulled the tiller over and set the course once more. They were as happy as children being let out of school for summer vacation. The trade wind bellied the patched, much-repaired sail and a few hours later found us riding the swells off shore.

"As we drew nearer, we could see a thatched house set in a grove of coconut palms. It appeared to be deserted. I quietly slipped the revolver out of my pants and dropped it over the side. With a fair breeze I steered the dugout straight in. The last breaking wave shot the canoe forward, depositing us on the sandy beach in a welter of foam.

"My four companions leaped out eagerly, but they were so weak after fourteen days at sea that they sprawled on the sand like drunken men. I crawled out also and with three others managed to drag the slimy dugout up out of reach of the waves.

"Several Negroes who were fishing with nets along the shore eyed us warily but would not come close. Jacques called to them in French and English to help, to climb please some nearby trees to get us some coconuts. The fishermen did as requested but would only roll the nuts down the beach toward us without coming any closer. One of them threw his machete toward us, and I used it to whack off the tops of several nuts so we could drink the good, sweet milk from them before digging out some of the meat to eat. I thought it was the best food I had ever tasted.

"The earth seemed to rise up and down under us as I and my four companions staggered toward the hut under the trees. It would take some time before our land legs would return. In the hut we found a pot of fish and rice prepared for somebody's supper. We dug our hands into it and ate like the starving men we were. Then we lay down on the floor and slept like we'd been drugged. No one bothered us.

" 'We must go turn ourselves in to the authorities,' I said when everyone awakened a short time later.

" 'Maybe we should stay here and eat and forage for food and get our strength back,' Jacques suggested.

" 'I'm afraid we'll be arrested,' André said. 'Let's wait a while.'

" 'No,' I said. 'It's better that they not hear of our arrival from someone else. Let's go.'

"The four reluctantly followed me as I led off through the coconut grove on a narrow dirt road. We met several groups of Negroes talking in broad English accents, some of them leading loaded donkeys. But these people gave us a wide berth as we passed. I could imagine what the five of us must look like . . . sunburnt, ragged scarecrows from the sea.

"After two hours we reached the hamlet of Moruga which, we discovered later, was the administrative center for the southeast coast of Trinidad. We went directly to the police station where we stood before a huge Negro in a military uniform. After questioning us, he asked where we were going.

149

" 'To the United States,' I answered, speaking for all of us, since I had the best command of English.

" 'Why have you stopped on Trinidad?' the official asked.

" 'We have been at sea fourteen days in a canoe and have no water or food.'

"The official wrote some information on a piece of paper with a black pen. Then he made a list of some sort on a separate sheet and handed it to an assistant.

" 'Get fifteen loaves of bread, five pounds of sugar, five pounds of coffee, five pounds of codfish, and three pounds of tobacco.'

"Then he turned to us. 'Know that the law of Trinidad provides that no French convict escaping from Devil's Island and reaching these shores will be arrested by any authority, unless he breaks some law here or disturbs the peace. If any fugitive arrives by boat, he will be given food and allowed to rest before embarking again. If his boat is not seaworthy, he will be transported to Port of Spain on the north coast by a police officer, given a more seaworthy craft, and allowed to proceed on his way. Do you have any questions?' he intoned as if reciting a familiar regulation.

"Tears of joy were filling my eyes at these words, but I managed to answer: 'No.'

" 'You will be locked up in our guardhouse for now, but you are not under arrest. This is only a precaution to keep you safe from the French consul while we look into your case. I will send someone to examine your boat to see if it is seaworthy.'

"I wiped my eyes on a ragged sleeve as we were led outside. It had been a long time since I had been treated with any decency or respect . . . a very long time. We were still a long way from the United States, but we had gotten our foot in the door of freedom, and I had a good feeling that this time we were going to make it. And we did make it, even though it took several more months," Marcel Dupré concluded his narrative. "Thank God for freedom!"

Silence fell on the three of them as he finished. Jay McGraw and the priest sat quietly assimilating all they had heard. It was an amazing tale of daring, endurance, and good luck. Jay had to shake his head and look around to reëstablish a sense of present time and place. He had been drawn so completely into this compelling story he felt as if he had actually been there, experiencing Marcel Dupré's cruel world, so foreign to his own.

"And all of this is in your manuscript?" McGraw asked. "Including the naming of corrupt officials?"

"*Oui.* All of what I told you, and more."

McGraw whistled softly. "No wonder the French don't want it published."

There was silence again for a few seconds.

"You still want this manuscript published in English in this country?"

"Yes. For two reasons. First, I'm hopeful that publishers in other countries will then buy and publish it also. Then there may be an outcry from all the civilized countries that will force France to close the penal colony with all its corrupt brutality. And the other reason is that this book will give me some money to live on until I can find a job."

"If you're allowed to live in this country," Father Stuart counseled.

"I am hoping that will happen."

"We can't be sure if it will," Jay said. "If you are deported to Guiana. . . ."

"No! I will never go back!" Dupré interrupted.

Jay McGraw imagined he could almost see the fire flashing from those eyes.

"I will fight to the death before I will go back there!"

"Then you will allow me to take your book to a publisher in New York?" Jay urged, taking advantage of the moment. "That way it will be in safe hands no matter what happens."

Dupré did not reply for a few seconds. "We will talk more about it tomorrow," he finally answered. "I am tired from all this talk. I need some rest."

"I think we all do," Father Stuart said.

They walked in silence back into the church through the side door, and Father Stuart relighted the lamp he had left just outside the door. Abandoning Dupré at his sleeping blanket in the baptistery, they went back to the priest's quarters.

"Do you think he'll give up that manuscript?" Jay asked as Father Stuart sat down heavily on his bunk, rubbing the heels of his hands into his reddened eyes.

"I don't know," the priest answered. "Marcel Dupré is a tortured man. He has lived these past few months clinging to one hope . . . freedom in the United States. And he has lugged that heavy manuscript with him through storms on the ocean and through the jungles of Panama. He has carried and protected that thirty pounds of paper like it was his own child. I think it became something tangible for him to focus on . . . a goal to see it published in this country. I got the feeling from talking to him that he's not seeking just freedom for himself but a more humane and just prison system for the men he left behind and any future criminals sentenced to Guiana. This book is his only hope of producing reform in the penal system . . . starting with the closing of the French Guiana colony. Whether he will put that hope in the hands of a stranger from Wells Fargo is a decision he alone will have to make."

Chapter Eleven

The crack of a shot woke Jay McGraw from a sound sleep. Before he was fully conscious, he was rolling out of his blanket and instinctively reaching for the holstered Colt near his head. He lay propped on his elbows, gun in hand, and listened. There were no more shots and, after a time, he began to wonder if it had really been a gunshot that had awakened him. Perhaps he had dreamed it. Daylight illumined the empty room where he had spent the night on the hard floor with his saddle for a pillow. He glanced out the arched window opening at the early rays of sunlight slanting down into the quadrangle and guessed it had to be after eight o'clock.

The dead silence stretched out in a continuous string until he felt compelled to break it by scuffling to his feet. He buckled on his gun belt and stepped, barefooted, to the door connecting the adjacent room and lifted the latch. The *padre* looked up as he entered.

"Good morning," Father Stuart greeted him. "Sleep well?"

"Was that a shot I just heard? Are they shooting at the buildings again?"

The priest shook his head. "Not this time. That was Santiago securing our dinner. We're having roasted goat." He grinned at McGraw's look of distaste. "Actually, goat meat is quite good, if it's prepared properly with limes, Cayenne pepper, and garlic. Unfortunately, we don't have any of that. I hope it's not too tough. I asked him to get us a sheep, but the Mexican families managed to collect them all before they were driven away by our friends who have us under siege."

Jay holstered his pistol and rubbed his gritty eyes. "I'm hungry enough to eat a whole goat . . . hair, hoofs, and all. What time is it, anyway?"

"About eight o'clock, I would imagine. I was just preparing for Mass, if you'd like to attend."

McGraw considered for a moment. "Sure. Let me get my shirt and boots on."

Besides the priest Jay McGraw and Marcel Dupré were the only ones attending Mass in the corner of the cavernous, ruined church. Santiago paused in the preparation of the meal long enough to wash up and come in to serve Father Stuart. A candle flickered at each end of the homemade wooden altar as Father Stuart approached it.

"Introibo ad altare Dei," the priest began. "I will go to the altar of God."

"Ad Deum qui laetificat juventutem meam," Santiago responded in Latin, kneeling on the stone floor to one side. "To God, the joy of my youth."

As the priest and the server intoned the familiar Latin prayers and responses, Jay McGraw began to relax. He felt at home. It was all a well-known ritual to him. He prayed fervently that the situation they were in would somehow be peacefully resolved.

After the Mass Father Stuart put away the gold-plated vessels and folded up the vestments into a small box. "I'm using the wine very sparingly," he said. "Until this siege is lifted, we can get no more. We have plenty of water and an adequate supply of communion hosts."

McGraw followed Santiago into the quadrangle where the carcass of a long-haired goat hung by its hocks, being bled out. The old Indian proceeded to gut and skin the animal, but Jay didn't stay to watch. He went to check on his horse that was quietly cropping the sparse grass near a wall of the enclosure. The rest would do the animal good. McGraw only wished he had some grain to feed him. The bay was not an Indian pony that could thrive indefinitely on grass alone. He moved the picket pin to an area of fresh grass where the bay could be in the shade part of the morning but still reach the water. Then he went to the stone aqueduct, took a long drink, and soused his head in the rush of cool water. He stopped at the corner of the quadrangle and looked out front at the vast field that fronted the mission. It was deserted. He scanned the trees in the middle distance that had sheltered the guards. If any men were there now, they were keeping well out of sight. No smoke rose above the foliage to betray a cooking fire. But Jay still had to assume someone was watching.

His complaining stomach reminded him he

hadn't eaten since noon yesterday. About the same time he remembered the bread and cheese remaining in his saddle bags. He retrieved the one hard loaf of bread and the wedge of cheese wrapped in cloth and turned them over to the priest for all to share. Father Stuart accepted them with thanks and put them aside to have with the roasted goat meat that Santiago promised would be ready about mid-afternoon.

Jay had another drink of water from the stone channel to try to calm his hunger, took up his carbine, and scouted the perimeter of the enclosure, keeping out of sight as much as possible. Whoever might be watching the Saint Anthony Mission was staying hidden. There were no glints of sun off metal or glass and no movement that he could detect on any side of the property. He even padded across the debris-laden floor of the church and started to open the door to the outside but changed his mind when he saw a bar in place across the inside.

The partially collapsed roof and wall had created an opening for plenty of morning sunshine but not large enough for anyone to gain access or even to see inside without climbing about twenty feet of wall. Roosting pigeons flapped away to the outside at his approach. As Jay came back across the church, Father Stuart met him.

"What are you doing with the rifle?"

"Just looking around."

"I don't think we are in any danger of attack. I'm responsible for this man, and I don't want any shooting unless it's a last resort to save our lives."

McGraw was surprised at the sharp tone of command. "Sorry, Father. I had no intention of doing any shooting. This rifle is strictly a precaution."

"I'm serious," the priest continued. "Even if someone outside starts shooting into the walls or windows or down into the enclosure, I want no retaliation. This is a delicate situation. Those men would like nothing better than to provoke a violent response on our part. I don't want to give them any excuse to storm this place and take Dupré by force. As irritating as it is, we must remain passive in order for sanctuary to remain intact. We have to be like the turtle . . . just pull in our head and feet and wait."

"Right you are, Father," Jay agreed, realizing that this man who had been here from the beginning had thought out the situation much more thoroughly than he had.

As he strode off to store the carbine in the saddle scabbard in his room, his mind was occupied with how to persuade Marcel Dupré to give up his manuscript. He left the Winchester but kept his gun belt strapped on when he went back outside. The August sun was high and rapidly heating up the windless quadrangle.

Jay paused in a sliver of shade and rested his eyes on Santiago preparing the butchered goat across the enclosure. The Indian had scooped out a shallow trench and started a fire with some fallen roof timbers and dry brush. But McGraw's mind was not on this sight. If he somehow succeeded in persuading the refugee to give up his manuscript, how could he guarantee it would arrive safely in New York? The simple fact was, he couldn't. He could only do his best. If Waterloo Williams and his men caught him trying to escape with this package of heavy paper, he could be in for a very rough time. Not only might he lose the manuscript, but he might very well lose his life. These men seemed to have no qualms about killing. Yet, even if he lost the manuscript, Marcel Dupré would still be here to write or dictate another one.

He decided not to push too hard. He would bide his time and maybe mention the manuscript to Dupré again after they had eaten. He would like to practice a little diplomacy and allow Dupré time to get to know and trust him. The problem was Jay felt a sense of urgency. He had no idea how long they had before something broke this impasse. Then his, and Wells Fargo's, chance of conveying the manuscript would be lost.

Time dragged. Jay paced the grounds and through the buildings, making sure to stay out of the line of fire from anyone outside. Father Stuart was busy writing something in a journal at the table in his room, and Dupré was sleeping. McGraw himself was still tired. They had all stayed up very late. The quiet outside was so deceptive as to suggest that no one was still watching and waiting for Dupré to come out. McGraw knew better.

The heat became oppressive as the sun bore down, baking the earth. No wind stirred the leaves of the small trees that were growing wild near the edges of the ruin. However, inside the thick-walled rooms Jay discovered the air retained a surprising coolness when he entered the priest's quarters. The wooden shutters were closed, leaving only a dim light filtering through a few cracks.

"Sit down and relax," Father Stuart invited, closing his journal and pushing it aside. "You seem a little nervous."

Jay straddled the wooden chair, folding his arms across the back. "I guess I am. This waiting gets under my skin."

"Patience is sometimes an acquired virtue."

"I can't shake the feeling that something is about to happen. I just wish I knew what."

"Being upset about it won't help."

"I know. I know. I'm on edge, and I've been here less than a day. You've had almost two weeks here, so maybe you've gotten used to the waiting."

The priest nodded, leaning back in his chair. "Being in a place like this helps a person put time in perspective. These old walls have seen lots of history. This was the third mission in the chain, founded by Father Junipero Serra in Seventeen Seventy-One. But this present building wasn't started until about Eighteen Ten and finished in

Eighteen Thirteen, after they decided to move the site. That arched façade out front wasn't added until Eighteen Twenty-One. I don't know why they added it. It makes the front of the church look strange.

"In Eighteen Twenty-Seven the elaborate water system was built. This mission was one of the largest and most prosperous in the whole mission chain. In the early Eighteen Thirties there were ten thousand sheep here and six thousand cattle. Something like four thousand Indians were baptized here and over eleven hundred couples married here. You'd never know it to look at the place now. Secularization in Eighteen Thirty-Four put a stop to everything. The church was offered for sale in Eighteen Forty-Five, but there were no takers. It was finally sold but returned to the Church a couple of decades later. While the place was abandoned, people came in and plundered the buildings for anything usable. That's the main reason it's in the shape you see it now. Too bad," he said, shaking his head. "I'd like to see the old place restored. The Franciscans were in charge here until it was abandoned. About two years ago my bishop assigned me to come out here on Sundays to say Mass for anyone in the local area who wanted to attend. I think he has the idea that the mission will be restored someday and wants to show that the Church is interested."

"Who owns this property? Does it really belong

to some rancher now, like that guard out there told me?"

"The Church owns it. It was part of a big spread for a while, but the rancher deeded it back to the Church. For many years Santiago took it upon himself to come here from town and do what he could to take care of the church. After his wife died a few years back, he left his job as a cobbler and moved in out here. He says this has always been his spiritual home anyway. He does a few odd jobs for people to keep himself in food. He's a very frugal man . . . and very devoted."

"How did you get here? Where's your buggy or horse?"

"I came on horseback, but the animal was stolen by Williams and his men shortly after Dupré got here."

They fell silent for a few minutes, and Jay pondered the past glories of this mission, trying to picture what it must have looked like when it was thriving in its heyday a half-century earlier. This led him to wonder how and why Dupré had picked such a rundown ruin in which to seek sanctuary. "How did Dupré get here from Los Angeles?" he asked.

"He didn't give me all the details. Somehow he got away from the authorities in the city . . . he's obviously had plenty of practice at escaping . . . and fled north up the coast on foot. He told me he got a ride part of the way on a farmer's wagon, but he walked most of it, sleeping in fields and barns and avoiding towns. He had the name of a Frenchman living in San Francisco he hoped to find for protection and help. He got as far as Jolon when he found out someone was on his trail. He made a dash for the nearest church, which happened to be here. He stumbled in here one Sunday morning, exhausted and hungry, with Waterloo Williams and his men less than a half hour behind. Any other time this church would have been deserted, but Santiago and I were here, finishing up after Mass. A handful of people had just left. Then . . . well, you know the story from there." After a short pause, he continued: "Frankly, you shouldn't be too disappointed if Dupré won't let you have his manuscript."

"You don't think he will?"

"I just don't want you to get your hopes up."

Jay nodded. Then he rose and went back outside into the quadrangle, took a last look around, before retreating to the relative coolness of his room where he pulled off his boots, stretched out on his blanket on the floor, and dozed off.

The mid-afternoon meal of roasted goat meat, hard bread, cheese, and few green olives proved to be tastier than Jay had expected. Actually, he was so hungry he could have eaten nearly anything. The dark meat reminded him somewhat of lamb but a little gamier and tougher. His hunger provided the seasoning.

They ate in an empty room adjacent to the priest's quarters to avoid the full force of the August sun. The room was close to the fire pit where the meat was roasting. They sat cross-legged on the floor around a blanket and ate with their fingers or pocket knives, helping themselves from a small iron pot. They washed down the meal with water brought from the free-flowing aqueduct. Jay drank from his canteen, the priest from a tin cup, Dupré from a long-handled dipper, and Santiago from a calabash. It was almost a picnic atmosphere.

McGraw waited about an hour after the meal before he approached Dupré. The Frenchman was hunkered down in the shade next to a wall of the enclosure, smoking a cigarette he had rolled himself — the makings probably borrowed from Santiago. The old Indian was busying himself cleaning up the remnants of the meal a few yards away. Sweat glistened on his broad, seamed face as he worked around the pit of still-glowing coals. He was saving the remaining goat meat for one more meal.

By nature, Jay McGraw was not a devious man. If Wells Fargo management thought they were sending a subtle diplomat, they were far wide of the mark. On the contrary, McGraw was usually very direct, even blunt, especially when in a hurry. And now he was in a hurry.

"Well, have you made up your mind to let me take your book to New York and get it published?"

Dupré took a last puff on his nub of a cigarette and dropped it into the dust, snuffing it out with the sole of his sandal. "I want very much to have this manuscript published," he replied, looking up at McGraw, "but, if this manuscript goes anywhere, I go with it."

The implications of this answer flooded through Jay McGraw's consciousness. He felt overwhelmed and seriously considered abandoning the whole idea then and there. Escaping with the bulky manuscript would be difficult enough but, if he had to take Marcel Dupré with him, it would be well-nigh impossible. He ground his teeth in frustration. This whole project had come to naught — unless he could somehow persuade Dupré to stay behind. Jay would have to travel far and fast when he made a break from here with the manuscript in his saddle bags. Breaking through the cordon of surrounding gunmen was by no means a sure thing. But, if he could somehow get past the watching eyes just outside, he felt sure he could outrun or elude them. His rented gelding had proven to be fleet of foot over a short distance. Yet the animal would not be nearly as fast carrying double — even a man as small as Dupré. And if some shooting started, either of them could be hurt or killed. He had no qualms about risking his own skin — he had done so before, protecting company shipments — but, if Dupré stopped a bullet, it would be McGraw's fault. There would be hell to pay — an international uproar.

He tried not to let his disappointment show in his face or voice as he tried again. "I realize why you don't want to let that manuscript out of your hands but, if you stay here and keep it, there's a chance it will be taken away from you by the government and will never see print. If you and the manuscript and I all try to leave this sanctuary together before the U. S. authorities decide what to do with you, there's a good chance we'll be caught and killed and the manuscript destroyed. Wouldn't you rather let me take the chance of getting the manuscript into a publisher's hands? If I fail, you will be safe here and can always rewrite it."

Marcel Dupré considered this, his outward calm belied by the flash of icy fire from his blue eyes. "What you say makes much sense, but whatever may happen, I will not be separated from what I have written. I have brought it this far, and I am determined to see it delivered into the hands of a publisher myself. If events should prove otherwise . . . ," he shrugged and left the rest unspoken.

"But the Wells Fargo Company is even safer than the U. S. Mail," Jay argued, a hint of pride in his voice. "There's no need for you to worry about it. All you need to do is sign a statement making me, as an agent of Wells Fargo, responsible for the delivery of your manuscript. If you wish, Wells Fargo will even select a publisher for you, subject to your approval, of course."

166

Dupré shook his head firmly. "No. Where this manuscript goes, I go." There was a note of finality in his voice.

"I'd like to take a look at it," Jay said, mainly to hide his disappointment.

McGraw followed Dupré into the dim interior of his alcove. Dupré went to the old, wooden baptismal font that stood to one side. The white paint was cracking and peeling away from the dried wood of the domed top that covered the basin. The small cross on top was askew. Dupré lifted one edge of this lid and swiveled the top to one side. A thick, oilskin-wrapped package lay inside. Jay took it and set it on the floor to unwrap it. The pages were water stained and dog eared. He shuffled through them, noting the bold scrawl. Some of the penciled words were familiar, but his limited knowledge of French severely restricted his understanding of what was recorded here. The sheets of paper, some of them yellowed with age and of varying sizes, had apparently been salvaged from different sources. A number of the pages were even written on the backs of blank forms of some kind. He rewrapped the manuscript, carefully tying the heavy cord that held it together. He hefted the bundle as he put it back into the basin, estimating its weight at more than twenty pounds. It was a tribute to the power of words that this stack of paper held more explosive potential than several carloads of dynamite.

"Are you willing to try to escape with me?" Jay

167

asked, sliding the domed top back into place.

Dupré considered this for a second or two. "Escape to where?" he asked. "I have already been in the hands of the law, and they were going to turn me over to the French. Where do you suggest we go?"

McGraw was taken slightly aback but said quickly: "To New York."

Dupré nodded. "Maybe by the time we reach that city, the American authorities will decide that I will be able to live here in freedom."

Jay felt relieved that this was so easy. He had expected some resistance or at least an argument, but then he realized this man had never lived a secure life. Taking chances was nothing to him. The U. S. authorities were taking so long to grant him asylum that he probably thought there was no need to stay in this church any longer. If the American government was going to deport him, he might as well be on the run, giving himself a chance.

"Traveling in your country without being seen is very difficult," Dupré observed. "New York is a long way from here. How will we reach it without getting caught?"

McGraw had no idea. "I'll find a way," was all he said.

Dupré fell silent for a time. The silence lengthened to more than a minute. "Except for Father Charles Stuart, you are the only one who has offered to help me since I came ashore in this country. If we hear nothing by this time tomorrow, I will take the manuscript and go with you."

"Good decision."

But events were soon to take a twist that neither could have anticipated.

Chapter Twelve

McGraw went immediately to Father Stuart and told him the plan.

"No coercion was involved? He led me to believe he was content to stay here in sanctuary until the authorities in Washington made some decision."

In deference to the afternoon heat, the priest had stripped to a white cotton undershirt and an ill-fitting pair of work pants that could have belonged to Santiago.

"No coercion," Jay replied. "He wants his manuscript published but won't let it out of his hands. Rather than take a chance on a decision going against him by Washington, or being captured by that bunch out there," he jerked a thumb toward the front of the church, "he's told me, if there's no official word by this time tomorrow, he'll take a chance on busting out of here with me and the manuscript."

Father Stuart looked skeptical. "What's your real motive in all this? To help this man gain freedom he has paid for over the past twenty years of earthly Purgatory, or to gain more fame and glory for Wells Fargo and Company?" His voice and attitude were frank but carried no rancor.

"Actually, Father, I came here with the idea of getting the manuscript and not the man. I had only the company's interests in mind. But now that I've seen and talked to the man, I'm also very much interested in his welfare as well. I would certainly never do anything I thought might jeopardize his life. Of course, I told him getting past those men out there could be very chancy. But taking risks is nothing new to him."

The priest rubbed the stubble on his jaw. "I can't really agree with leaving here until we get a decision from Washington."

"If it's taking this long, it's liable to be bad news for Dupré."

Father Stuart shrugged. "Not necessarily. We have no way of knowing what's going on."

"But it will be too late to run when some deputy U. S. marshal shows up to arrest him."

"If they do, he still has sanctuary. Not even a U. S. marshal has authority to come in here. In fact, it was just because of repressive governments and rulers in the past that the concept of sanctuary was developed centuries ago."

"That may very well be," Jay conceded, "but Dupré can't stay here indefinitely. You'll eventually run out of food."

"We're close to it now," the priest agreed. "I wonder if the law knows that Waterloo Williams and his men have the place blockaded?"

"Not likely. But even if the local sheriff or a U. S. marshal knows, they can't actually arrest anyone unless Williams and his gang break some law, like maybe kidnapping. As long as they're just hanging around, there's not much the law can do . . . except maybe just watch the watchers." He shook his head. "This whole thing could get very confusing."

"Well, if Marcel Dupré decides to leave, I want to talk to him to be sure this is strictly of his own free will."

The racketing of gunfire somewhere outside interrupted him. Three, four shots in quick succession. There was a pause, then two more shots and a slug splintered the wooden shutter on the front side of the room, slamming into the opposite wall. Both men jumped back and crouched against the plastered brick wall on either side of the shuttered opening. McGraw had his Colt in his hand.

"Just harassment," the priest said. "Don't return fire."

Jay nodded but kept the pistol in his hand.

"Hullo, the church!" came a muffled cry from somewhere.

Father Stuart cautiously reached and unhooked the shutter and pushed it outward where he could see through the small opening.

"You, there, inside the church!" a voice yelled again.

"What do you want?" the priest shouted back.

"Rider coming in with a white flag. We want to talk. Don't shoot!"

"I guess they think we're keeping an armed guard," Father Stuart said under his breath.

Then, loudly: "Ride up to the front door!"

Jay and the priest went through the row of three rooms to the connected church. Santiago was already there, lifting the heavy bar from the double doors.

"Don't open it all the way," the priest cautioned. He positioned himself where he could see the approaching rider through the foot-wide opening. McGraw stood behind him where he was out of sight but could still look over his shoulder. Marcel Dupré stood several feet back to one side behind the door.

The horseman who came up slowly was none other than 'Loo Williams himself, carrying a white handkerchief aloft, tied to the barrel of his rifle. He stopped about ten yards from the door. The priest waited, standing sideways to make as small a target of himself as possible in the narrow opening.

"We haven't been bothering you folks much lately," he said. "We seem to have a stand-off here." Williams paused. "You know you're going to run out of food sooner or later. And I doubt that fella who rode in there the other night brought you much grub." He laughed shortly. "But why go through all this? Why not just have Dupré come on out and go with us?" He held up his hand as Father Stuart started to reply. "Hold it. Before you say anything, I have a confession to make, Father." He shifted to one cheek in the saddle and did his best to look embarrassed. "Actually, we've got ourselves in a bind here. The good Frenchmen who hired us will pay all our expenses. But they will pay us our fee only after we deliver Dupré to them. Problem is . . . ," he paused and grinned, "short of blasting our way in and taking him, we don't seem to be able to get our hands on him. And the Frenchmen who hired us have told us not to go in and take him. So where does that leave us? The longer we wait around, the better chance there is of the law decidin' he can stay in this country. If that happens, we stand to lose not only our fee but also our expenses. And we've run up one helluva saloon bill in Jolon, not to mention the tab for food, hotel, and feed for our horses in the past three weeks." He lowered the rifle with its white flag and allowed it to rest across the saddle. "So we figure to throw in our cards and lose our ante rather than to keep raisin' and lose the whole pot."

"What are you talking about?" Father Stuart asked.

"We're proposin' a compromise. You give up Dupré, and you have our word he won't be harmed. We'll turn him loose and tell the French politicos he got away from us. That way at least we gave it a good try, and we get our expenses paid. That's all we want out of this. Me and my men are tired of this whole business. We figure we got into a high-stakes game. Seems to us we stand to lose more than gain if we just wait. This way, Dupré goes free, this stand-off ends, and we at least break even for a few weeks of work.

I don't aim to welsh on a saloon and hotel bill like some penny-ante con man. That ain't my style. I just want to make expenses. When we started chasing him, we never figured he'd run into a church and hide, and there'd be a big stink about it all over the country." He paused and looked at the priest. "What do ya say? Couldn't ask for a squarer deal than that."

"He lies!" Santiago hissed from behind the door. "These are bad men. Do not trust them, Father."

"One minute while we have a conference," the priest said, stepping back and pushing the big door closed. "What do you think?" Father Stuart asked then, facing the others but looking at Dupré.

"It makes no sense," the fugitive replied. "How did they think to get me, if I just stay inside here? Starvation? I have lived on little food for so long in the past, I could outlast almost anyone. I require very little nourishment. No, they have something else in mind. I will not put myself in their hands."

"Yes, there is nothing to prevent them from murdering you and destroying your book," Jay McGraw agreed. "Then they could get their fee as well."

"I too think it's a trick," the priest concluded. "That's why I think it's foolish for you two to leave here tomorrow."

"The American officials might not grant me asylum," Dupré said. "I must be free to run if

175

their decision goes against me."

The priest looked from one to another of them. Their faces were serious, intent, and showed they were of the same mind. He opened the door slightly again and edged into the opening.

"No deal. Dupré stays inside."

Williams's face clouded and turned as dark as the blue-black beard just beneath the skin of the clean-shaven cheeks. "By God!" he exploded. "Refuse my good-faith offer, will you! You'll live to regret that decision, priest. Hide behind that collar if you want to. It won't protect you from everything!"

With that, he wheeled his horse and spurred the animal savagely, galloping away toward the distant trees. Father Stuart swung the big wooden door shut, and Santiago dropped the bar into place.

"Do you think they might try something?" McGraw wondered aloud as the four of them retreated through the church.

"That last sounded like some kind of threat," the priest said.

"Maybe we stand watch tonight?" Santiago suggested.

Jay had been thinking that very thing. "Good idea. I don't trust them. Sounds as if they mean to do something besides sit and wait."

It was about four hours until dark. If 'Loo Williams and his men planned a frontal assault on the mission, they would most likely do it when there was light enough to see — either just before dark or just after dawn. If, on the other hand, they planned a quiet sneak attack to get Dupré, it would more likely come at night. They had to be prepared for anything.

Jay saddled the gelding but left him picketed. He kept his rifle with him and emptied a box of cartridges into his pocket. He filled his two-quart canteen from the aqueduct and hung it on the saddle.

They gathered at dusk in an empty room just off the quadrangle to eat the leftover goat meat before it began to go bad in the heat. Buzzards would clean up the remainder that Santiago would pitch over the wall. The last of McGraw's cheese and hard bread were also eaten.

"Is there any safer place that Dupré can hide?" Jay asked as they ate. "Any cellar or attic or hidden room . . . something like that?"

The priest shook his head thoughtfully, chewing a mouthful of bread and meat. "I can't think of any place. Santiago, you're more familiar with the mission grounds than I am. Do you know of any good hiding place?"

"No cellar. Old grain mill is outside the wall. Not a good place to hide."

"Only place I can think of is the dry water tanks," Father Stuart said, "but they are also just outside the wall near the mill, and they're just rock-lined square pits in the ground with no tops. Dupré's probably better off where he is."

Jay nodded. "Then it probably is a good idea if we take turns standing guard tonight." He paused, thinking that he sounded as if he were giving orders. He didn't want to give that impression, being the latecomer here. The priest sipped some water from a tin cup, saying nothing. "I'll take the first three hours," Jay offered when nobody said anything. "Maybe nothing will happen but better safe than sorry."

"I won't sleep," Dupré said. "Give me one of your guns, and I'll help."

"It might be better if you stay in the baptistery and let us do it, rather than expose yourself."

"They come in here, I kill them," Santiago stated flatly, flinging a rib bone out the open door toward the hot ashes in the fire pit.

Father Stuart looked somewhat distressed by this talk of a violent confrontation. "I believe they were bluffing. They've respected sanctuary here so far, and I think they'll continue to do so," he said.

Jay McGraw did not agree but could not think of a diplomatic way of saying so. "Best be ready, though," was all he said. "I'll take the first watch until midnight, then I'll wake you, Father. Santiago can take it from about three until daylight, if that's agreeable to everyone."

It was.

When twilight came down between eight and nine o'clock and the winking stars began to appear, Jay McGraw gave his Colt to Marcel Dupré and then took his carbine and hunted for some vantage point high enough where he could view

178

most of the grounds. Aside from the impossible task of climbing to the rotten roof of the church building, the next best place seemed to be the top of the wall around most of the quadrangle. The only other choice was the low, red-tile roof that stretched out from the side of the church, forming a continuous roof for the row of rooms they were all using. This, in turn, formed the front side of the quadrangle. This roof sloped toward the front and would be a very exposed lookout perch. He looked longingly at the darkened coastal hills that rose behind the mission. On this clear night with a partial moon he would have an excellent view of the grounds. But, if he saw anything, he could not get back here fast enough. He finally decided to roam the grounds, not staying in one place.

The night proved to be quiet. Jay padded as softly as his boots would let him around the grounds, staying in the shadows, stopping at broken gaps in the corner to survey the expanse of moonlit field. He had no feeling of anything amiss. After two hours of this, he began to wonder if Waterloo Williams and company had gone back to their hotel in Jolon. The threats had probably been only a sudden burst of anger.

When the hands of his engraved pocket watch pointed at five minutes past midnight, he went softly into the priest's room and wakened him without lighting the lamp. Father Stuart sat up on his bunk quickly in the pale moonlight that streamed through the open window. He immediately got up, reaching for his trousers on the bedpost. He moved as if he had been awake when Jay came in.

"All's quiet, Father." He handed over the carbine. "If you need me, I'm throwing my blanket out in the grass near that back wall. I don't feel like being closed in tonight."

"This is probably not necessary," the priest said, slipping his arm into a shirt.

"Probably not," Jay agreed, "but. . . ."

"I know." He took the rifle and disappeared out the door.

Jay McGraw's unconscious mind must have decided that their precautions were an overreaction, or he wouldn't have slept so soundly. When he rolled into his blanket on the soft grass in the deep shadows of the wall, he heard the quiet snuffling of his bay a few yards away, and then he knew nothing.

Chapter Thirteen

Jay McGraw was dreaming that he was imprisoned alone in a large enclosure. Each time he attempted to climb the adobe wall to escape, a grinning Waterloo Williams appeared at the top to throw him back inside. A ripping thunder rumbled through his dream, shaking him. Then someone was shaking him, and the dream vanished as he opened his eyes a slit. Abruptly he started up, wide eyed in fear. Mother Earth was shaking him.

The rumbling noise was not atmospheric thunder. It was the ground and buildings and walls grinding and cracking. Jay jumped up, swaying, and then fell back to his hands and knees. His senses were reeling. A gray dawn illumined the mission.

The ground heaved in a long undulation, and the wall near him buckled with a grinding crash, adobe bricks falling in a shower of dust. His horse emitted a low, moaning sound, and McGraw looked up quickly. Through a pall of dust he saw the animal standing with all four legs spread and braced, his head hanging down.

He heard some shouting and tried again to get to his feet. The trees outside the wall were thrashing, but there was no wind. A shot exploded, and he saw Santiago running heavily toward the corner of the quadrangle, Jay's carbine in hand. The ground stopped shaking, but McGraw could hardly tell, since his knees were trembling as he staggered toward the front wall, fighting down a queasy feeling in the pit of his stomach.

Just as Santiago reached the corner of the broken wall, a horseman galloped through the opening. The horse hit the old Indian and spun him to the ground, the rifle clattering against the wall. The horseman slid his mount to its haunches and hit the ground running. He yanked open the door to Father Stuart's room. Just as he started inside, gun in hand, he jerked backward out the door, sprawling on his back in the dust, a red stain spreading down his face. The priest stepped out the door, the leg of a chair gripped like a club. He saw Jay McGraw.

"They're after Dupré. Took advantage of the quake!" he yelled, pointing toward the church.

Jay snatched at his empty holster before he remembered he had given his Colt to Dupré. He dashed toward the side door of the church. He lifted the latch and jerked, but the door didn't move. A jagged diagonal crack in the wall indicated the building had been shifted enough to jam the door in its frame. He ran back toward the priest's quarters, leaped over the unconscious raider, and into the room.

"Check on Santiago . . . and get that rifle!" he yelled over his shoulder.

The doors to the adjoining rooms proved to

be no problem. But just as he came through the door to the baptistery, someone entered from the church side. With a yell of surprise, the man raised his gun and fired. Jay was too quick. He jumped back and flung the wooden door closed the instant the raider began to raise his arm. The slug buried itself harmlessly in the thick wood. A quick glance around the room showed nothing he could use for a weapon; the small room was empty. He was prepared to run or block the door if they came after him, but he heard a scuffling and a yell from the next room. Two shots exploded almost simultaneously. More yelling. A muffled curse from somebody. Just as Jay finally decided to open the door to find out if they had killed Dupré, Father Stuart came in the opposite door with the rifle.

"Santiago's all right. Just bruised up," the priest panted, handing Jay the carbine. "He's guarding the wall with his pistol, but I think the rest of them are coming around the other side. Part of the church wall crumbled so they can climb in over there."

"Get ready to swing that door open," McGraw ordered, levering a round into the chamber. "Okay? Now!"

The priest yanked the wooden door inward, and Jay fired from the hip at a figure across the room, going out the opposite door. The man yelled, grabbed his arm, and dove into the church out of sight. A second man turned and fired in his direction, but Jay was already on the floor, working the lever. The tiny baptistery was obscured with choking, acrid powder smoke. Jay fired again, but the dim figure was already out the opposite doorway and into the church. A quick glance under the swirling smoke told him the room was empty. They had gotten Dupré. He hoped Dupré hadn't been killed by one of those first shots. He crept into the room, his ears ringing from the blasting in the confined space, and crouched behind the wooden baptismal font. Would he be ambushed if he made a dash into the church? Or had they gone out the door with their captive?

Then he realized the domed top was still in place on the font by his head. They had not found the manuscript. He slid the lid to one side and put his hand inside. The package was still there. He lifted it out and looked around.

"Father, take this and put it in my saddle bags."

The priest took the bulky package and disappeared. From the direction of the quadrangle, Jay heard two shots. Were they attacking from that side, too? Maybe they intended to kill all the witnesses, now that they had gotten Dupré. Then he heard a third shot and decided the shots might be coming from the old Army Colt of Santiago's. Maybe he was trying to pick them off as they left the mission. Jay heard no horses, but the walls were so thick he doubted he could. He heard nothing from the church either, so he decided to take a chance.

He levered another round into the chamber, took a deep breath, and leaped through the doorway. He hit the floor on his stomach and elbows, swinging the barrel in an arc. Toward the far end of the nave, a portion of the partially collapsed side wall had fallen the rest of the way down, creating a huge opening in the outer wall of the church, choked with an eight-foot pile of adobe bricks and rubble. It was up and over this pile that two men were helping two other men who were apparently injured. Jay recognized the slight figure of one of the injured as Dupré.

"Hold it!" he yelled, and fired a warning shot that struck a puff of dust from the adobe pile about three feet to their right. One of the men immediately fired back, but the snap shot went wide.

"Let him go!" Jay shouted.

The only reply was a faster scramble to drag Dupré and the man with the wounded arm up the pile. McGraw cursed under his breath but took dead aim at the man who had hold of Dupré. Just as they reached the top of the pile, he fired. The man screamed, grabbed his thigh, and stumbled backwards out of sight. The other man fired with his pistol, and Jay felt the bullet fan his cheek. He rolled to one side as a second shot struck the floor and ricocheted, stinging his face with chips of stone and dirt. He was momentarily blinded. He rubbed the dirt from his eyes. Through blurred vision he saw only one remaining raider struggling to drag the obviously unconscious Dupré with one arm while pointing his Colt in the general direction of Jay with the other. The two wounded raiders were already outside.

Afterward, McGraw would remember that picture of Dupré and the raider as if frozen in a photograph. Because it was at that instant that everything changed. A sudden, sharp aftershock jolted the ground, and the building shuddered. With a sharp crack one of the roofbeams parted and, with a crashing roar, the back section of the roof gave way. The outlaw heard it coming, let go of Dupré, and bounded over the rubble pile to the outside.

Jay felt a wave of panic and sprang up, instinctively looking for a way out. The earth gave another, sharper jarring, and the church, strongly-built as it was, seemed to sway dangerously, stones grinding against stones, bricks against bricks, with a sickening noise. McGraw's head was reeling as the whole room filled with fine dust.

Dupré! He had to get Dupré! He lurched to his feet and staggered toward the collapsed wall. The floor was trembling under his feet. As he reached the pile of adobe bricks, plaster, and wood, he began to cough and choke on the thick dust that hung in the air. For a second as he dropped the rifle and scrambled frantically around, he thought Dupré had been buried alive. Suddenly his hand caught a human arm and then he saw the head and torso, so powdered with dust he looked like part of the pile. Jay scrabbled frantically to pull the unconscious man free. He failed. He dug with both hands, throwing bricks and dirt to both sides like a badger. Everything continued to tremble slightly.

McGraw finally got enough of Dupré's body uncovered to grasp him under both arms and heave him out. He flung the small man over one shoulder, retrieved his carbine, and half ran with his burden toward the baptistery. In a matter of less than a half minute he was back into the quadrangle. The aftershocks had stopped for the moment. Father Stuart was trying to catch the bay gelding that had pulled his picket pin loose and was galloping wildly around the quadrangle. Jay set the unconscious man on the ground, checking quickly to make sure he was still alive and breathing.

The quake had ruptured the stone aqueduct, and water was gushing out into the enclosure. McGraw's horse lunged away from Father Stuart, and the dragging picket pin snagged under one of the dislodged stones. The horse was brought up short at the end of the line.

Jay flinched as a shot exploded, but it was just Santiago firing past the end of the wall at something outside. Jay went for the horse, slipped in the mud and fell to his knees, sprang up quickly, and he and Father Stuart were able to corner the panicked animal whose picket pin was still hooked.

"Where's the manuscript?" Jay yelled, getting

a grip on the bridle of the still-saddled bay. The priest jabbed a finger at the oilskin-wrapped packet on the ground several yards away and instantly ran to get it.

In the few seconds it took him to retrieve it and return, Jay had begun to quiet the plunging horse. The gelding was still walling his eyes and prancing, but the priest was able to jam the pack into the left saddle bag. Jay led the horse toward the aqueduct to give the line some slack, and the priest jerked the pin loose and threw the pin toward McGraw who caught it with his free hand. He leaped into the saddle and spurred toward the prostrate form of Dupré. He reined up, looping up the slack picket line and stuffing it into the right saddle bag. Father Stuart had caught up and was crouching by Dupré who was coming around and attempting to sit up.

"Is he okay? Can he ride?" Jay asked, glancing back to where Santiago was still guarding the broken wall.

"Yeah, I think so. Nothing broken that I can tell. Got a gash on his head."

"Lift him up here and throw me that rifle, will you?"

The priest complied. Jay pulled the semi-conscious man up and positioned him astride in the saddle, while he slipped out over the cantle to ride behind, holding him in place.

"Thanks for everything, Father!" Jay yelled. "You'll be hearing from us."

For the first time that chaotic morning, Father Stuart grinned, his even teeth showing white in a face covered with dust and grime. He turned and pointed at a V-shaped break in the back wall of the quadrangle. Jay raised his hand in salute, then jerked his horse's head around, and spurred him toward the opening. The bay, bursting with nervous energy, didn't hesitate as he leaped the low notch and galloped out the back of the mission enclosure.

Jay had no idea where to go, but on instinct he circled wide and headed east, away from the coastal mountains behind him. Fortunately the valley was fairly level and partially wooded, and he struck straight cross-country. He only vaguely knew that the Southern Pacific Railroad cut the central part of the state from north to south. If his horse could somehow reach the railroad, just maybe. . . . Maybe what? He would surely not be lucky enough to arrive just as a train was available to take them aboard. But at a depot — if he could find a depot — there would be a Western Union telegrapher. He could send a message to his boss, another to the *San Francisco Chronicle*, and one to the nearest town that had a law officer. Then, depending on how fiercely Waterloo Williams wanted Dupré, maybe he could hold them off from the depot with his rifle until help came.

Would they be pursued? Jay had stung two of them, one with a bullet in the arm and the other with a bullet in the thigh. And Father Stuart had laid out one with a chair leg. He had no idea if Santiago had hit anyone with his old cap and ball revolver. But the Waterloo Williams gang had been hurt. It would either discourage them or make them madder and more determined than ever. He had to assume pursuit would be coming. He had not seen Waterloo Williams. Maybe he had sent his men on ahead to do the dirty work. After all, 'Loo had been the spokesman yesterday. Perhaps he was serious when he said he wanted Dupré so he could let him go and then collect his expenses from his French employers. It was hard to figure. These men could have shot Dupré in his room and then carried his body away. But they were trying to capture him alive. Were they really meaning to let him get away later, or did they just need him alive until they could force him to tell where the manuscript was? From the French point of view that manuscript was nearly as important as the man. Then again, maybe Williams actually intended to turn him over to the French for deportation.

These thoughts ran quickly through McGraw's mind as the bay thundered east into the dawn. When they had covered about three miles, he eased the horse to a walk. The animal was lathered and blowing. Jay tried to shift to a more comfortable position. Sitting behind the saddle and reaching around put a strain on his back and legs. He wanted desperately to dismount and rest but knew they had to put more distance between themselves and any pursuit.

He thought suddenly of arms. The Colt Jay had given Dupré to defend himself was gone. They had only the carbine, and what shells remained in the saddle bags and in McGraw's belt loops and pockets — a sufficient number unless they were in an all-out battle.

Dupré had not spoken a word since regaining consciousness and being lifted to the saddle. But, in spite of whatever injuries he had sustained, he clung to the saddle horn and kept himself balanced without the use of the stirrups or much help from McGraw's arms that encircled him, holding the reins.

Once the bay had recovered from his hard run, Jay urged him to a lope until he spotted the cottonwoods and willows bordering a watercourse. He rode until they were well under cover of the foliage before reining up and sliding off. He reached up to help Dupré down, but the Frenchman needed no help. He was off the bay and down on his hands and knees in the shallow water among the willows before Jay could slip the bit from the gelding's mouth. Man and beast slaked their thirst in the sluggish stream. Jay would have preferred the clear water in his canteen, but he assumed they would need that later. He pulled off his boots and they both rolled, fully-clothed, in the refreshing water, washing the dust and sweat from their bodies.

"Here, let me take a look at that head," McGraw said, noting the clotted blood matting the hair on the side of Dupré's head. He soaked and rinsed it gently and revealed an oozing wound that was long and shallow. It would be sore as hell but should heal in time if the dirt were kept out of it. He got the canteen off the saddle horn and bathed the gash in clear, clean water. It was the best he could do, not having any whiskey or carbolic. He also had no clean bandages. The wound would have to stay open for now. He didn't even have a hat to give Dupré, since he had lost his during the fight at the mission.

"Did they hit you with something, or is that from a bullet?" Jay asked.

"Something hit me. I don't know if they did it, or something fell on me." He reached up to press gently around his injury with his fingertips. He winced. "Is it bad?"

"A sizable gash but not dangerous. It should scab over and heal okay. Does your head hurt?"

"Like a thousand devils hammering on the inside trying to get out."

Jay grinned in spite of himself. This wiry little man would take a lot of killing.

"I'm sorry I lost your gun, *mon ami*," he said. "They took me by surprise. The earthquake wakened me. I knew from a few days ago what was happening, and I was going out when they came in."

"That's okay. We still have the carbine and plenty of ammunition. And the main thing is both you and the manuscript are out of their hands."

"They came in. They did not respect the sanctuary."

Jay nodded. "Yeah, I had a feeling they would do that, sooner or later. They aren't the type to respect much of anything. That earthquake gave them a good excuse. They caught us all off guard. Except Santiago. But he couldn't do much against all of them."

"I hope the old man is all right."

"Both Santiago and the priest were when we left."

"I hope they will not be harmed. They were very kind to me. They probably saved my life."

"We'd better get moving. Feeling better?"

"Very much."

Jay pulled the horse from the browse he was cropping and slipped the bit back into his mouth.

"You sit in the saddle," Dupré said. "I will sit behind and hang on."

They mounted up, and McGraw walked the horse out of the copse of trees then kneed him down into the stream and across.

"I hope there is a sheriff in King City," Jay said over his shoulder. "I don't remember seeing a sheriff's office when I rode through, coming down. If so, he can take you into protective custody, and I'll go on with the manuscript. Maybe I can fool them long enough to get to New York."

"You don't sound as certain as you did before."

"I'm not even sure we're being pursued.

Maybe Waterloo and his boys have given you up as a bad job." Jay secretly wished he felt as confident as he sounded. They rode in silence for a few minutes. "I hope I can remember where King City is," McGraw resumed. "Since we're not following the road, I'm just guessing at the direction."

"Even if there is a law officer there, I will stay with you."

"Why?"

"I do not trust the law officers in this country. The Los Angeles police were ready to turn me over to the French. When I get official notice from your government in Washington that I can stay in this country, then I will trust the law officers."

Jay could understand and sympathize with this view. However, it certainly complicated things as far as he was concerned. As Dupré saw it, he had nothing to lose by running. Either the law or Waterloo Williams would turn him over to the French. What Jay had failed to convince him of was that the Williams gang intended to kill him and destroy the manuscript. The fact that they had not immediately killed him back at the mission apparently strengthened Dupré's belief that the gang was only trying to capture him for delivery to the French and deportation. As they rode east, cross country, Jay wracked his brain for some kind of a safe haven where he could leave Dupré while he attempted to get the manuscript into a Wells Fargo express box then on a train for the East Coast. But he could think of no plan other than getting him north to San Francisco where Anthony Artello would probably provide shelter. But he didn't dare entrust the fugitive to any other Wells Fargo agents, some of whom he knew casually, because they had not been privy to the mission he was on.

He had been riding with a view to striking King City but, since Dupré had let it be known that he would not accept protective custody from any law officer, there was only one reason to find King City — food. McGraw's saddle bags were empty of any provender, but he had money to buy something, if he could find a store. If this was going to settle into some long chase, he had to have food, especially for the fugitive whose strength had not completely returned. He guessed they had outdistanced any immediate pursuit and had bought enough time to stop at a store, provided he could locate one. King City had been the only town he had passed through on his ride south, but the longer he rode the more convinced he became that he had somehow missed it. Perhaps the stream they had stopped at was the Salinas River that he had earlier forded at King City. But they had gotten to it so quickly, it had to be some other stream. He tried to remember what the Salinas had looked like. With a sinking feeling he realized it was very much like the stream they had watered at which was already almost two miles behind them. Since they had ridden almost due east, they had to have crossed the Salinas River a few miles south of King City. He had not been aware of crossing any north-south road, the road that led south from King City another forty miles to the San Miguel Arcángel Mission.

"Reach into that left saddle bag and get me that map," he said over his shoulder.

The Frenchman complied, handing him the thick, folded paper. As the bay proceeded at a walk, Jay unfolded the map and studied it. It was not at all detailed, but it did show the thin line that was the road running along the Salinas River through King City and on south. So it was the Salinas River they had crossed. Looking at the map, he estimated they had passed about ten miles south by east of the town. *Oh, well,* he thought, *there was no going back now.* There were a few towns marked on the map, but in this part of the state they were many miles apart. They were riding toward the vast central valley of California. A hatched line split the San Joaquin Valley lengthwise, representing the Southern Pacific Railroad line. He estimated they had ridden about twelve miles but were still many miles from reaching the railroad. The land was becoming more open now, with fewer places to hide, should the need arise.

He had to make a decision, and he did. He reined the bay north. He might not make it to San Francisco, but he might as well head in that direction. He would stay off the road and hope they were not seen.

The sun rose in a blue August sky, and the day grew sultry and hazy with no wind. Sweat ran down his face, and the wet clothes began to itch. He put the discomfort out of his mind and spurred the bay to a lope. After a few minutes of this, he settled him back to a walk for a quarter hour before running him again. He hoped in this way to cover a lot of ground without tiring the animal too quickly. Dupré stuck to the back of the horse as if he had been born on horseback, with only one hand on the cantle and one on McGraw's belt. He did not complain. He didn't speak at all.

After two hours they stopped to rest the horse and themselves. Since Jay had no hat to use as a bucket, he instructed Dupré to pour some water from the canteen into his cupped hands for the animal to drink. In a few minutes they were on their way again.

Jay had put his gold-plated watch, carefully wrapped in a large bandanna, in the saddle bags for safe-keeping, and when he thought to ask Dupré to get it out for him, he realized he hadn't kept it wound. It had run down and stopped. He hooked the chain through a buttonhole in his shirt and put the timepiece in the watch pocket of his trousers anyway. He glanced at the sky, trying to estimate the time. Early afternoon — maybe one o'clock or a little later was his guess.

He urged the bay into a gallop. But in less than a quarter mile, the gelding broke stride and pulled up, favoring its left foreleg. With a sinking feeling, Jay dismounted. He lifted the forefoot and examined it. Nothing was visible. He ran a finger around the frog and pressed here and there. The animal stood patiently, giving no sign of pain.

He dropped the foot and, taking the reins, began to lead the horse. The animal followed reluctantly and walked with a decided limp, favoring the left foreleg or foot. *Maybe a stone bruise*, Jay thought, *or maybe he hit a depression in the ground the wrong way and cracked a bone in his leg*. Jay was no expert when it came to horses, but he knew this one wasn't going any farther carrying even one rider, much less two.

"I don't know what's wrong, but he's gone lame," he said.

Dupré needed no explanation and silently fell in beside McGraw. *Not a man for idle conversation*, Jay thought, *but then English was a second language and probably not as easy for him, even though he was very articulate in it*.

Jay McGraw was glad to be walking, stretching his cramped muscles and loosening the still-damp clothes clinging to him. But, after about two hours of walking, he was wishing he could be back in the saddle. Dupré, uncomplaining as usual, was scuffing along, his sandals kicking up puffs of dust. Then, quite unexpectedly, McGraw found himself standing on a faint track of road, running east and west. The wagon road that cut through the dry grass showed a moderate amount of use, and he wondered where it led.

Surely, there must be a town at one end or the other, but how far? Then, again, it might be just a private road to some ranch house several miles away. Jay would not admit to being lost even to himself, but he had only the vaguest idea of where they were. He had seen no sign of pursuit all day, but that made him even more nervous. It was like not seeing an Apache, yet having that skin-crawling feeling that they were there. Jay didn't consider 'Loo Williams and his men as dangerous or unpredictable as the Apache renegades he had encountered in the Arizona Territory, but one enemy could kill you just as dead as another, so he had no reason to relax his vigilance.

He checked the bay's foreleg and foot again. If anything, the animal was favoring it even more than before. Jay pondered his next move. He should unsaddle the horse and turn him loose to fend for himself. Just as he straightened up to tell Dupré he had decided to do just that, he heard the thudding of hoofs and the jingling of trace chains as a wagon came down the road behind him. He looked up quickly and put his hand on the stock of the carbine protruding from the saddle scabbard. He saw the dust as the tail of a wagon disappeared briefly into a swale in the landscape. Jay pulled out the carbine and stood behind the horse, ready for anything, although he doubted their pursuers would be driving a wagon. The team of horses trotted up out of the dip in the road, and Jay let the rifle dangle from his hand as the dark green wagon approached.

"Whoa! Hold up, there!" a rough voice came from the wagon seat as the driver hauled his team to a stop. He had little choice since the road was blocked. The driver leaned out to the side and looked at them. "You boys having trouble?"

"Horse went lame," Jay said, walking toward the man, still carrying the rifle.

"Where you headed?" the driver inquired, pushing his hat back and eyeing the rifle.

"North. To San Francisco."

The driver shook his head. " 'Fraid I can't help you there. I'm headed east to the railroad. If you want a ride that far, you're welcome. You can tie the horse on back if he can keep up." He eyed Dupré curiously. "Ridin' double, were ya?"

"Yeah," Jay answered without offering an explanation. "How far's the last town back?"

"King City's about twenty miles. That's where I just come from. A good far piece to walk on a hot day."

"We'll take you up on that offer for a ride. I'll turn my horse loose. I don't want to take a chance on injuring him any further. I'll just be a minute getting the gear off."

Jay slipped the rifle into its scabbard then stripped off the saddle, blanket, saddle bags, canteen, and bridle. "I'll come back for him later," he said, dumping the load into the back of the wagon. Dupré climbed into the back, and Jay stepped up onto the hub and sat on the seat next to the driver.

"Heyah!" The driver slapped the lines over the backs of the team, and the wagon lurched forward.

"By the way, my name's Clarence Moats, but everybody knows me as Boomer."

"Jay McGraw. And this is Marcel Dupré," he gestured over his shoulder. "Boomer is an unusual nickname."

"Not so unusual. I'm a telegraph operator. Retired. But I used to be a drifter, a floater. I practiced my trade whenever and wherever I took a notion. And I mostly took a notion where the pay was the best. I didn't hold allegiance to no company. Back in the 'Fifties and 'Sixties there were a lot of telegraph companies. A good man with a key could move around a lot. And, not bragging mind you, I was one of the best. In the profession fellas like me were called boomers. Don't ask me why. I don't know how it got started. Anyways, it was a good life, and I made a good living at it. But then Western Union began to buy up all these other companies, and in a few short years they pretty much had a monopoly. You've heard of monopolies, haven't you?"

Jay nodded as the old man went on.

"Well, sir, when an outfit gets too dern big and runs off all the competition, they generally go hog wild, and Western Union was no exception. They commenced t'cuttin' salaries and dictating working hours . . . no extra pay for Sundays and all that. Then it got even worse when that robber, Jay Gould, and that union-bustin' sidekick of his, General Eckert, got control of Western Union. That's when I had to get out. I wasn't there for the second big strike the telegraphers had last year, but I was in sympathy with the union nonetheless. 'Course the strike failed in a few weeks, just like the first one did in 'Seventy. The company helped bust the strike by bringing in a lot of the boomers like me to man the keys when the union operators went on strike. But not me, no siree. I wasn't a union member, but I wasn't about to hurt my fellow telegraphers . . . men and women. Yeah, bet you didn't know there were a lot of women telegraphers too, mostly in the big cities," he said, glancing sideways at McGraw, his hooked nose not looking so big from a frontal view.

Normally, McGraw would not have been particularly interested in this recitation of the old man's past, but he himself had applied for a job as an apprentice telegrapher in Iowa some four years earlier, in 1880, but hadn't gotten it. Instead, he had gone west looking for adventure. Yet, telegraphy had continued to fascinate him as a romantic profession, and he had always intended to try again. Other events and other circumstances had intervened. He had found more adventure than he ever bargained for and had wound up as an express messenger for Wells Fargo & Company. He mentioned to Moats that he had a lingering ambition to be a telegrapher. A grin split the leathery face.

"It was a good life in the old days, but I'm not so sure now. You know, in Eighteen Seventy an operator in a big office was expected to handle between a hundred and a hundred and twenty-five messages a day. By last year he was expected to handle from three hundred to three hundred and fifty messages per day . . . at about twenty percent less pay."

"You've almost convinced me I was lucky to get turned down for that job," Jay grinned.

"You're dern right, the way things are now, in spite of everything the Brotherhood of Telegraphers can do. But there'll come a reckoning one of these times, you can bet on it."

The old man drove the team in silence for a short time, apparently mulling over the injustices between labor and management. His lantern jaw was working as if he were chewing tobacco, but he never spat. *More likely chewing on past grievances,* Jay thought. Surreptitiously he studied the man. Moats was probably sixty or past, with iron gray hair flaring out from either side of a sweat-stained felt hat. He was lanky and rawboned with big hands and a long face with a strong crook in his nose. He had sparkling blue eyes. Knobby wrist bones protruded about three inches beyond the cuffs of the blue shirt he wore. A well-worn leather gun belt circled his lean hips. His speech sounded like nothing Jay had ever heard.

"Where you from, originally?" McGraw asked,

more to start the conversation again than for information.

"Chattanooga, Tennessee. I was a telegrapher there during the war. Later I moved out to New York, Boston, Cincinnati, and finally wound up out here. I like the wide-open spaces, and the climate agrees with me. Some o' those Yankees are hard to work with. Wife and I never had no kids, and most o' her family was killed in the war, so she didn't mind movin' around with me. She liked seein' new faces and new people. She's got kinda tired lookin' at me these past two years since I quit work and took up a little farming." He chuckled and slapped the reins over the backs of the team that was slowing to a walk. "That's one reason I'm heading for Colson, a little whistle stop on the Southern Pacific. My brother-in-law is a telegrapher there. He took sick last week, and Western Union shut the office down 'cause they didn't have another telegrapher to send. Anyway, since this earthquake has torn Ned all up and down the coast, they need a good man to relay messages down the line for them." He grinned again. "I swore I'd never go back to work for Western Union if it hare-lipped the governor, but they offered me more than a month's pay for a week's work, so here I go."

McGraw saw a crack of daylight for their escape. Father Stuart would say Divine Providence had thrown Clarence "Boomer" Moats in their path, a heaven-sent telegrapher. And Jay would have agreed.

"I'll need to send a message to San Francisco as soon as we get there," Jay said. "Do passenger trains run pretty regularly up and down that line? Maybe we could catch the cars to San Francisco," he added casually, trying to keep any urgency out of his voice but nevertheless glancing over at the driver as he spoke.

"Don't rightly know what their schedule is," Boomer replied. "The S. P. hauls a good deal of freight on that line too, I understand. 'Course they're run off on sidings to highball the passenger trains." He looked over at McGraw. "Your friend doesn't talk much."

"No, he's pretty quiet," Jay agreed.

Boomer Moats looked his curiosity at McGraw but then averted his gaze and didn't pursue it. His years of living and working with all kinds of people had obviously taught him not to pry into someone else's business or past, unless the information were volunteered. *More than likely he thinks we're on the run from the law,* Jay thought, since it was apparent he kept watching their back trail. Since McGraw was not inclined to talk further, the conversation flagged. Moats alternately walked and trotted the horses.

"We'll have to stop for the night and rest the team," Boomer finally said. "We'll have to camp out, if that suits you. No towns close. I was just planning to sleep in the wagon. If we get started by first light, we can be there before noon."

"Fine."

The long, hot afternoon wore away, and Moats

let the team have their head at a walk the last few miles. They stopped for the night northeast of the Kettleman Hills on a small creek that gave enough water for the horses to drink and for the men to splash over their heads and necks to wash off some of the trail dust and sweat.

"Creek's mighty near dried up," Moats observed, glancing at the red and gold that was washing the western sky behind them to end the hot August day. "I wasn't expectin' company today, but you're welcome to share the vittles my wife made me. She wanted to make two sandwiches, but I've been watching my weight lately so I just took one. You want half?"

It took all of McGraw's will to say no for himself, but he did take the half and gave it to Dupré.

"*Merci, mon ami,*" the Frenchman murmured. He ate slowly and washed it down with water from McGraw's canteen, declining the offer of lemonade from a gallon jug Moats had. Jay knew the one or two bites of food would not be nearly enough to begin to satisfy his hunger and that it would be just enough to get the gastric juices flowing and make him feel worse. So he contented himself with several sips from the canteen.

Clarence Moats stretched out in his wagon bed, after the horses were secured on a long line to a wheel. Jay noted that he kept his gun belt close to hand. McGraw and Dupré slept in the open under a black velvety sky and millions of winking stars. It was a warm night, and Dupré used the saddle blanket for a pillow.

There had been no one in sight all day. As one hour stretched into another, Jay had begun to relax. No one was after them. As he lay on his back in the dry grass, his head propped on the saddle, he began to picture Waterloo Williams telling his French employers how he had made a valiant attempt to capture Dupré, but the earthquake had interfered, and Dupré had gotten away in a hail of gunfire. He would show them his wounded men as proof and whine that the French should at least pay his expenses. Jay smiled to himself at this imagined interview. From their brief contact with Williams, Jay had concluded that the gang leader was the type who wanted reward without danger, payment without confrontation. Nothing could have been further from the truth.

Chapter Fourteen

The wagon rattled into Colson an hour before noon the next day. Clarence Moats halted the tired team at the stock tank. As Jay McGraw climbed down stiffly from the hard seat, the only sounds in the stillness were the snuffling of the horses drinking and the squeaking of the large windmill barely turning in the light air. The tiny town, set down along the railroad track in the midst of the vast San Joaquin Valley, reminded him of many whistle stops on the prairies of the midwest. The small depot with the overhanging roof and wooden platform was painted yellow with brown trim. Just across the dirt road behind the depot was a three-story frame house. A roof shaded a big porch and a picture window that was backed with lace curtains. A barn of almost equal size loomed behind the house.

In addition to these three buildings, a massive round water tank squatted on heavy legs between the windmill and the tracks. A railroad equipment shed was on the other side of the water tank. A four-foot high stack of spare ties next to the shed gave off a resinous odor in the midday sun. A string of empty gondolas and box cars were parked on a siding just south of the depot. McGraw saw about eight or ten other houses and stores straggling along the one dirt street. Windows were broken out and a general air of desolation pervaded the place.

"What happened to all the people?" he asked Moats. "I saw several farm houses this morning as we were coming that were empty, too. I thought this was a great grain and cattle country."

"Cotton, too," the telegrapher agreed. "But all the settlers were run out of here four years ago when they had that big ruckus with the Southern Pacific railroad. They were squatting on land near the railroad that the S. P. claimed as its own. Immigrants mostly. Some sheepherders. Some farmers. Railroad told 'em to buy the land, at a good stiff price mind you, or move off. Some of them had been here for years. Freight rates and fares on the S. P. were sky high anyway, so feeling was pretty much against the big, rich bully. Ever hear of the Mussell Slough feud? No? A bunch of ranchers organized themselves into something called the Settlers' League to fight the Southern Pacific. The railroad, under an Act of Congress, was trying to take possession of every odd-numbered section along this newly-built line. The ranchers and a bunch o' the sheriff's men who were tryin' to evict them had a shoot-out a few miles north of here in the spring of 'Eighty. As I remember, five ranchers and two deputies were killed and seventeen league members went to jail. Damned shame. The railroad got that land free. And those were good, hard-working settlers. Seems like they could have worked out some kind of reasonable compromise. Now a lot of good, productive people have been run off the land, and the average farmer hates the railroad, even though a railroad is good and necessary for this valley." He shrugged. "All you have left of Colson is what you see here . . . the depot and the station agent's house. Tulare is about twenty miles north. It's the Division Headquarters for the S. P. roundhouse and repair shops and offices and all that. Town caught fire last year and mighty near burnt down. Poetic justice, some folks say. Anyway, what you see is what's left of Colson. Used to be a right busy little town."

Jay looked around. Except for the line of poles running north and south along the tracks and supporting a single telegraph wire, the only other man-made structure in sight, besides the abandoned shops and houses, was a pole corral and loading chute.

"If you're in the notion for a meal, there's the Nelson's place," Boomer said, taking off his hat and mopping his face with a large, blue bandanna. "Missus Nelson sets a mighty good table. You can get a bed for the night, too, if you're of a mind to sleep between sheets. Carl Nelson's the station agent. His wife rents rooms, mostly to the section hands who come to work around here. Keeps her from going crazy from loneliness here, Carl says. Real nice lady . . . motherly type. Even wants to mother an old man like me," he

210

grinned. "I don't know if any of the section hands are around in the middle of the day, but I'm guessin' she's got something good on the stove. And that's where I'm headin' as soon as I get this team unhitched and in the barn with some grain."

Moats looked toward the depot just as a man stepped out onto the wooden platform. He wore sleeve garters and galluses and a green eyeshade. His white shirt looked as fresh as if it were a cool day.

"I was looking for you last night, Boomer," Carl Nelson greeted him.

"It's a bit far to make in one day. Didn't want to push the team in this heat."

"You needn't have hurried anyway. The line's dead."

"Damn! If I don't work, I don't get paid. Dead, you say?"

"Yeah. I'm no telegrapher, but you know I've been pressed into it a time or two in emergencies. Almost wish I'd never learned Morse code. I try the key every hour or two, but it's been down since just after the Western Union supervisor sent for you a couple of days ago. Must have been one of the aftershocks up north that took the line out. I'm sure they've got a crew out working on it. Maybe I can get some news from the next train. There's a southbound freight due in about four hours. In the meantime both of us have light duty. I was just getting ready to have some lunch. Come on over. Martha's got some leftover stew.

There's nobody else at the house just now."

"Great idea. I think she might want to set a couple more plates." Moats looked at McGraw and Dupré.

Jay nodded. He was reluctant to leave his only weapon, the carbine, in the saddle scabbard in the wagon but didn't want to arouse any suspicions or be forced to answer any questions. Since his Colt had been lost, he unbuckled the gun belt and left it in the wagon with the rifle.

As they were ushered through the parlor and into the big dining room, McGraw caught a glimpse of himself in the mirror above the sideboard. He was shocked at his grubby, unshaven appearance. And Dupré looked just as bad. Moats had to be wondering if they were fugitives from the law, but he treated them as if they had been boarders at the Nelson house. They probably didn't look or smell any worse than some of the laborers who maintained the rails and roadbeds. Jay still had money he had brought with him on this trip, so he had no worry about paying for the meal. He and Marcel Dupré had not eaten since their second meal of goat meat the night before last. McGraw was ravenous, and the aroma of hot stew tied his stomach into knots.

The four of them sat around the end of a long, varnished table. Moats introduced McGraw and Dupré to the station agent, a stocky man of about fifty with salt-and-pepper black hair and then to his wife, Martha, a buxom woman, probably in her late forties, with a flushed, round face and dark brown hair piled on top of her head in deference to the August heat.

The southerly breeze was barely stirring the curtains at the open window, but Jay forgot all about the weather when he dug into the stew. Three bowls later he was beginning to feel full as he wiped up the last of the gravy with yet another piece of homemade brown bread. Dupré was keeping pace with him, and Moats and Carl Nelson, who were leaning back and picking their teeth, were staring at them in open amazement. Jay could easily have eaten more but was embarrassed to ask for it.

"Been a while since you boys had any victuals," Moats observed.

"Yeah, haven't eaten for about a day and a half," Jay replied, wondering if he should make a clean breast of who they were and what they were doing. Instinct told him not to. He had no way of judging what these men might do. They might try to make themselves famous by holding the two for the law, or they might try to help. But his story was so fantastic, Jay doubted it would be believed at all. He glanced around the room but saw no newspapers anywhere. With the telegraph down for more than a day, there was no way these people could know they had escaped from the Mission San Antonio de Padua. They might be aware of the standoff there but that would be all. McGraw decided the fewer people who knew about this, the better. He would let it ride for now. Moats would be wise soon enough if the telegraph line were fixed quickly since Jay would have to send word north — he had not made arrangements with Anthony Artello for a coded message.

"Any idea how long it'll take to fix that line?" Jay asked, wiping his mouth with a white napkin. "I need to get a message to San Francisco."

Carl Nelson shook his head as he got up and selected a cigar from a humidor on the sideboard. "Depends on how bad a break it is, if any poles are down, or when they get a crew out there to find it and fix it. Could be a few hours, or it might be days."

"I hope it's not days, or I drove all the way over here for nothing," Moats said.

"Well, I don't know," Nelson replied, striking a match to his cigar. "You and I haven't had a game of cribbage for a good while. We've got some catching up to do."

McGraw smiled his thanks at Martha Nelson who appeared silently and refilled his coffee cup from a large pot. She topped off Dupré's cup and disappeared into the kitchen once more. McGraw sipped at the scalding brew and stared out the window at the garden in the side yard that was beginning to go rank with weeds between the tomato plants. As dry as it was, the green plants indicated someone either carried water to the plot or piped it from the well. Jay could also see the corner of a chicken coop toward the back lot to one side of the barn.

Moats and Nelson were still talking, but

McGraw was preoccupied with his own thoughts and ignored the talk of the two older men. He paid Mrs. Nelson three dollars in greenbacks for their meal, and he and Dupré walked outside. A high, hazy overcast had dulled the ferocity of the sun, but the early afternoon was still hot with only a slight, intermittent breeze out of the south.

It was apparent to McGraw that their only means of early escape from here was the next train. He almost wished he had not accepted the ride with Moats, but he had had no idea Colson was such an isolated spot. And, considering the fact that they were lost, on foot, and miles from any houses or towns, they really had little choice. The food and coffee were beginning to revive his flagging strength and spirits. He was feeling much better.

"I'm going to shave," he told Dupré. "You can borrow my razor if you want to."

"Merci. That would be good."

Jay retrieved the razor and a bar of soap he had wrapped in a towel in his saddle bag. He stropped the razor on his leather boot and let Dupré shave first. Then he again stropped the blade, wet his face in the stock tank, lathered his cheeks, and carefully removed several days of growth. He splashed water over his head and neck and ran a comb through his hair. As he dried off in the hot air, he felt fresh and relatively clean again. Now he could concentrate on the job at hand — getting to San Francisco and then on to New York under the protection of Wells

Fargo & Company. He almost wished someone had been sent to help him on this mission, but the next moment he was thankful he had come alone. He was proud he had gotten this far successfully, although he knew luck had also played a big part. He looked back up the road as he wiped his face with the shirt he had taken off. The wagon track that disappeared across the dried grass of the big valley lay deserted under the late summer sun.

"I don't think they're coming after us," he said to Dupré. Yet he had a nagging doubt he couldn't shake. The sooner they were out of here, the better. He slipped the shirt back on, buttoned it, returned the razor to its tiny case, and wrapped it up with the soap. Dupré was hunkered down in the scant shade of the depot and made no comment.

Boomer Moats and Carl Nelson had come out of the house, crossed the dirt street, and gone into the depot. Jay clumped across the wooden platform and went through the depot door into the small waiting room. Two pew-type benches faced each other about twelve feet apart, separated by a black, pot-bellied stove. Tarnished brass cuspidors were on the floor at either end of the benches. The room smelled faintly of old wood and tobacco smoke and coal oil. He was in the middle room of the three-room depot. To his right, through a closed door, he guessed was the storage room for freight and baggage. To his left, enclosed in multi-paned windows above the waist-high wainscoting, was the combination office for the station agent and the Western Union telegrapher. He opened the bottom half of the Dutch door that served as a ticket window and went in. Nelson sat in a swivel chair behind a massive wooden desk that took up most of the floor space in the room. The desk blotter was stacked with papers and invoices and what appeared to be a timetable. A calendar hung on the far wall depicting a large drawing of a locomotive under a full head of steam. Beneath it were the words: **Ship On the Southern Pacific**. The calendar sheet showing below was the month of September. With a start Jay realized August had somehow slipped past, and he had no idea what day of the week it was, much less what day of the month. He shook his head and turned to Moats who had flipped off the circuit closer on the key pad and rattled the telegraph key expertly with some sort of signal.

"She's deader'n four o'clock, all right," he confirmed, sliding the circuit closer switch back into position.

"I'm used to hearing messages passing up and down the line," Nelson said, indicating the sounder near the telegraph key. "When it was quiet for a few hours, I tried the key."

"Did you look for any breaks close by?" Boomer asked, scrutinizing the wire that led down from the outside pole to a glass insulator at the top of the wooden window frame and then down inside to the base of the key.

"Yeah. I went up and down the line about a mile each way but didn't see anything out of the ordinary."

"Wonder if I oughta wait around here for them to fix it or maybe drive the wagon up the line to Tulare and see if they know what's wrong."

Nelson shrugged. "Not much point in it, unless you're just too nervous to sit still. Break's likely way on up north, if they got a heavier jolt than we did here. A man learns patience on a job like this." Nelson got up from his desk and walked around to the bay window where he folded his arms and stared out at the empty track and the vacant land beyond. "In fact, if things don't start picking up around here, I look for the company to close down this depot and ship me somewhere else. There's been some talk about it."

"Hell, you may have the title of station agent, but you're a one-man show around here . . . porter, ticket seller, caretaker for that windmill, water tank, cars on the siding, storage shed, not to mention husband to the lady who feeds and houses section hands. Doesn't matter that you don't have any passengers or very little freight," Moats responded.

Nelson shrugged. "All of that could be transferred about twenty miles north to Tulare, once they get all the facilities rebuilt after that fire. They could send someone down the line to check the windmill. That apparatus doesn't require much maintenance. Just a little grease now and again."

Jay McGraw had been leaning against the wall, waiting and listening. Finally, Nelson turned to him with a questioning look when he asked: "When's the first train north?"

"Normally, there's a northbound through here every evening about six o'clock. But without a telegraph to confirm, I don't know if it's on time or even if the southbound freight is coming. The engineers are on their own. I'll watch for it and flag it. You can get your ticket now if you want. Where you going?"

"San Francisco."

"Two, one way?"

Jay nodded, reaching for his billfold.

Nelson moved back to the desk and prepared the tickets. He stamped and handed them to McGraw, who paid him out of the remaining greenbacks. It left him with only ten dollars and some coins. Nelson was pulling a cribbage board out of a desk drawer as Jay slid the tickets into his pants pocket. He glanced at the wall clock as he turned toward the door. It was 1:40. He reset and wound his watch.

The distant, rhythmic chugging of a locomotive broke the afternoon stillness and roused Jay McGraw from a fitful doze. He sat up on the bench of the back platform and squinted at the sun that was sliding down the western sky. He got up, stretched, and looked down at Dupré who was sprawled on his back nearby, his head on the saddle. Jay dug out his watch. Its hands pointed at 6:10. Their train was here. But then he realized the sound was coming from the wrong direction. By the time the southbound freight ground to a halt, McGraw, Dupré, and Carl Nelson were on the trackside platform to meet it.

"Where you been?" Carl Nelson called out even before the engineer swung down from the cab. "You're four hours late."

"Trouble up the line," the lean engineer said, coming up to them and pushing his cap back on his head. "Quake weakened a few of the small trestles. They had to be shored up with some timbers before we could cross, and then we had to take it real easy. I was holding my breath. The line's down so we couldn't signal you."

"I know. The quake get it too?"

The engineer nodded. "Somewhere up between Oakland and Stockton, I think. They've got a crew out trying to track it down and fix it."

"The six-o-two's due through here any minute, if she's on schedule. Better shunt you off onto the siding just in case."

"Right. Lemme back her up and take on a little water first. The northbound'll have to stop for your passengers anyway."

Jay didn't wait for more. Clarence Moats was watching and listening at the open window by his key, and McGraw went into the office, reaching for a pad of paper on the desk.

"Here's a message I want sent as soon as the

line's back in service," he said to Boomer as he began writing.

"Not much telling when that'll be," Moats responded.

"Doesn't matter. Just send it as soon as you can. I'll pay in advance," Jay said, pencil poised as he sought the most economical combination of words that would convey his urgency to Anthony Artello.

He finished and handed the message to Moats who counted the words and charged him accordingly. Jay saw him scan the message briefly and thought he noticed a flicker of surprise on the telegrapher's face, but Boomer said nothing. He had probably learned discretion during his years of sending and receiving messages.

As McGraw turned, he happened to glance out the back windows of the depot. He froze, a sinking sensation seizing him. The dark figures of three horsemen were coming slowly toward Colson from the west. They were still upwards of a mile away, moving at a walk, their elongated shadows stretching out ahead of them across the short, dry grass.

Moats noticed his reaction and followed his gaze. "Looks like we're going to have company. Probably somebody to catch the northbound. But they're not in any hurry."

They were too far away to recognize, but the horses were plodding, heads down, as if they had put many miles behind them this day.

"We need to get out of sight somewhere until

221

we see who that is," Jay said quietly to Moats.

"Figured you were on the run from somebody," Boomer said.

"It's not the law. A gang of killers is trying to get their hands on him." He jerked his head toward the platform outside where Dupré was waiting.

"Why?"

"He's a French escapee from Devil's Island. He was holed up in an old mission church, and I just helped him escape. The French want him dead so he can't embarrass their government."

"What's your connection with this?"

"I'm with Wells Fargo, like the telegram says." He was staring out at the approaching riders. "Look, I haven't got time to talk now. Is there a place we can hide?"

Moats looked around thoughtfully. "Those old, empty houses are boarded up. If those men are the ones after you, they'll look all the obvious places, like the Nelsons' or the baggage room or the empty boxcars on this train and the siding." He fell silent as he looked around again while Jay nervously watched the bobbing figures following their lengthening shadows toward Colson. "That's it! The water tower. They'll never think of looking there. Quick. Get your friend and come on."

Jay dashed outside, grabbed his carbine, and slung the saddle bags over his shoulder. "C'mon!" he said urgently to Dupré. "We've got to hide. They're coming!"

Dupré asked no questions as he followed Jay and Boomer around the building between the storage shed and the depot to the base of the water tank. Nelson had walked about fifty yards down the track to the south, flag in hand, looking intently for any sign of the expected passenger train.

"Here," Moats said, pausing at the base of the ladder. "They won't see you climb up because the Nelsons' house and barn are between you and them."

Marcel Dupré was already half way up the iron ladder, agile as a monkey. Jay followed him, carbine in one hand, saddle bags still over his shoulder. The catwalk around the base of the huge, cylindrical tank was a good twenty feet above the ground. Once on the catwalk, McGraw saw Moats was right — he could not see the horsemen approaching. He followed Dupré around to the opposite side of the huge water tank, holding the narrow iron handrail. The westering sun was striking the top half of the dull red tank.

Two trainmen looked up curiously at them from the side of the mogul locomotive as they swung the big metal spout into position with a thin chain to take on water. Standing, flattened face to the side of the tank, Jay reflected that he was going to look very foolish if the incoming riders turned out to be just some farmhands or ranchers from somewhere in the valley. But he dared not take a chance. He and Dupré lay down on the narrow catwalk.

"Stay here," he whispered to the Frenchman as he began to worm his way forward, gripping the carbine. He edged along until he could just see the street between the depot and the Nelsons' house. Nothing there. He waited, and then waited some more, the seconds dragging interminably. He wiped his sweating palms on his pants and gripped the rifle again. Had the riders stopped or turned off somewhere? But finally the long shadows appeared, sliding jerkily along the ground, followed by the sound of hoofs, and then the three horsemen emerged from behind the building and turned their mounts toward the stock tank, almost below where he lay. His heart sank. The leading horseman was Waterloo Williams himself. The other two he didn't recognize immediately beneath their hat brims, but the bulky form of the outlaw leader was unmistakable, as was the way he sat his horse.

Jay held his breath and watched through a two-inch wide space between the boards in the catwalk as the trio dismounted almost beneath him. Williams removed his hat and wiped a bandanna over his face as his tired horse plunged his muzzle greedily into the water tank. Williams's face was covered with a thick stubble, and his clothes were powdered with a fine dust. He turned and said something to one of his men standing just out of McGraw's vision. Jay didn't catch the words, but Williams pointed toward the depot.

"Where the hell's the saloon around here?"

came a rather high-pitched voice from one of the men. "My tongue thinks it's just come from a seven-year drought."

"There'll be no drinking until we get what we came for," Williams growled in a low voice. "If you're so damned thirsty, try a little of this here water." He followed his own advice by stepping away from the horses to the pipe that was pouring a small stream of water into the tank. He filled a double handful and drank. He repeated this three times, then scooped his hat full of water and slammed it back on his head, the water cascading over his face and soaking his shirt to the waist.

"Whew! That's a lot better than whiskey when you're dry," he exulted, water dripping from his short hair.

As each man in turn followed his example, Jay could see them through the crack. He could not remember seeing either man before, in the barroom at Jolon or during the wild battle and flight from the mission, but then he hadn't really been studying faces at the time. There was nothing distinctive about either of these men from their outward appearance. They both looked to be in their late twenties or early thirties. As they removed their hats, he saw one was blond, and the other had dark brown hair. The blond man was leaner and slightly taller, and he wore tan canvas pants, a plaid shirt, brown vest, and brown hat. The dark one was slightly shorter and stockier, dressed in faded Levi's, white collarless shirt, leather vest, and sweat-stained gray felt hat. Their boots were scuffed and worn, but the blond one sported large-rowelled silver Mexican spurs that jangled when he moved. Other than that the only part of their apparel that was the least ostentatious were the sidearms they wore. The blond man had a tooled Mexican gun belt and holster with the carved ivory butt of a nickeled Colt protruding from it. In addition, another pistol with an ivory grip was tucked into his waistband. From where he lay, Jay thought the weapon looked very much like his own missing Colt.

The darker man wore a black gun belt with the polished walnut grip of a Colt in the holster. Except for these low, tied-down gun rigs, a casual observer might mistake these men for itinerant cowhands. But Jay was no casual observer, and he went cold in the afternoon heat at the sight of them. He wondered what these two were like. He could read very little in their faces. If he could only observe them moving and talking for a short time, he would have a pretty good handle on what they were like. Waterloo Williams was a man plain to read, and Jay read him to be forthright, bullying, and slightly below average intelligence which he compensated for with an animal-like cunning. One thing about his character that Jay had grossly misread was his tenacity. McGraw would have bet his lunch that Williams would not come after them. Perhaps it was wounded pride that spurred the gang leader to track them — more the idea of revenge than to satisfy any agreement with his French employers.

Whatever the motive three of them were here. It was three against two, and Jay itched to have it out with them here and now. He was tired of hiding and running. Actually, it was three against one, since he and Dupré had only one carbine between them. He was glad the three outlaws ignored the train that was watering up because the two trainmen were casting occasional glances in their direction. But the trainmen, whatever they thought, had other things to do and went about their business without yelling up at them.

The three men below let their horses drink another minute then followed Williams as he pulled his mount toward the hitching rail at the back of the depot. Boomer Moats had gone outside to the platform and waved at Carl Nelson who was down the track a way with his signal flag. Nelson came back to the depot, still looking back over his shoulder south along the empty track. The northbound passenger train was late.

Jay lay flat on the catwalk, watching Williams and his men trooping through the empty depot toward Nelson and Moats on the trackside platform. He hoped Moats was warning Nelson to keep his mouth shut. McGraw hugged the rough wood of the catwalk, not daring to move now for fear of being seen. All the men on the platform needed to do was raise their eyes, and he would be visible. He hoped Dupré was staying well out of sight on the other side of the tank.

The quietly panting engine below him obscured the words he strained to hear from the men on the platform. Undoubtedly Williams was asking if they had been there. Jay wondered if they had found the abandoned horse somewhere near the road and guessed the two fugitives had caught a ride toward the railroad rather than back toward King City. But then, the tracks in the seldom-used road would have been plain to read. There had been little wind and no rain in the past few hours to erase them.

McGraw was perspiring freely, and sweat was tickling the side of his nose. He gritted his teeth and remained motionless. Moats shook his head and glanced at Carl Nelson who shrugged and said something. Whatever he said apparently angered the volatile Williams who raised his voice, although Jay could still not distinguish the words. After a minute or two of this, Williams stomped through the depot with his men, and the trio started across the street toward the Nelson house. A small sign Jay had not noticed before advertised board and room. He hoped Mrs. Nelson would have the presence of mind not to say anything about having seen them. But then, she would have no way of knowing and would probably answer any questions they put to her. He went cold at the thought. As soon as the screen door slammed behind the outlaws, he sprang up and looked down the track. How he longed for a sight of the northbound passenger train! But the track to the south was as empty as ever.

The men on the locomotive had finished watering and swung the counterbalanced metal spout back up into place. McGraw found Dupré just as he heard his own name called. He looked down and saw Moats motioning frantically for him to come down. He glanced toward the Nelson house. If any of the outlaws happened to be looking out the window, they would be in plain sight. But they were probably in the dining room beyond the parlor. He fervently hoped so as he and Dupré quickly slid down the iron ladder, hardly bothering with the steps. They followed Moats back to the depot.

"We've got to hide you somewhere else until the train gets here," Moats said.

Nelson looked at them curiously as if undecided whether or not to believe this strange story.

"Maybe the baggage room," Boomer suggested, glancing at the locked door leading off the waiting room.

"No," Jay said. "If they suspect we're in there, we'll be trapped."

"Where, then? It'd take too long and make too much noise to tear off the boards from one of those empty houses and get you inside."

"We need to keep moving and stay out of sight until they leave."

"They're not leaving any time soon. I don't think they swallowed my story that I hadn't seen you two. They asked about your saddle on the back platform. I told them it was mine. And there was no way we could warn Martha. She may be telling them all they want to know right now. I've taken a chance on believin' your story, fantastic as it is. And after seein' those three, I'm even more inclined to believe you. They tried to let on they were lawmen, but they wouldn't show me any badges."

"They're not the law," Jay assured them.

"The six-o-two's already a half hour late," Nelson said, looking at the wall clock inside his office. "And it won't be dark for another two hours."

"The tower's no good," Moats said. "If they spot you up there, you're sitting ducks."

"Is there an empty boxcar on that freight?" Jay asked, looking out at the locomotive that was puffing and steaming its way onto the siding. "We could hide in there until the other train arrives."

"Good idea," Nelson said, "but I'm sure they'll search the passenger train when it gets here. They might even take it into their heads to search this freight. I think they're convinced you're around here somewhere."

"Get down! Here they come!" Moats hissed.

McGraw and Dupré immediately sank to the floor of the waiting room where they were standing and scuttled toward the open door of the office. By the time McGraw was hidden under the big desk in the middle of the room and Dupré squeezed in beside him, he heard boots clumping on the wooden floor outside.

His heart was pounding as he tried to shift the carbine in the constricted space so as to have it ready. The barrel was wedged on something and, as he jerked it free, it banged against the underside of the desk. The noise was deafening in his own ears, and he caught his breath, listening.

"What the hell was that?" a voice asked, sounding close.

"I didn't hear nothin'," Moats replied. "Just that freight bangin' around outside."

"Where are they?" 'Loo Williams demanded.

"Where are who?" Nelson asked.

"Don't play dumb. Your missus told me there were two men eating in her dining room no longer ago than lunch time today."

"Oh, I guess they were the two section hands who stopped in. They headed south a few hours ago," Nelson replied.

Jay could almost imagine Williams's face clouding up. "Those were no section hands!" he exploded. "I asked her to describe them, and they're the same two men we're after. Now, I don't know what yarn they spun you, but you're obstructing justice by harboring these men. They're dangerous fugitives. They'd just as soon kill you as look at you." Williams was obviously trying to control the emotion in his voice as he unconvincingly played the part of a lawman. "We found the abandoned horse they were riding double, and we scouted around a couple of miles to see if they were anywhere close by on foot. They had to have come here. We tracked a wagon here.

231

Probably that very wagon out front."

"Sure. I just got in about noon today from King City," Boomer replied evenly. "I'm a telegrapher. Didn't see a soul between here and there."

There was a pause, and then Nelson said: "Hey, mister, there's no call to draw a gun on us."

"I'm gonna give you about five seconds to give me some straight answers or. . . ." Williams left the threat hanging.

"If you're really lawmen, you wouldn't shoot us down," Moats affirmed.

"And if I'm not?"

"Figured as much," Boomer said.

"Okay, then, where are they? And you better think about it before you tell me you haven't seen them."

"All right. I guess we can't hide the truth from a man as perceptive as yourself," Moats said with feigned resignation.

McGraw's legs were beginning to ache where the circulation was cut off as he squatted under the desk.

"I gave them a ride when I found them on foot yesterday," the telegrapher continued. "Didn't know anything about them except they were in trouble because their horse had gone lame. Brought them here and they ate at the house and then decided to start out walking the tracks towards the next town south of here. They thought they could probably buy a horse there."

"Why south instead of north?" Williams asked suspiciously.

"You'll have to ask them that question. If you get going, you can probably catch up with them. With a four-hour head start, they probably aren't more'n twelve or fifteen miles ahead of you."

Good old Clarence "Boomer" Moats, Jay thought. *Trying his best to throw them off the track and protect us. And he hardly knows us.*

"I don't believe you," Williams said. "I think you're lying. They're still around here some place. I can feel it."

"I tell you, they're gone. They were in one helluva sweat to get goin' for some reason. They acted half starved, or they wouldn't have even taken time to eat."

"They're still around here some place," Williams insisted. "I know it."

"You can see for yourself there's nobody else here," Nelson put in. There was a pause. "If you'll excuse me, I have to go hoist the signal for the northbound express."

"Then you won't mind if we search the place," Williams said with a sarcastic tinge to his voice. "We'll start with your office."

McGraw held his breath and inched the carbine around to be ready without the barrel visibly protruding. Dupré was jammed in against him, and McGraw's squatting legs were dead from lack of circulation. He doubted he could spring quickly if he had to. He would have to rely on the element of surprise. He would have to take the first man, whichever one of the three it was, and then. . . .

The floor vibrated under the steps of heavy boots. At the same moment in the distance Jay heard the mournful wail of a steam whistle on the approaching northbound.

Chapter Fifteen

Jay McGraw had had the presence of mind to pull the big rolling chair back into place after they squeezed under the desk. He could hear men moving about in the office and prayed he could get off the first shot, since he knew it would be only a matter of seconds before he was discovered. He saw a scuffed boot toe appear a few inches from him as the big outlaw leader paused next to the desk.

"Huh! Not in here. Andy, bust that padlock offen that baggage room door and look in there. Ty, get outside and start checking those freight cars. They could be hidin' out there somewhere."

The toe disappeared as Williams moved away, and Jay let out his breath slowly as he heard the footsteps moving out of the office. Yet he dared not move. He trusted Dupré to remain silent. He was sure the little man had been in tighter places than this. He could feel the warmth of his body, but he couldn't even hear the Frenchman breathing, he was so still.

McGraw knew he would have to move soon since the squatting position was taking a terrible toll on his muscles. He wondered how baseball catchers could remain in this position. No wonder most of them were slow afoot. He himself had been a swift, skilled outfielder for his college team, so skilled and so hard-hitting, in fact, that only an untimely ankle injury had prevented him from being hired to play for the professional Cincinnati baseball club. How fate seemed to turn on small hinges! Except for that minor injury, he might be playing for pay right now in some eastern city before crowds of cheering people instead of crouching under a desk, fearing for his life in some god-forsaken railroad stop in central California.

The wail of a steam whistle sounded again, much closer. McGraw wondered if Nelson was going to signal the passenger train to highball right on through, since it was already late, and he wouldn't dare stop it for McGraw and Dupré. But no. In less than a minute Jay heard the heavy chuffing and the bell clanging of the locomotive as it slowed for the depot. Maybe Nelson had some mail or freight for the express car. And suddenly Jay realized there might be a Wells Fargo express messenger aboard this train. His heart leaped at the thought, and he took the chance of pushing the chair back and crawling out from under the desk, groaning as the blood rushed back into his numbed legs, making him slightly dizzy. If there was an express car, he would fight his way aboard, if necessary. Once aboard, they would be safe. It would be the answer to all their problems. They would then be under the protection not only of Wells Fargo but also of the Southern Pacific Railroad. They could ride north to Oakland, report to Anthony Artello, and then connect with the eastbound to Chicago and on to New York. The three outlaws outside would have to be very desperate to attack a locked express car while it stood in the station with other armed railroad men all around.

There was plenty of noise outside to mask their movements as McGraw crawled to the open door and put his eye around the edge. Dupré was right behind him with the manuscript in the saddle bags.

"You didn't have to bust the lock off of it," Nelson was saying to the blond outlaw as he emerged from the baggage room just across the waiting area. "I had a key and had to open it anyway."

The outlaw ignored him and went outside as the passenger locomotive came to a stop just beyond the platform with a squeal of brakes in a cloud of steam. Nelson turned and spotted McGraw's head and cautiously signaled him to stay down. Then he casually approached the office door, pretending to be writing something on a pad of paper in his hand.

"Stay out of sight until I can divert them all outside," he said in an undertone. "Then get over to the house and tell Martha I said to hide you in the root cellar, or one of the upstairs closets. She'll know best."

"No. We've to get away from here," Jay whispered back. "Is there an express car on this train?"

"Baggage and mail car only. No attendant. It's locked from the outside. I have a key but no chance of getting aboard without being seen," he answered without looking their way. Suddenly he glanced up and said aloud: "Ah, I see you've searched everywhere around here and didn't find them. You can see we were telling the truth."

McGraw and Dupré were flattened against the wall behind the door inside the office as Nelson walked away through the waiting room, taking the brown-haired outlaw called Andy with him. The outlaw only grunted.

"Why don't you men go on over to the house and get some supper? I'm sure Missus Nelson's got something pretty tasty whipped up by now." They passed out of earshot, and Jay chanced another peek through the crack between the door and the wall. He could hear something going on outside and men's voices. Moats was apparently helping load whatever mail and few freight items the train had stopped to pick up. No passengers got off, and there were none to get on except McGraw and Dupré. There had to be some way to get aboard. Jay risked raising his eyes above the lower sill of the window. Williams and the blond man whom he had addressed as Ty stood on the platform with their backs to him, watching the passenger train, the conductor, the engineer, and the man helping Moats load a mail bag and a half dozen small parcels through the sliding door of the baggage car. Even as Jay watched, the baggage door was slid shut and a padlock snapped into place. There was no messenger aboard, and the locomotive was not going to water up here. It was a quick stop. Jay saw about a dozen passengers scattered along the windows of the two coaches. The baggage car was next and then the caboose. Even as McGraw watched, the conductor waved to the engineer and swung aboard the rear step of the last passenger coach just as the engineer opened the throttle. The wheels spun briefly and then took hold. Gray smoke whooshed from the diamond stack as the train pulled away. McGraw's hopes went with it. There was no way they could get aboard. He dropped down and crawled back behind the desk.

As the sound of the departing train diminished, Jay could hear Williams yelling at his man, Ty, to hurry up and finish checking the freight cars so they could eat. Jay was careful to stay out of sight but was banking on the fact that the outlaws would not check the office again. He was right. In a couple of minutes Williams collected his men, and they trooped across the street to the Nelson house. The outlaws were apparently satisfied that McGraw and Dupré were really gone, or else they were just taking a break for some nourishment before continuing their search.

McGraw briefly considered getting Nelson to smuggle them aboard the southbound freight as the train began to pull off the siding back onto the main line, but he was determined not to go south. Somehow he had to work his way north.

He would not go any farther out of his way than he absolutely had to.

He had another idea. The three outlaws had left their horses saddled and tied to the hitching rail. They were either very negligent of their mounts, or they were planning to move on shortly. He guessed the horses had to be very tired, but if he and Dupré could steal them and head north, leading one horse, they could at least put the outlaws afoot. Williams might commandeer any horses available and come after them, but it would be dark in about two hours.

Keeping low, he and Dupré crept out of the office to the waiting room and sat on the floor behind one of the wooden benches while Moats and Nelson lounged on the bench above them as if talking to each other. Jay whispered his plan of stealing the horses.

"I know there will be hell to pay for you if we get away," McGraw said regretfully. "That's the only reason I hate to try it. You two have saved our lives already, and I hate to ask you to do more or bring any harm to Missus Nelson."

"You let us worry about that," Nelson said.

"Forewarned is forearmed," Boomer added. "We may not be gunmen, but I don't think any man in the world is going to try to draw on another man who's holding a cocked gun on him." He shifted on the bench to toss a casual glance toward the Nelson house. "Those horses have been watered, but they've got to be tired, and I don't know when they last had anything to eat. But they should be good for a few miles if you take it easy."

"We'll have to make a run for it at first. If you can just keep them off us until we get a head start, we'd be obliged."

"You can bet on it." Moats almost grinned. "Surprise! That's how we'll do it. Just like a few of us captured the telegraph from the Yankees at Calhoun, Georgia, during the war. But just so we'll know what's really going on, how about telling me and Carl a little more of your situation."

Jay quickly briefed them in as few words as possible. He told of his own involvement, the siege, and the escape. He stressed the international implications.

"Whew!" Nelson breathed. He ran a hand across his forehead where some beaded drops of perspiration had collected.

The sun was down. Though there was still plenty of light, Nelson got up to pull down the coal oil lamp from the ceiling and strike a match to its wick. The wall clock in the office pointed at four minutes to seven.

"I don't know how to thank you two," Jay said.

"Don't worry," Boomer replied, patting the worn black holster on his thigh. His blue eyes were positively glinting with expectation of what was to come. "Are you up to this, Carl?"

The station master nodded, tight lipped.

"Maybe we'd better wait a few minutes until they're done eating," Moats said. "That way we'll catch them coming out and not put your wife in danger. And it'll be a little closer to dark when they make the break."

Nelson nodded again, saying nothing. He glanced around toward his office. Then he said: "I think I'll go to the house and get my shotgun. It's upstairs in the bedroom. I don't think I can do much against three gunmen with only my Colt. My hand might not be steady."

"Good idea. Just don't tip them off."

"I'll meet you in the parlor in five minutes, and we'll stop them as they come out of the dining room."

Nelson got up and went outside and across the street to his house.

"Stay out of sight until I step out on the porch and give you the high sign," Moats told them. "Then grab those horses and go like hell."

"Wouldn't it be easier if we just quietly walked those horses away while they're at supper?" Jay asked.

"Might work," Boomer admitted, "but if one of those horses should whinny or make any kind of noise, it'll ruin our play. I've seen men like them before. They live on the ragged edge. They're not like normal folks. They live by the gun, and they're always attuned to danger. It's a survival instinct. If one of their horses so much as snorts wrong, they'll be up from the table, guns in hand. Better wait 'til we get the drop on 'em".

And so the very simple plan was carried out.

At 7:15 Boomer Moats stepped out of the Nelsons' front door onto the porch and gave them a thumbs-up signal. McGraw quickly checked the cinches on the three saddle horses, loosed their reins from the hitching rail, and he and Dupré swung into the saddles. Jay took the reins of the third animal, and they kicked their mounts into a gallop, heading north. They followed the tracks and the row of telegraph poles that stretched toward Tulare about twenty miles away. But, after only a quarter mile, Jay knew these horses were in no shape to run, and they slowed to a walk. He looked back but the little town of Colson appeared deserted. The three outlaws were probably still being held at gunpoint inside the house. He felt a strong urge to get as far away from there as quickly as he could, but on this flat terrain they would be visible for several miles. He wondered if Moats and Nelson would disarm the outlaws and maybe lock them in the root cellar or the baggage room. Then he remembered the lock had been broken off the baggage room door.

The horses were still blowing from their sudden exertions as they plodded along, heads down. Dupré carried the carbine so McGraw could have a hand free to lead the third horse. The saddle bags containing the precious manuscript and the extra ammunition were draped across the pommel of McGraw's saddle.

A long, lingering twilight was settling over the vast valley. Jay found himself wishing for darkness to hide them on this treeless landscape. He felt vulnerable and exposed, in spite of being confident that Moats and Nelson had carried out their end of the plan.

Just as he was contemplating what might have happened back there at the Nelson house, he heard a distant, muffled explosion that sounded very much like a gunshot. There was only one place it could have come from, and Jay twisted around to look back at Colson. Had Moats or Nelson been forced to shoot one of the outlaws? Or had one of the gunmen had a hide-out gun he had somehow brought into play? The thought sickened him as he strained to listen for any more shots. None came. He began to regret his decision not to steal aboard the southbound freight and quietly slip away. This had put Moats and Nelson, and very possibly Martha Nelson, at risk, two men he and Dupré had just met who believed their story and, for whatever reasons, had decided to endanger their own lives to help total strangers escape. Maybe they just didn't like the odds and, with the Westerner's penchant for siding with the underdog, had taken up their cause. Or it could have been the decent man's aversion to everything lawless. No matter. It was done now. Moats and Nelson had three mountain lions by the tails. He trusted they would figure out what to do with them. The telegraph wire was still down, so no calls for assistance could be sent out to the law.

They plodded on into the gloaming, Dupré

leading and McGraw following with the trailing horse. Jay had thought to fill their canteen and bring it, even though they had no food. But it didn't matter just now; they had filled up at lunch, and Jay wasn't really hungry yet. Speed and distance were the main things. They were safe for the moment. It was midnight before they knew their plan had gone awry.

Chapter Sixteen

The outlaws' horses were more spent than even Jay McGraw had supposed. At a slow walk they often stumbled with fatigue. He and Dupré dismounted and led them for a time and then alternated riding and walking. By about two hours after dark the animals, one after another, absolutely refused to go any farther. Dupré's mount went down and would not get up. They discussed putting a bullet in the brain of each since the three seemed to be going down for good. But, since there might still be some hope for their survival, if left to rest and graze, Jay finally settled for just unsaddling them by cutting through the cinches, thus rendering the saddles useless. Besides, as Dupré pointed out, they shouldn't take the chance of any shots being heard.

They slipped off the bits and bridles and regretfully went forward on foot, carrying the rifle, canteen, and saddle bags. Clouds obscured any moon there might have been as they trudged along the roadbed beside the tracks. They settled into a monotony of putting one foot ahead of the other — on and on with nothing to vary the numbing sameness of it, until Jay was almost falling asleep on his feet. The wiry little Frenchman was tireless. Years of deprivation had hardened him to nearly anything. It seemed to McGraw the little man could keep up this pace forever — and walking in homemade sandals at that. *Maybe that was part of the answer,* Jay thought, looking down at his own heavy boots. He regretted not having worn shoes when he left San Francisco.

Jay estimated it was nearly midnight when they finally halted to rest for a few minutes. McGraw sank wearily to the ground while Dupré set the saddle bags down and sat on one of the iron rails. Jay noticed a slight breeze out of the west, and a few ragged clouds were scudding across the starry sky, borne on some stronger wind aloft. As they sat there in silence, he fancied he could detect a change in the smell of the air. It was the scent of rain. He had no idea how far they had come but felt the town of Tulare could not be that far ahead.

He got up to move on, and Dupré followed without question or comment. After a few minutes, Jay caught sight of a dark lump about forty yards ahead. When he reached the darker blot, it turned out to be a stack of spare ties with a pole car tipped up against it. His heart leapt.

Just as he opened his mouth to tell Dupré, he heard the sound of hoofbeats. He froze then looked, straining his eyes into the darkness. Nothing. The thickening overcast had completely blotted out the stars. He turned his head this way and that, hoping the breeze would bring him the sound again, but after a few seconds he became convinced he had not actually heard hoofbeats.

"What is wrong?" Dupré asked, noting McGraw's movements.

"Ssshhh! I think I hear horses."

He held up his hand in warning. They stood silently for several seconds. Then the sound came again. It was behind them to the south. It faded as the wind shifted then came again. Jay wished he had been mistaken, but he had not. It was the rhythmic, staccato sound of several horses, moving fast.

"Get down!" Jay pulled the smaller man behind the stack of crossties, where he knelt on one knee, his carbine ready.

As they waited, McGraw felt a strong sense of having done all this before. It seemed he had been running and hiding for weeks. The sound of hoofs grew louder, but Jay could see only vague forms. As the riders approached, he could distinguish three mounted men, trotting a few rods outside the row of telegraph poles. As they drew almost abreast of them, he was startled to hear the voice of Waterloo Williams.

"Hold up, boys. No sense killing these horses, too. We'll catch 'em soon enough. They can't be much farther ahead."

The three outlaws reined their mounts back to a walk.

"Damned shame we don't have any moonlight, chief," one of the men said. Jay recognized the voice of Andy.

"Doesn't matter. Just keep a sharp lookout.

248

They have to be following the tracks. There's no other way to go if they want to find a town. There're no roads out here."

The sound of their voices began to fade as they moved on past, and McGraw could no longer make out what they were saying. There was an emptiness inside of him. How had the three outlaws escaped? Had they killed the three good people of Colson? It must be Moats's and Nelson's horses they were riding. And now the outlaws were between them and Tulare. He thought for a few moments. He would let them go on ahead while he and Dupré rested here for an hour or so. Then they could set the pole car on the tracks and pump themselves along toward Tulare. By the time the little car caught up with the outlaws, maybe they would have stopped for the remainder of the night to rest. If they were very lucky, McGraw and Dupré might be able to pass them in the dark and keep going. Yet he had to discount the possibility the outlaws would stop to sleep. These men were tenacious, and he would not again make the mistake of underestimating them. He posed his plan to Dupré.

"You know best in your own country," the fugitive deferred.

"We'll try it, then."

Jay was not at all sure his judgment was the best, but he was simply reacting to one situation after another. He could have ended this thing at Colson when the three were just below him and he had a rifle in his hands. As he stretched out on the ground next to the stack of crossties, he knew there were two reasons he hadn't ambushed the pursuers from the water tower. First, the three men, even though surprised, would have been very fast and accurate with their six-guns and very likely would have gotten him before he could put all three of them out of action. The second reason was the fact that he couldn't bring himself to shoot a man down from ambush. Besides, he thought as he closed his eyes and relaxed, that kind of a shoot-out could have brought on all kinds of legal problems, even including accusations of murder and probably arrest and trial. At the very least a coroner's jury would have been convened. He likely would have been cleared on testimony by Father Stuart and Boomer Moats, but . . . well, enough of what "might have been." Back to reality. He would just rest his eyes a few minutes, and then they would go on.

"Jay!"
He awoke with a start at the sound of his own name in his ears.
"Is it not time to go, *mon ami?*"
"Yes, yes. Didn't mean to fall asleep. I'm glad one of us is alert. I wonder what time it is?"
He had no matches by which to check his watch. The wind was kicking up, and the blackness was thicker than ever. He could smell the rain coming, and it wasn't far away.
It took considerable struggle and effort, with

several stops to rest, but the two of them finally wrestled the pole car onto the tracks. The thing was surprisingly heavy for its size, but Dupré was strong for a man of his size. And durable. McGraw, the athlete, was built for explosive speed and short bursts of coordinated action. Dupré, the small fugitive, was built for endurance and staying power. So far they had made a good team. Jay hoped it stayed that way.

The rest of that stormy night into the gray dawn and most of the next day were only a dim nightmare to McGraw. The rainstorm held off for about thirty minutes, preceded by a fantastic display of lightning flashes illumining the whole sky and then flaming out, leaving the valley in blackness as deafening cannonades of thunder rolled and crashed down. They sat spraddle-legged, facing each other on either side of the vertical lever that stuck up from the center of the flat, wooden platform of the tiny rail car. Each man grasped this pole from opposite sides and pumped it back and forth, rocking from the waist.

The rain came sweeping out of the darkness and hit them while they were driving the handcar along the level track at about fifteen miles an hour. Jay averted his face from the stinging blast that was coming out of the west. Cold and un-comfortable as it was, he was glad the wind was not heading them to slow their progress and make the laborious pumping even more tiresome. As it was, he didn't know how long he could last.

While the hours wore on, they settled into a rhythm that drove the car along at a steady eight to ten miles an hour, not fast but better than walking. The rain soaked them, washing the sweat from their faces, hour after hour. McGraw's back went from aching to numb and stayed that way. He knew, if he ever stopped pumping, he would stiffen up and never get started again. The exercise kept the blood pumping and warded off the chill that would have come from being wet through.

Tulare came and went. Jay saw only two lights in the small town. If there was anyone awake here, they were staying in out of the weather. But, from what little he could see of the place, the rebuilding of the burned-out town had not proceeded very far. There was no point in stopping.

"Drive right on through to the next town!" he yelled across at Dupré who sat with his back to the direction they were traveling. The Frenchman's only response was to continue pumping — back and forth, forward and back, like a perpetual-motion machine. In the windy, thundering darkness a train could have borne down on them without their ever seeing or hearing it, since Jay had his eyes slitted nearly shut most of the time. They saw and heard nothing more of the three outlaws who may have holed up some place to ride out the storm. Jay hoped so.

When the gray dawn broke, the rain stopped, leaving a heavy overcast. They continued pumping in a hypnotic trance of motion, now and then passing the canteen back and forth for sips of water without ever breaking their rhythm. The sky cleared in the late morning, and the wind dried their clothes. By mid-afternoon they both ran out of fuel. Exhaustion caught up with them about the same time, and they both quit pumping as the handcar approached a slight upgrade. The sound of the flanged wheels against iron rails slid down to silence as the car rolled to a stop. For the first time they could hear the west wind rustling the dry weeds along the right-of-way.

McGraw thought his back would break if he tried to stand up. He rolled over and off the edge of the car and down the slope of the slight embankment where he lay in a half-conscious stupor. Dupré was in a similar state a few feet away. Jay's back was aching fearfully, but he was cradled and cushioned by the thick grass and weeds at the base of the embankment. He had to get up, his mind told him, and tip the polecar off the track, but first he would lie here for a few minutes in the warming sun and rest his tired back. He closed his eyes.

The next thing he knew he was jarred rudely awake by the squeal of brakes and the clanging of a bell. He jumped up and gasped with pain at his stiffened back. His shirt and pants were wet again from the soaked ground under the dry grass. He staggered up the embankment to see the fireman and the brakeman of a freight that had stopped a few feet away. The two trainmen were walking toward him. By then Jay realized they had not stopped for them; they had stopped to clear the track of the polecar he and Dupré had left standing on the main track. The lean, dark fireman reached him first. He was dressed in overalls, cotton shirt, and sported a huge black mustache that hid his mouth. He gave McGraw and Dupré a look as if they were two hobos who had tried to sabotage the Southern Pacific.

"Who put this car on the tracks?" he demanded, glaring first at one then at the other. Jay knew they must look like the scum of the earth, muddy and sunburned. He stepped over to the handcar and retrieved the saddle bags and carbine he had left when they stopped. He saw fear in the short brakeman's eyes as they focused on the rifle. Neither of the trainmen carried any visible sidearms.

"We have to get north to San Francisco," McGraw said, slinging the saddle bags over one shoulder and trailing the gun at his side by the barrel to show he meant them no harm.

"Did you steal this polecar?" the stoker asked as he and the brakeman took hold of either end of the car and strained to tip it off the tracks and out of the way.

"Had to borrow it yesterday," McGraw confirmed. "We missed our passenger train, and we have to get to San Francisco as fast as possible."

"You missed your passenger train, is that it?" the stoker said sarcastically.

254

Jay dug into his side pants pocket and produced the creased and damp pasteboard tickets. The lean stoker looked at them and then reached out and took them for a closer look.

"You did have tickets." He glanced up at McGraw with renewed interest. "These are from Colson to San Francisco."

Jay nodded.

"When did you buy these?"

"Yesterday at Colson."

"We came through there a few hours ago, and there was nobody around. We stopped to water up, but there wasn't a soul to be seen."

Jay's heart sank at the news, but he didn't feel like going into any long explanations with this man. Instead he said: "Carl Nelson sold us these tickets yesterday, but we fooled around and missed the northbound passenger train. The train was late anyway."

The stoker nodded. "The quakes the other day have played hell with the schedules. I reckon Carl and his wife have just gone off somewhere. Not like them to leave the depot unattended like that, though, even when there's no trains due. We're runnin' about six hours behind as is. The highball signal was up, so we came on."

"Mister, we really need to get on north. We've got urgent business. Any chance we could hitch a ride with you? I've got a little money. Maybe split it with you and the crew?" he said, glancing at the short brakeman who stood listening.

The lean fireman stroked his mustache thoughtfully, looking back at the locomotive that sat, panting quietly, a few yards away. "If it's okay with the engineer, it's okay with me. We've got one boxcar that's not quite full you can ride in. Keep your money. You've already paid for the ticket."

The engineer thrust his head out the side window of the cab. "What's the hold-up? Let's get rolling."

The light breeze was swirling smoke around them from the straight stack.

"How far you going?" Jay asked the stoker as they strode toward the train.

"Through to Stockton and Sacramento. We're carrying a load of lumber and a lot of other stuff the folks up there need to start rebuilding from the quake damage."

Jay's spirits soared. If they could get to Sacramento, they could connect with the Central Pacific and Wells Fargo. They could get back to San Francisco or send a telegraph message to Artello and wait for instructions. It would be easier to catch the express car on the overland at Sacramento and on to Chicago and New York. Artello could authorize some expense money by wire. It looked as if they had finally shaken their pursuers and were home free.

"Third car back," the stoker directed. "The side door's already slid open a piece."

McGraw and Dupré wasted no time in scrambling into the boxcar with the saddle bags, rifle, and canteen. In spite of being sore, tired, and hungry, Jay felt better than he had in days. The end wasn't yet in sight, but the road to it seemed assured.

Chapter Seventeen

When Jay McGraw had time to think about it four days later, he was not able to figure out how Waterloo Williams and his two gunmen, Ty and Andy, had been able to get ahead of them, indeed to know where they had gone. It had to be a lucky guess or a hunch that paid off. When Jay pondered it, he decided the crafty outlaw chief had questioned people along the railroad line who may have seen them pass through on the handcar. They had probably continued following the tracks north until they discovered the abandoned handcar where McGraw and Dupré had picked up the freight. But how had they gotten ahead? Somehow they were waiting in Galt when the freight was sidetracked there for a passenger train to pass. There had been two other delays down the line — one for a washed-out section of track that had been repaired quickly and another for the shoring-up of some damaged pilings on a small trestle over a creek. This last stop had cost them several hours. Undoubtedly the outlaws had passed them in the darkness again without knowing it, as they had done the first night out of Colson.

By the time they were sidetracked at Galt, McGraw and Dupré had been two days without food, and they slipped out of the boxcar to find something to eat in the little town. There appeared to be only a few hundred residents in the little community that was surrounded by vineyards and orchards. But they hardly saw any of this as they headed for the nearest saloon — the only saloon, as it turned out, on the wide, dusty street. The available food was the free lunch at one end of the bar. It consisted of pickled eggs, a block of cheddar cheese, and some smoked ham.

McGraw and Dupré had eaten two plates full and drained two mugs of draft beer each before they even slowed down. Seeing the rate at which they were consuming the food, the bartender was pushing the sale of two more beers, keeping a wary eye on them as he would on any tramps who entered the back door of his place. Jay blew the foam off his third beer and took a long draught, hoping the bartender would mistake them for just two more dirty migrant workers in the valley. Not that it mattered. Their money was as good as anyone else's, and the salty food was free to all takers. McGraw and Dupré stood at the bar rather than use one of several empty round tables. They were stoking their famished, tired bodies with food as fast as possible, not knowing how long the freight would remain on the siding. It was their only transportation to Sacramento and security.

McGraw had leaned the loaded rifle against the bar near at hand, and Dupré had set the saddle bags on the floor next to the brass rail. Just as Jay lifted his mug to his mouth, he saw in the back bar mirror the silhouettes of three men push through the batwing doors into the room. The mug stopped half way to his mouth, and he set the glass down carefully on the bar and reached slowly for the carbine beside him. He nudged Dupré. Williams and his men had found them. The only thing that saved them both was the fact that it took a few seconds for the outlaws' eyes to adjust to the dim interior after stepping out of the bright afternoon sunlight. In that several seconds McGraw and Dupré grabbed the saddle bags and rifle and bolted for the back door.

Just as they went through it, there was a shout behind them, followed by the blast of a shot. Jay later remembered being amazed at how fast the small man was. Jay considered himself an excellent sprinter but was barely able to keep up for the first twenty yards. He saw immediately they could not run directly for the train. There was nothing but an open field behind the saloon toward the railroad siding. They would be gunned down in the open. He had to slow them down. He slid to a stop, whirled, and fired the carbine twice from the hip, working the lever as fast as he could.

There was a shout of surprise, and Ty stumbled back into someone behind him as the bullet shattered the glass in the door. That should slow them up some, as he and Dupré veered away, dodging down a small alley next to the general mercantile. They were out of sight of their pursuers for a few seconds. No one was on the street as they came out from between the buildings. A wagon stood in front of the mercantile, two mules hitched to it and patiently twitching their ears. Some sort of a lumpy load in the heavy wagon was covered with a white canvas. There were no humans in sight on the street.

"Quick! In here!"

McGraw led the way for Dupré and dove into the wagon, burrowing under the canvas cover. He squeezed between two wooden kegs and pulled Dupré in after him. The wagon bed was full of boxes and bags, apparently a combination of groceries and cloth and tools. It was a tight fit, but Jay wiggled down so his carbine was in position for quick use, if needed. He muffled his harsh breathing in the crook of his elbow to keep as quiet as possible. Dupré lay flattened in front of him, both facing the closed tailgate. Now it was a matter of waiting. It seemed a long minute before they heard the thumping of boots and muffled voices.

"Hell, yes, they've got to be around here close. They haven't had time to get far."

"Did they have horses?" another voice asked.

The sounds were coming closer to the wagon, and Jay gripped the carbine, his breath still not steadied down and his stomach uncomfortably full from the food and beer he had consumed so quickly. Dupré did not have to be reminded of his peril. He had melted into the cargo in the wagon and was completely motionless.

"Look around back. I'll check this store. They're probably hiding close."

"If you see 'em, give a holler."

"What's all the shooting about?" Jay heard another, fainter voice ask.

The wagon rocked slightly as if someone had climbed up into it. McGraw tensed, waiting for the canvas cover to be thrown back. He would come out shooting. He would not hesitate this time. He knew these men were out to kill them both.

But suddenly he heard a sharp command and the wagon lurched forward. The first thought in McGraw's mind was that one of the men knew they were in here and had decided to drive the wagon out of town where they could then take them prisoner or kill them without witnesses. Whose wagon was this, anyway — the storekeeper's, a customer's, some drummer's?

Dupré arched his neck to look back at McGraw. Jay motioned for him to lie still and stay quiet as the wagon kept rolling at a steady pace. Whoever was driving was not in any hurry. They would stay still and await developments. As the seconds and minutes dragged by, they heard nothing but the rumbling, grinding of the steel-shod wheel rims rolling on packed earth. There were no more voices, no more shouts. Jay grew restless. He wanted desperately to sit up, throw back the cover, and see where they were and who was driving. But he forced himself to lie still. He would be patient. It might be one of the outlaws at the reins.

He squirmed around until he could reach his watch in his pants pocket. He popped it open and held it in front of him. Lucky it hadn't been damaged from everything it had been through in the past few days. He waited a full fifteen minutes before he made a move. Then he signaled to Dupré that he was going to throw the canvas back and jump up. The Frenchman nodded his understanding.

Jay drew his legs up under him and got to his hands and knees. He hesitated, listening intently. Were the outlaws riding alongside, just waiting their chance? Waiting for him to pop up so he could be shot? Over the rumble of the wagon he could hear no other sounds. It was time to take a chance.

With his free arm and the gun barrel he threw back the rear half of the loose canvas cover and sprang up, swinging the gun barrel in an arc. There was a yell from the front of the wagon as the driver nearly fell off, twisting around to see what had happened.

"Oh, my God! Who're you? Don't shoot! You can have whatever you want!"

The startled driver had dropped the reins and had his hands in the air as he faced around. Jay found himself pointing the carbine, hip-high, at a lean figure in a brown felt hat, leather gloves, red plaid cotton shirt, and wearing a gun belt.

"Stop this wagon!" he commanded.

"Whoa up, there!"

The span of mules came to a halt.

While this was going on, Dupré was up out of the wagon bed at his side. McGraw looked around quickly while the driver was busy with the team. They were somewhere out away from the town of Galt that was visible in the distance behind them. There was no sign of the outlaws. There was also no sign of the railroad. The sun was behind them. They were going east.

He turned his attention back to the frightened driver. McGraw didn't really know what to say next. He hesitated, looking more closely at the driver. Then it was his turn to be startled. The driver was a woman. She wore a man's clothing — Levi's jeans, boots, gun, and hat, but her form and face clearly identified her. The skin of her face was deeply tanned and fine lines of crows feet fanned out from the corners of her brown eyes that were now wide with fear. There was just the hint of parentheses of smile lines framing her well-formed mouth, but she was not smiling now. She appeared to be in her very early forties, probably a farm woman in town for supplies. And without knowing it, she had saved their lives.

"Where are you going?" Jay asked. She did not reply at first, staring down at the carbine he still held on her. "Put your hands down. We're not here to rob you," Jay assured her, realizing how frightened she was. "But unbuckle that gun belt and put it on the seat, all the same."

She moved quickly to obey, her hands trembling.

"Now, I asked you where you were going."

"Back home."

"Where's that?"

"About a hundred and twenty miles east of here." She gestured vaguely over her shoulder.

Jay pondered the situation, looking at Dupré who stood quietly at his side, apparently leaving the decision up to him.

"We'll ride along with you for a ways," McGraw said, climbing over the side of the wagon onto the wheel hub and stepping down.

"Who are you two?" she asked as McGraw and Dupré stepped up onto the seat beside her. With an apprehensive glance at them, she moved her gun belt to the floorboards near her feet and took up the reins again, clucking to the mules and popping the lines over their backs.

"Just keep driving. We'll explain on the way," Jay said, looking back at the distant town. He sat sideways, rifle ready, watching for any sign of pursuit. That had been a very close call. Their meeting with the three outlaws had apparently been totally by chance, but it had very nearly proved fatal. Not only did the outlaws now know approximately where they were, but this unlucky encounter had ruined their chances to ride all the way to Sacramento in the relative comfort of the freight car. Waterloo Williams and his men had guessed correctly that they would be following the rail line north. He and Dupré would now have to change their plans and take a detour. If they couldn't reach San Francisco directly, they would somehow keep bearing north and might be able to strike the east-west Central Pacific line somewhere east of Sacramento. Possibly then they could flag a train going either east or west. McGraw didn't know what Anthony Artello would say if he showed up at the Wells Fargo office with both the manuscript and Marcel Dupré. Artello had seemed to be giving him the entire job of getting this manuscript and taking it east to a publisher. If he could reach a telegraph that was working, he might be able to communicate with his superior by wire for some further instructions. In the meantime. . . . He glanced over at the woman who was driving. Dupré sat between them.

"What's your name?"

"Edna Woods."

"Where'd you say you lived?"

"In the mountains. Just this side of the Nevada border."

"You drive a long way for supplies. Why didn't your husband come?"

She seemed to hesitate, whistling and cracking the line on the offside mule. "I'm a widow. Jason died in a logging accident near six years ago now."

"Sorry."

"You needn't be. I've learned to take care of things alone."

"Any children?"

"One boy. Grown up and gone down to work on the railroad near Bakersfield."

"What town are we going to?"

"We?"

"We may ride with you all the way if there's a Western Union office there. Unless, of course, we pass through a town between here and there that has one."

"No offense, but I don't fancy your company all the way home." She had apparently recovered from her fright.

"You come all the way to Galt to do your shopping? You must have a special reason. Seems Placerville or somewhere like Carson City would be a lot closer."

"My business," she said shortly. "I don't favor big towns. Besides, I like the scenery down this way, and it gives me a chance for a trip two or three times a year. About once a year I'll take the wagon on down to Bakersfield and see my son, Robert."

"He doesn't come to see you?"

"He does. About once a year. We trade visits." She smiled at the thought. "But it's a long way."

"You live alone?"

She nodded.

"What's the name of the town?"

"No town. I have a place in the woods up in the mountains above Carson City."

"Sounds like a real lonely life."

"I prefer it." She glanced sideways at him and then at the Frenchman between them. "What's wrong with your friend? He doesn't talk?"

"My name is Marcel Dupré, *madame*," the fugitive said in his soft, flowing French accent, inclining his head slightly toward her.

"Oh? A Frenchman?"

"*Oui*. And may I say it is a pleasure to be in the company of so lovely and charming a lady?"

Her cheeks went slightly red under her tan. Holding the reins with one hand, she took off her hat with the other and shook her chestnut hair loose. What had been tucked under the hat fell, loose and thick, to her collar. Jay noticed for the first time that this woman, in spite of what had probably been a demanding life, had retained a good measure of the beauty she had apparently been blessed with in her youth. She looked again at Dupré with interest.

"You are from France?"

"I am."

"What are you doing in this country?"

"Mine is a story which will take some time to explain."

"It'll take us about four days to get home," she replied. "I'd like to hear it from you." She included Jay in her glance, but her attention was obviously on Marcel Dupré.

McGraw briefly sketched in the tale of how they happened to be in her wagon. Her face blanched slightly when he related how they had been chased by the gunmen in the saloon.

"I heard two or three shots while I was in the general store, and the clerk ran outside to see

268

what was going on. I saw these men running around with guns in their hands, but nobody seemed to know what was going on. We thought at first the bank had been robbed. But then the clerk said it was probably just a couple of drunks who got into a fight."

"Where did the men go?"

"They went into the Post Office and the mercantile and the bank like they were looking for someone. I just got into the wagon and drove off."

"Thank God for that," Dupré said.

"You took us right out from under their noses," McGraw added.

"Who were they?" she asked.

Jay backtracked and gave her their story from the time he had been sent to the mission church. She heard him out without interruption, looking at the two of them now and then, her eyes wide with wonder at what she was hearing.

"I've heard some wild tales in my time, but I believe that about tops them all," she remarked when he had finished.

"I can assure you, every word of it is true, *madame*," Dupré said.

"Call me Edna," she said, glancing at him as if she really enjoyed the formality of the title but was somehow still rather uncomfortable with it.

"Edna," he agreed, smiling at her.

Chapter Eighteen

Four full days it took them to reach the widow's house in the mountains. They had plenty of time to get acquainted on the way, and Jay McGraw was somewhat amused at the way she and Marcel Dupré struck a harmonious chord. From the beginning he had seen the spark between them and, as a way to pass the time and to cement the woman's trust of them, he had encouraged conversation between Dupré and Mrs. Woods. He needn't have bothered. Even counting the night at the mission when the Guiana fugitive had first recounted his tale to him and Father Charles Stuart, Jay had never heard Dupré talk so much. The reticence he had displayed during their flight from the mission until now was broken, and a torrent of words came pouring forth, all tinged by his soft French accent and animated with expressive gestures. Years of hardship and confinement in a penal colony had not diminished his natural charm that was being brought to the fore by this attractive woman.

They wound upward from the valley through the foothills on a deserted road, seeing only a few empty gold mining camps from earlier years before the placer gold ran out. They stopped a night at one of these abandoned camps, cooking up bacon and beans and corn cakes over a camp-fire while Dupré answered a flood of questions from Edna Woods concerning his life in France and the long years in French Guiana.

"You mean those Negroes wouldn't even help you when your canoe landed on Trinidad?" she asked, handing him a tin plate of smoking beans.

Dupré shook his head. "I don't know who they thought we were. Maybe drowned seamen come back to life. Some of those fishermen are very superstitious. And I know we must have looked frightful . . . ragged, thin, burned by the sun, unshaven." He chuckled at the recollection. "We must have looked like ghosts."

"I don't know how you had the courage to keep going."

Marcel Dupré reddened slightly. "It was hardly courage. We were desperate men. And desperate men will do anything."

"And the British authorities wouldn't let you stay there?"

"Only long enough to eat and get our strength back. But they did furnish us with a twenty-foot sailing boat, stocked with food and water to continue."

She paused with a piece of corn cake and bacon half way to her mouth as she eyed him critically. "You still look awful skinny."

"I'm a small man, but I have not eaten much lately." He smiled thinly.

"I'll take care of that. You supply the appetite, and I'll supply the grub. When we get to my cabin, I'll be able to whip up some proper meals. Something that will stick to your ribs."

He looked slightly embarrassed yet pleased by her personal concern as he ducked his head and dug into the hot beans. After a few moments he looked up again.

"In my daydreams in the solitary cell, I created a situation almost like this," he said, chewing thoughtfully, "where I was free, had plenty to eat . . . and was sharing it with a beautiful woman like you."

It was the widow's turn to blush.

During their days on the trail, McGraw discovered that Edna Woods was indeed capable of looking after herself without help. She could hitch and unhitch a team of mules with as much dexterity as she could build a fire or cook up a delicious meal. The fare was plain, but her judicious application of garlic or onions or red peppers could bring out the savory taste of beans or sliced potatoes with the skill of a gourmet chef.

Marcel and Edna took a walk together after the evening meal to explore the abandoned mining camp. In the quiet twilight Jay sat alone by the campfire and listened to the picketed mules grazing nearby. Now and then he could hear the musical sound of Edna Woods's laughter in the distance. There was no accounting for human behavior. An attraction between these two disparate people was the last thing McGraw would have imagined. A stranger happening upon their camp would never have guessed that Edna

Woods was an unwilling traveling companion — almost a captive — of these two men.

Jay harbored a grain of doubt concerning Edna Woods. Was she only feigning a romantic interest in Dupré to insure her own safety until she could be rid of them? Certainly the fugitive was not physically attractive, being very small and toothless and seemingly aged beyond his years, but he did have a certain vitality and charm. Jay was in the dark as to what this widow found appealing.

Dupré chopped firewood with a small camp axe, fetched water from the creeks, washed the tin plates and cups, helped with the mules, and practically pushed McGraw out of the way to make himself useful to Edna Woods. He even relieved her of most of the driving, though he was not as adept at handling the team as she was.

Once they reached the mountains, the going was rougher and slower, but the scenery was spectacular. The nights were much colder, and McGraw and Dupré shivered around the camp fire inside fire-reflecting windbreaks of pine boughs they cut and stacked as lean-tos. Mrs. Woods had come prepared with a soft buffalo robe she rolled herself into at night. Finally, they skirted the south side of the crystalline Lake Tahoe and went several more miles to the widow's cabin. She insisted she was a Californian, but Jay wasn't so sure she didn't live on the Nevada side of the line. In any case, she was isolated from any human habitation.

Even as they helped her unload the wagon of sacks of dried beans, potatoes, onions, dried apricots, kegs of flour, yeast, salt, yard goods for making clothes, and dozens of other items, McGraw's mind was leaping ahead, wondering where they would go from here. The map he still carried in his saddle bags was sadly lacking in detail for this part of the state, but he gleaned enough from it and from his own knowledge of general geography to know that he was no more than thirty-five miles south of where the Central Pacific main line crossed into Nevada. They could rest up a day or two here at the widow's place and then start northeast on foot to intersect with the railroad. It would be a hard two or three day trip through the mountains, but they should be able to do it. Providence had seen them through this far, and Jay was hopeful, even confident, that it would continue with them to their goal.

Edna Woods's home was a stoutly-built three-room log house her late husband had constructed while working for a nearby lumber company some fifteen years before. She also had a small stable for the mules, built of sawn lumber. The remnants of a vegetable garden were behind the house.

"The soil is poor, the growing season too short, and not enough sunlight gets down through the trees," she told them as they sat down to supper the night of their arrival. "But I keep trying. Mostly, if I want fresh vegetables, I have to hitch up the team and travel down out of the mountains to buy them."

"How did your husband die?" Dupré asked as the three of them were digging into some delicious beef pan pie fresh out of the wood-burning cook stove.

Edna Woods set her fork down and took a deep breath. "More coffee?"

Both men indicated their willingness for a refill. She rose to pick up the blackened pot with a hot pad.

"He was crushed by a huge log that fell on him. It came loose and rolled off one of those rail cars. He just happened to be in the wrong place at the wrong time," she said with a slight tremor in her voice.

"I'm sorry. I should not have brought it up," Dupré said.

"It's all right," she replied, setting the pot back on the hot pad and wiping her eyes with the back of her hand before turning back to the table. "He was a good man and a good provider. I still miss him but not as bad as the first few years."

"Why do you stay here? How do you live?" Dupré asked, voicing the same questions that McGraw hesitated to ask. But she and Marcel, in the short space of a few days, already seemed like old friends between whom there were no secrets.

"Even though my husband was only one of the laborers, he had invested some money that he had inherited from his father. During the big silver boom in Nevada, lumber was needed by the millions of board feet to build the towns and for timbering to shore up the mines. The Washoe Lumber Company he had invested in boomed, and his investment paid off handsomely after his death. But the mines fizzled out about three years ago, and the demand for lumber dried up pretty quickly. I've been stretching out what little money still comes to me by doing a good bit of sewing and dress-making. I'm a good seamstress, if I do say so myself. Come by it naturally, I suppose, 'cause it's so easy for me. You saw the yard goods I brought back from town."

"Don't you get lonesome up here all by yourself?" McGraw asked.

"Actually I like the beauty and solitude of the mountains. It gets pretty cold and snowy up here in the winter. The winters are also too long. I get out and do a little hunting in the woods now and then. Occasionally bag a deer and that keeps me busy curing meat for winter. And, when the weather's decent, I go down to Carson City to sell my dresses. Then I have a few neighbors who live about ten to twelve miles from here, so it's not all that bad." She smiled at them, as if to say that her life was a fairly happy one, if somewhat rigorous. "But I may have to move to town next year. Used about all the money I had left to buy that wagon load of supplies. I can get a job in Carson City," she added.

The conversation turned to the canning and preserving of fresh vegetables and fruits for the winter. She and Marcel Dupré got into a detailed discussion about the various methods of food preservation. Marcel was telling her about some of the food the Guiana prisoners were fed.

Jay pushed his chair back and let the conversation slide by him as he began thinking again of what their next move should be. He felt they were at last safe from pursuit by Waterloo Williams and his men, but he could not shake a nagging doubt. After all, he had thought they were safe at Colson. And he had thought they were safe at Galt. Had someone at Galt seen them jump into the wagon? The outlaws would persist and question everyone they could find who might have seen anything. And there were bound to be merchants in town who knew Mrs. Woods and where she lived. Waterloo Williams might eventually conclude that this was the only possible way they could have vanished so quickly and so completely. It would pay not to get too relaxed.

He watched Edna Woods and Marcel Dupré in animated conversation and wondered. The man seemed to have blossomed since he had met the widow. Maybe it was just the fact that he had not been in female company for a long time. Then again. . . .

Edna Woods provided them with blankets to ward off the September chill when they went to sleep in her son's bedroom. There was a feather tick on the bed, and McGraw insisted that Dupré sleep there over the objections of the Frenchman.

"There's a little more meat on my bones, so

I'll just wrap up and sleep on this hooked rug. Throw me a pillow, and I'll be fine."

The next morning the widow was up and had breakfast ready for them when they arose just after daylight. As they ate, she requested that they cut some firewood for her before they moved on. In a lean-to at the back of the house rested a cross-cut saw, a double-bitted axe, and a splitting maul with wedges.

"I'm not quite up to cutting wood like I used to be," she explained. "At least not in the amounts that my stove and fireplace use."

It was a chilly, windy morning, but McGraw and Dupré took the tools and set out into the nearby woods where deadfalls were plentiful. For two full days they worked without letup, sawing, chopping, splitting, and stacking wood in usable lengths. It would not be enough to see her through the winter, but it would be a good start. While they were at it, she cooked and served them three full meals each day, in between working at her treadle sewing machine. At night the two men slept like the dead, exhausted from their labors. Jay kept his loaded carbine at his side at all times, even while working in the woods. It never hurt to be cautious. On the morning of the third day after their arrival, McGraw told her they needed to be moving on.

"I haven't seen a newspaper or talked to anyone else, so I don't know what's being said about our escape from the mission, the French ambassador, or our Washington politicians. It's probably dropped out of the news by now. They may think we're dead."

McGraw had resigned himself to the fact that Mr. and Mrs. Nelson and Clarence Moats had probably been murdered by Waterloo Williams and his men. If someone had found the bodies by now, he wondered if any connection had been made between their murders and Jay McGraw and Marcel Dupré. Probably not.

"I wish I had time to make you boys some coats," Edna Woods said as they sat at the breakfast table. "Can you at least stay long enough to let me wash your clothes?"

Jay had to admit that they were sadly in need of washing. They were sweaty, muddy, and generally in bad shape with buttons missing and tears here and there. They agreed. They hauled water from a nearby mountain stream and built up a fire to heat it.

While the widow soaked and scrubbed their clothes, they wrapped up in blankets and waited. Afterward, she hung them on a rope near the fireplace to dry. McGraw and Dupré then took turns bathing in a tin washtub in front of the fire, using homemade lye soap. Jay had almost forgotten how luxurious and refreshing a good hot bath could be. They shaved and retrieved their still-damp clothes that Edna had repaired. By the time all this was finished, more than half a day had passed, and by unspoken agreement they decided to put off their departure until the next morning.

"Since I don't have time to make you coats, I'm going to make two ponchos out of the blankets you've been using. You can belt them around you and stay fairly warm until you get down out of the mountains," Edna Woods told them when they had cleaned up and dressed again. "I'm sorry I don't have any hats for you."

"Considering that we forced ourselves on you, you have done more than enough," Marcel Dupré told her. "We don't deserve it."

She looked wistfully at him. "I wish you didn't have to go."

She made no pretense of including Jay McGraw in her remark. As it turned out, they almost stayed permanently.

Chapter Nineteen

Apparently, Waterloo Williams and his two gunmen were not sure McGraw and Dupré were in the log house or the outlaws would very likely have set up an ambush as the two left the next morning. As it was, they rode up in the cold, foggy dawn, dismounted, and rapped at the door.

"Ah, that must be Zeb Jarvis, my nearest neighbor. He usually brings my mail up from Carson City about once a month," Edna Woods said, dropping a hot stove lid back into place and wiping her hands on her apron as she went to open the door.

McGraw, who had just come in from using the privy out back, didn't have time to warn her to ask who it was before she flung open the door. There stood the bulky form of Waterloo Williams. He and Jay McGraw saw each other at the same time. With a roar of surprise and anger, the outlaw leader reached for his gun.

"Look out!" Jay yelled, hitting the floor behind the table as Edna Woods slammed the door. She shot the bar into place just in time to keep the door from being flung open again by the weight of a heavy kick.

McGraw scuttled across the floor to reach his rifle, propped against the wall. A shot broke a pane of glass in the window, and the slug buried itself in the back log wall. Edna uttered a cry and ran to crouch behind the cast iron stove. Dupré had jumped back into the doorway of the adjacent bedroom.

"Come on out, you two! There's nowhere to run. You can't hide behind a woman's skirts this time!" came the booming voice of Williams.

McGraw's mind was racing. There was a back door, but they might have it covered already. He aimed his carbine and fired a return shot through the broken window.

"Might as well make it easy on yourselves," the yell came again. "You can stay in there if you want to, but you have five minutes, starting now. Then we burn the place down around your ears. Do you want the woman hurt, too?"

The outlaw leader was not going to make the mistake of storming the house or coming through a window where he or one of his men would run into a deadly hail of lead. Or they might climb onto the roof and block up the chimney, relying on the smoke from the fireplace and the stove to force them out. Dupré sprang past McGraw to crouch beside the widow next to the cook stove.

"Are you injured, *ma cherie?*"

"No," she replied in a frightened voice, looking at him with wide brown eyes.

"We can fight them off, can we not?" Dupré asked McGraw. "We have much ammunition for the rifle, and Edna also has a rifle. We will fight them this time, yes?" That unquenchable fire was ablaze in his eyes again, Jay noted.

"Not if I can help it," McGraw replied. "This is not the time or the place. There has to be some way out of here."

"You have four minutes, Dupré!" came the shout from outside.

McGraw said: "Edna, take your rifle and stay back in that corner by the stove. If they bust in that door or through a window, shoot them."

"What are you going to do?" she asked.

"We're going out the back door. There's heavy forest close by. If we can elude them and get into the trees, we may be able to lose them. It's barely daylight, and there's plenty of fog this morning. The clouds are practically enveloping the tops of the mountains."

"Three minutes, Dupré!" Williams yelled. There was almost a note of glee in his voice.

"There may be another way to escape that is quicker," Edna Woods said. "But it's probably too dangerous."

"It couldn't be any more dangerous than what we're facing right here. What is it?" McGraw asked.

She hesitated.

"Tell us . . . quickly!" Dupré urged.

"There is a water flume that starts a quarter-mile from here and runs about fifteen miles down into the Carson Valley where there's a mill. Logs were floated down out of the mountains when the Washoe Lumber Company was in business."

"Yes, I know what a flume is even though I've

never seen one," McGraw interrupted her. "Is there water in it? Can it carry two humans?"

"There is a narrow boat, like a canoe, that the men used to send supplies and things down the mountain . . . things they didn't want to carry down or wanted to get to the valley in a hurry."

McGraw and Dupré looked at each other. Jay knew the Frenchman was game for it.

"Two minutes, Dupré!" the voice outside boomed.

"Can you lead us to it?"

She nodded.

"It will be too dangerous for you," Dupré said. "Just point the way."

"No. I know where the boat is stored and the sluice gate that diverts the water from the stream into the flume."

Jay gripped his carbine and crept to the back door and opened it a crack. Then he opened it wider and looked out. The cottony mist was as thick as a San Francisco fog. The damp, cool air blew into his face. There was no sign of the outlaws. All three of them were confident. They were still out front.

"Come on," he whispered. "We can make it now."

The three of them slipped cautiously out the back door and crept through the swirling cloud mist to the side of the stable and then a few yards into the thick pine forest beyond. Running quietly on the carpet of pine needles, Edna Woods led them toward the cluster of abandoned buildings that marked the head of the flume. The huge pines had long since shaded out all undergrowth and, except for windfalls and dead snags of lightning-blasted trees, the forest floor was fairly clear of obstructions.

The quarter mile she had estimated turned out to be more than twice that distance. They arrived, panting and sweating, clammy from the condensed moisture of the fog. The widow ran directly to the iron wheel that controlled the sluice gate. The mountain stream was rushing and foaming over the rocks on its way to the valley far below. She gripped the two-foot wide wheel and tried to turn it. It didn't budge.

"Oh, no! I think it's rusted shut," she wailed.

She, McGraw, and Dupré all formed a circle and gripped it. McGraw said: "Okay, ready? One, two, three, *heave!*" They threw their combined strength into it. The worm gear groaned and gave a few inches. "It's not rusted tight. Again!"

They heaved with all their power. The gear turned again. It got slightly easier with each effort, and at last the wooden sluice gate began to slide down into its long-neglected groove and block the water of the rushing stream. By the time the gate was all the way down, it effectively dammed the rushing stream as the water was diverted at right angles into another trough and then out into the flume.

McGraw's eyes followed the course of the flume as it snaked down the steep slope, made a turn, and disappeared into the mist fifty yards away. In spite of his efforts he was shivering with cold and anticipation. The icy water was now directed down the mountain, contained only by the warped boards of the flume that was running full to the top. Small streams of water were spurting and dribbling out in dozens of leaks in dozens of places. His stomach contracted when he looked at the spidery network of boards and logs that supported the old aqueduct.

"Where's the boat?" Dupré demanded.

"Oh, please don't do it!" Edna Woods pleaded, clasping her hands and staring at the same thing McGraw had just been looking at. "You'll be killed. It's probably rotted and broken in a hundred places."

"The boat . . . quick!" Dupré ordered.

She tore her gaze away from the steeply-gushing torrent and ran to a shed nearby. The door was fastened with a rusty padlock. Dupré looked around quickly and found a rock bigger than both his fists. He pounded on the lock three, four times. It held firm.

"Stand back," McGraw ordered. He raised the rifle.

"No! They'll hear you," Dupré warned.

Frustrated, he looked around. "If I use the barrel as a crowbar, I may bend it."

They attacked it with the rock again and finally managed to tear the heads off the rusty screws that held the hasp to the wood. Two boats stood on end in the storage shed when they finally got the door open. They had V-bottoms and were blunt at one end, pointed at the other, and were about eight feet long. The two men quickly hoisted one out and set it down where the water was rushing into the head of the flume.

"Please don't go," Edna Woods said. "It's too dangerous. You can start down the mountain on foot. They won't be able to track you."

"They've tracked us this far when I never thought they could," Jay answered.

"See if you can strike a deal with them," she tried again. "I've seen too many men killed in these lumber camps, including my own husband. They were floating an injured logger down this thing to the doctor in the valley a few years ago, and he was killed on the way down. Shot right off one of those curves." Her voice was anguished.

"We'll make it, Edna," Marcel Dupré told her in his soft accent. "I have come too far and endured too much to die now. And I have more to live for than just revenge on the French penal system," he put his arms around her and drew her close. She was at least three inches taller than he was.

"Spread out. I know they came this way. The back door was left open."

They all jumped at the sudden sound of voices.

"I knew we should have shot our way in. That house was too wet to burn, anyway."

"Hey, chief, there're some buildings up ahead."

"Go!" Edna said urgently.

"It will have to be this way," McGraw said, looking toward the boat.

"No. We cannot leave you to those men," Marcel Dupré said to Edna.

"They don't want me. Go on! I'll just slow them up. They won't catch me. I know these woods, and they don't."

McGraw and Dupré sprang toward the boat on the ground. Two men emerged from the fog, leading their horses. Edna Woods snatched up her rifle, worked a round into the chamber with one quick motion, aimed, and fired. The slug knocked a chink from the pine tree about two feet from Andy's head.

"There they go!"

There was some wild yelling, and then three shots were fired. McGraw and Dupré had the canoe in the trough. The rifle and saddle bags were already in it. Jay snatched one quick look back, and then they both leaped in simultaneously, McGraw in front. They let go of the sides, and the boat shot away as if from a catapult.

All thought of the outlaws and possible danger to Edna were swept away in an instant as they plummeted down the first precipitous drop before leveling off. McGraw's heart was in his mouth as he unconsciously gripped the sides of the boat and looked ahead, trying vainly to pierce the fog ahead to see what was coming next.

They swept into a long curve, and the boat bumped along the sides of the old flume.

McGraw was sitting in the bottom with his legs out in front of him, and he could feel Dupré stiffen behind him as the trough straightened out and began to tilt downward again. He recoiled in horror as the boat dropped toward the wall of a rocky cliff. At the last second the flume dipped under an overhanging lip of rock, and McGraw fell back into Dupré as the rocky projection flashed past his face. Then, just as suddenly, they were away from the cliff and bending out over a chasm on a tall, spidery framework of trestle that looked too flimsy to hold them. They passed over the chasm, slowing somewhat, and Jay found himself gasping, not realizing he had been holding his breath. They had come out below the cloud cover of mist that blanketed the top of the mountain.

Before McGraw could recover from his fear or catch his breath, the flume led through a rocky declivity then tilted downward with a sickening drop, and the rushing water accelerated. Jay's stomach rolled and seemed to be left behind as they plummeted. The green landscape whizzed by in one long, filmy blur. McGraw clung to the sides of the boat in sheer panic. His senses were reeling, and he knew they were doomed. They had to be traveling more than a mile a minute — faster than any express train he had ever ridden. The wind tore at them, whipping hair and clothes, stinging tears from their eyes.

Then they were banging and bumping the sides

as the flume curved and flattened out. Suddenly they shot out over a tumbling, foaming creek, wet ferns and greenery hanging all around its edges. The flume bent into a curve in the opposite direction, and they darted over another creek, cascading down the mountain. It was the same stream, lower down, as the flume swept into another bend and plunged downward once more. Jay had no idea how long they had been in the boat. As the flume flattened out and they slowed somewhat, he chanced a look over the side. Far below, in the bottom of the cañon, were logs that looked like matchsticks — timber that had apparently jammed up and gone over the side at some earlier time and now lay, unrecoverable, in the bottom of the cañon. The flume curved in to run along the edge of a cliff face with pine trees growing in rocky crevices and leaning precariously out over the yawning chasm.

McGraw saw it coming at the last second — the low-hanging branch of an oak. He threw himself forward, bending his head to his knees and yelled a warning at Dupré. But it was too late. Dupré was knocked out the back of the boat. The little man turned a flip and landed in the trough behind the boat. He was swept along, headfirst, banging and bumping, until he could scramble, cat-like, to his feet. He ran after the boat, stumbling and splashing in the V-bottomed trough. Jay tried to slow the boat by grabbing the sides of the flume but jerked his hands back, needled with splinters. Finally, as the boat slowed on a flattened section, Dupré threw himself forward and McGraw, reaching back, caught his hand and dragged him back over the transom into the boat.

McGraw did not know how much farther it was to the bottom or what awaited them when they got there, but it was too late to worry about it now. The water was roaring and rushing as it swept them along another cliff edge with dizzying speed. The rocks rushed past only a foot or two away. Jay was giddy and looked away from the rocks to steady himself, glancing at the spindly trestle ahead where the flume curved out over a deep gorge and — and ended! A spout of water plunged off the broken end of the flume into space, spilling into the gorge more than a hundred feet below.

"Out! Out the back! Quick!" McGraw yelled. He grabbed the saddle bags and shoved Dupré. The little man tumbled backward over stern into the water again, followed by Jay. The shock of cold water took his breath. They were still being swept along, nearly keeping up with the empty boat. McGraw was in front of Dupré, sliding feet first on his back, trying to brace his boots against the slippery, moss-covered sides of the flume, but he slowed their progress only slightly as the force of water swept them inevitably toward destruction.

He saw one last chance. Just where the flume curved away from the rock face of the mountain about fifty yards ahead, a stunted pine tree was tilted out at a sharp angle, its bushy limbs within reach.

"Grab the tree and hang on!" he yelled to Dupré.

McGraw heaved one end of the saddle bags over the edge of the flume and threw his arms and shoulders on top to drag down their speed. Dupré's shirt was being shredded from his arms as he grabbed the other tilted side, but their progress was slowed enough so that some of the icy water was flowing around and over them. The pine tree limbs were still rushing at them, but McGraw had somehow to hang onto the saddle bags and grab the tree at the same time. He would have only one chance. He slid the saddle bags even farther over the edge so one bag was only slightly in the water. He would have to let go of it to get the limb.

"Get ready! Here it comes!"

They rolled and stumbled to their knees in the swift, shallow water and both lunged at the low-hanging branches at the same time. McGraw hung on desperately as the bristly needles raked his face, and he felt Dupré's body slam into him. His hands slipped a few inches, but he threw a leg over the edge of the flume, and Dupré grabbed the other leg as he lost his grip on the tree and was being swept past. They came to a stop, McGraw hanging to the limb and Dupré clinging to one of Jay's legs and lying prone in the rushing current. The tree bowed with their weight, but its resilient strength held. McGraw gradually worked his grip upward and felt with his right foot until he hooked his heel on the framework of the trestle. With the strength born of desperation, Dupré clawed his way up until he got hold of McGraw's belt and then was able to reach and climb out over the other side of the flume.

The saddle bags were sliding slowly along, half in the water, and Jay let go of the tree to retrieve them, while he straddled the edge of the trough. His hands were bleeding from many splinters, and he was soaked with icy water, but he felt nothing as he gasped for breath, knowing they were still alive for the moment. He looked down. They were a good eighty to a hundred feet from the ground, just at a point where the flume trestle curved away from the cliff and sloped out over a rocky gorge that dropped away into a jumble of boulders and trees. He motioned to Dupré a few feet away from him on the opposite side of the flume.

"We've got to climb down. Be careful!"

Dupré nodded that he understood and began to work his way down the timbers. McGraw flung the saddle bags over one shoulder and stepped backward and down, hugging one of the slick, wet, supporting timbers. Water was dribbling down on his head from several leaks. He suddenly remembered the rifle that had gone down with the boat. No matter. They had saved their lives and the saddle bags with the manuscript. If they could get their feet on solid ground, they could walk the rest of the way out to Carson City. It couldn't be that far.

He stepped carefully on a stringer, and the board gave way under his foot. He instinctively hugged the big upright in front of him and slid down several inches, raking his face and feeling more splinters stab his hands and arms. When he caught his breath, he looked across at Dupré and saw him making his way farther down, agile as a monkey.

Suddenly there was a wild yell above, and he threw his head back. At first there was nothing visible. Then he saw arms flailing over the edges of the flume as an unseen boat shot past overhead.

"I missed the tree!" a voice screamed.

"Get out! Get out!" the booming voice of Waterloo Williams roared.

The voices subsided as the boat tobogganed down the flume toward the jagged break over the gorge. The boat, with two men in it, hurtled out into space from the end of the flume, followed by another figure, kicking and turning in the air.

Abruptly dizzy and faint, McGraw closed his eyes and hugged the thick timber in front of him. When he finally looked again, there was no sign of the boat or its occupants. Smashed to pieces somewhere below in the trees and boulders. All was as before. The waterfall still gushed out the end of the flume, feathering into a spray as it fell and fell and finally disappeared.

Shakily he resumed his climb down, being extremely careful to test each foot and handhold before putting all of his weight on it. He felt no sense of relief, only a sickening horror at the sight. Outlaws for monetary gain they certainly were, and possibly even murderers, but Jay couldn't rejoice at any man's death. Although it meant he and Dupré were no longer in danger, he could only pity the three humans who lay crushed in the bottom of the mountain gorge.

Dupré was there to meet him when he finally hung by his hands and dropped the last few feet to the stony ground. They were scratched and torn and bleeding, and their wet clothes were plastered to them in shreds but, as they looked at each other, they both broke into grins.

"It is destined that we survive all this, yes?" Dupré asked in his flowing accent, his blue eyes smoldering with unquenchable fire.

"Yes!"

Chapter Twenty

They followed the cleft of a foaming stream downward, slipping and sliding and banging their shins on the mossy boulders. The weight of fear and responsibility for keeping them both alive had been lifted from Jay McGraw's shoulders, and he felt giddy with relief. Carrying the saddle bags over one shoulder, he bounded down the slope, leaping from rock to rock, outdistancing Marcel Dupré as he threaded his way toward patches of sunlit green in the valley several miles below.

When they paused for breath after nearly a mile, it occurred to Jay that maybe they should have climbed down into the gorge to confirm that Waterloo Williams and his men were all dead. He didn't see how any human could have survived that fall but, by some outside chance, one of them might have done so and could be lying there, gravely injured. He glanced back up the steep slope into the mist that hid the tangle of greenery and rocks, debating whether to go back and see. But they might not be able to get down into that gorge without the help of some long rope or climbing gear. As a good athlete he knew the rush of adrenaline he was feeling now would soon ebb, leaving him with maybe just enough energy to get down out of the mountains before dark.

"Do not concern yourself, *mon ami*," the Frenchman panted, halting beside him and giving Jay a searching look. "They have all gone to the judgment."

McGraw thanked him with a sad smile. They would not burn any daylight or strength going back.

"Let's move," he said.

The late afternoon shadows were long when two ragged, blood-stained men made their footsore way into Carson City. Marcel Dupré, especially, was limping badly on bruised, sandal-clad feet. From some loafers in front of the International Hotel they got directions to the sheriff's office, and a few minutes later they sat in the lawman's presence as he ate his supper. They were hardly seated in the two wooden chairs in front of his desk when he wiped his mouth and threw down his napkin irritably.

"Hell, it's gettin' so a man can't even take a supper break around here. Can't it wait? My deputy'll be back tomorrow."

" 'Fraid not, Sheriff," McGraw replied, his stomach grumbling at the delicious smell of the roast beef.

The lawman sighed. "Okay, then, go ahead. I'll eat while you talk."

Jay made it brief, omitting most of the details. The sheriff paid little attention at first, then McGraw saw the startled look in the lawman's eyes as if he suddenly realized the potential for personal fame and prestige in the words he was hearing.

"Damn! This thing is big!" He pushed back the chair and rose quickly to his feet. But then he stood, irresolutely, chewing the last bite, cake crumbs falling from his mustache. "Too late to get a search party up there before dark. If they kilt the widow Woods, it's too late to help her now, anyways. We'll have to wait 'til morning. Can't have men and horses stumbling around up in them cañons in the dark."

He continued talking, a blank look in his eyes, as if he were thinking out loud and had forgotten their presence for the moment. "The bodies'll keep. I'll round up a few of the boys and deputize them so they'll be sober and ready to head out at first light. Might even have 'em ride down the trail a ways tonight and camp so they'll have more time to get up there and bring out the bodies. Gonna take some work. That's rugged country. Waterloo Williams and two of his men, you say? Hmm. . . . Good job. Save the cost of a trial. Dangerous bunch. Been terrorizing California and Nevada for years. But they were more into robbin' stages. Wonder how they got mixed up in this business? Stages gettin' scarce, I reckon. That'll teach 'em. Man should stick to what he does best, even if it's outlawin'. Good riddance, I say. . . !"

The sheriff was still mumbling to himself as he grabbed his hat off a peg beside the door and started out. Then, as an afterthought, he stopped and said: "You boys look pretty tuckered out. We got a good hotel just down the street. Tell the manager to bill your room to the sheriff's office. And don't forget to mention in your report to your bosses how the law in Carson City cooperated in this matter. My name's Tom Mahlon. That's spelled M-a-h-l-o-n." Then he was gone out the door, a long-legged stride carrying him diagonally across the street toward the saloon where he would presumably recruit his search party.

Jay McGraw heaved his tired body out of the chair, reflecting that it seemed about a week since the confrontation with the outlaws in the misty mountain morning. He was achingly weary and knew that Dupré must be, too.

"First thing I have to do is find a Western Union office and get a message off to my boss," Jay said. "Then we'll go to the hotel and get checked in before we hit that bathhouse down the street."

"I hope Edna is safe," Dupré said as they went outside into the gathering dusk.

"She had a rifle, and she's quick and knows those woods," Jay assured him. "They didn't get her. They were too close behind us in the flume, so I know they didn't waste any time chasing her. She's fine. Don't worry. She can take care of herself."

McGraw found the telegraph office on the same block, next to the hotel. He took a pad and pencil and composed a short message to Anthony Artello, stating succinctly what had happened and where they were. He wanted his boss to have the facts before the story hit the newspapers, probably in some sensational, garbled fashion in the next day or so.

At some earlier time Jay might have asked for instructions from the District Superintendent but not now. He had been through too much and used his own judgment in critical situations to ask what to do next. He simply stated they would arrive in San Francisco on the first available train and would bring the manuscript.

"When are you going into politics?" Fred Casey asked Jay McGraw as the two of them sat in Boyle's Saloon, sipping their steam beers.

"Not me. I've had enough of political intrigue to last me a lifetime."

"I'd think you'd at least run for mayor of San Francisco or maybe governor of California. Better yet, you'd probably make a good senator. That's it . . . the Honorable Jay McGraw of California. I can hear it now in the senate chamber . . . 'I defer to my esteemed colleague from California . . . !' "

"Enough. Enough." McGraw raised his empty mug for the waiter to see. "Ready for another beer?"

"No. As soon as I finish this, I have to get home. I have to work in the morning. It's not like when I was on night patrol in Chinatown.

300

I'm on a regular day shift as a detective."

Jay accepted the foamy mug the waiter set in front of him. "I guess it did turn out pretty well after all, though," he conceded.

"I wouldn't be for visiting Paris anytime soon, if I were you," Casey said with a grin.

"Yeah. I guess Dupré and I are *personae non gratae* there since the publication of his book. They may not abolish the French Guiana penal colony right away as a result of that embarrassment, but I think they'll have to close it eventually if they want to continue doing business with other civilized countries."

"With all the upheavals in France, you and Dupré may just be responsible for bringing down the French government."

Jay shrugged. "I don't know anything about politics, but I guess that wouldn't be all bad. They may come up with something better."

They sat silently for a few moments with their own thoughts.

"How in the world did anyone read that manuscript after the soaking it got?" Casey asked then.

"If it had been written in ink, the translator probably couldn't have," Jay replied. "Luckily, all Dupré had to work with was pencil. After we got it dried out, it was smudged and faded some but still legible. Dupré was there to fill in the blank spots. Carter & Son got that book into print in record time, considering it had to be translated, edited, printed, bound, and distributed. The newspaper headlines and stories provided all the publicity they needed to sell it. It was only a matter of weeks from the time we got to New York and negotiated a contract before it showed up in the bookstores here in San Francisco. They did a great job on it. And Dupré got good money for the magazine version before the book came out."

"Regardless of the money he got, I think the greatest thing for him was being allowed to stay in this country and apply for citizenship," Casey said, draining his beer and wiping the corners of his black mustache with the back of his hand.

"Next to his freedom, I'd have to say the most important thing in his life was his engagement to Missus Edna Woods," McGraw observed. "He's never had much money and, to him, it's only a means to an end. As soon as he gets back from visiting her, he's booked on a lecture tour . . . twenty-one cities in thirty days. The money from it, along with proceeds from the book, will set him up financially for years to come, if he doesn't spend it all trying to get his friends out of Guiana."

"He's going to lecture with no teeth?" Fred asked.

"He's used to talking that way," Jay grinned. "But I know of at least one dentist who's offered to make him a set of dentures for half price, just for the publicity. I don't think he'll be toothless for long. You can bet he'll be eating steak before the wedding."

"Well, I have to go," Casey said, rising and

stretching. "Some of us have to work, you know. When's your next trip to the East?"

"Two days from now. And I'll sure enjoy the rest between now and then."

"If you can avoid the reporters."

"I think that's finally starting to die down. This being treated like a hero is a lot of nonsense. What they write about me makes me more inclined not to believe anything I read in the newspapers. The credit should be given to people like Father Stuart and Santiago at the mission, and to Carl and Martha Nelson, and Clarence Moats, and Edna Woods. Thank God the Nelsons and Moats weren't killed. They were foremost among the ones who saved us."

"Yeh. Boomer Moats was even able to send your telegraph message to Artello after Moats got himself loose from that root cellar."

"Yeah. I still haven't figured out how Boomer and Carl let those outlaws get the best of them."

"Artello got that telegraph message two days after you escaped from Colson, so I guess it took that long to get the line fixed. Moats even sent a message of his own to the police department here. After that you two just vanished for more than a week. The newspapers were speculating that you were dead, until you came walking into Carson City looking like somebody had locked you in a cage with an angry cougar. I damned near took leave from the force to come looking for you myself."

"Next time you can go in my place, and I'll

303

stay here," Jay said, rising and dropping some coins on the table.

"By the way, did the company deduct the cost of that rented saddle horse out of your bonus?" Casey asked with a grin.

"Believe it or not, Wells Fargo actually paid the livery for it, less my deposit. Some rancher in the San Joaquin Valley probably has a good horse by now, if its leg wasn't broken. I did lose the Colt and Winchester I bought, though."

The young, black-haired Irish police detective and the lean, athletic Wells Fargo messenger walked out of the saloon into the foggy street. Jay looked up at the gas street lamp making a fuzzy ball of light in the thick mist. A bright red and gold cable car clanged up the street in front of them. He took a deep breath of the chill, damp night air.

"It's sure good to be home again," he breathed.